BILLION
Dollar Date

BELLA MICHAELS

BILLION DOLLAR DATE

BELLA MICHAELS

1

ENZO

"*D*on't look now. Three o'clock."

Which is the one thing Hayden could have said to guarantee I *do* look. That's human nature for you. Or at least it's my nature. Someone tells me not to do something, and you can guaran-damn-tee I'll do it anyway. And worse, he knows it.

Even in the dimly lit restaurant, I can see Giovanna clearly, and our eyes meet because she's staring straight at me.

"Shit," I mutter, looking away. "She caught me looking. There's no way she's not coming over now."

Hayden makes a sound that I can easily decipher after more than ten years of his antics. It's somewhere in between *better you than me* and *I'm going to thoroughly enjoy this.*

"If I can't navigate this," I whisper as the restaurant owner's daughter starts sidestepping through the tables to reach us, "say goodbye to Wednesday dinner. She's getting more and more aggressive."

Hayden's drink pauses midair. Eyes narrowed, he waits to see if I'll forgo diplomacy just for the sake of sticking it to him. It would serve him right for deliberately attracting the attention of the woman who's been pursuing me for months.

But I'm no idiot—if I mess this up, we'll lose out on the best Italian food in Tribeca.

"Evening, gentlemen."

Regular patrons of Faustini's are used to the owner's daughter. But the two tourist couples sitting next to us openly stare at her. I don't blame them. Giovanna Faustini is gorgeous in a way that turns heads, from her dark hair to her signature red lipstick. She's a razor-sharp attorney who has nothing to do with her father's business, yet she always seems to make an appearance on the one day a week Hayden and I frequent this small restaurant. It's not a secret we eat here every Wednesday. When the press figured it out, we nearly had to find a new weekly dinner spot.

"Hi, G," I say.

"Good evening, Miss Faustini. You're looking lovely, as usual." Hayden's playing with fire, encouraging her with his tone. I warn him with a look, but he doesn't take the hint.

"Congratulations on the Merrick settlement. Well done."

Hayden hasn't lost his touch with the ladies. He could charm the habit off a nun.

Giovanna smiles, but not at my friend.

She's stunning. Smart. But nothing stirs in me as she flashes her pearly white teeth—a lovely contrast to her red lipstick. I could easily picture those lips wrapped around me, but still, nothing.

"Thank you." She waves her hand as if such a high-profile victory were commonplace. The opposing counsel is considered the best in the business, his track record, off the charts. "So, Enzo."

Here it comes.

"I hear you've just been approved in Switzerland. You must be thrilled!"

It's obvious the comment is addressed only to me, never mind the fact that my business partner sits across from me.

"Quite. Hayden's going there in a few weeks for the launch."

My tone clearly communicates that the conversation is over. Most people respond to that tone, but G, as she insists I call her, is a pit bull. She won't be put off so easily.

"Maybe a celebration is in order?" she asks. "This weekend, perhaps?"

Hayden bites the inside of his cheek to stop from laughing.

Asshole.

I lift my wine, the beginning of a polite but firm dismissal. "Unfortunately, I'm out of town this weekend."

"Oh? Somewhere good, I hope?" she says, dropping into an accent she sometimes pulls out like a pair of expensive shoes. She might be second-generation Italian, but G was born here, not in Italy.

"Home," I say. "For the opening of my brother's restaurant. Please give your father my compliments on the risotto. It's especially good tonight."

I don't intend to answer any follow-up questions, so I bring the wine glass to my mouth and take a long sip, pointedly shifting my attention to Hayden. Finally, after an excruciating few seconds, she walks away.

"Home?"

Screw a sip. I might need another glass.

"I thought you said you weren't going?"

The bell over the door rings, catching my attention. The old-school bell is a nice, kitschy touch—a sign that despite the red velvet cushions and chandeliers, Faustini doesn't take himself too seriously.

Except he definitely takes his daughter seriously. Did she leave? Did I offend her with my borderline rudeness?

One of these days, I'm going to piss off Giovanna enough that she complains to her father. And I really, really don't want that to happen.

Wednesday night at Faustini's is the bright spot in a week filled with work and more work. According to everyone I know, I work too much. They're not wrong, but I don't plan on stopping anytime soon, which is the exact reason I planned to miss my brother's opening. I really can't afford to take time off, but the guilt train conducted by my mother and occupied by my brothers and sister, not to mention Hayden, has been gaining steam these past two weeks.

"I wasn't. Changed my mind."

Hayden takes a bite of mushroom risotto and groans. His overdramatic enjoyment of food hasn't changed a bit since college, except now his performance involves slightly more refined food than the ramen noodles we lived on back then.

"Seems kind of an extreme way to avoid a date with G."

Out of the corner of my eye, I see her coming from the kitchen. I'm relieved that I didn't drive her away after all, and even more so that she doesn't look our way.

"Maybe, maybe not."

He cocks his head. "And maybe you should just do what every other red-blooded male in this restaurant wants to do with her."

"Everyone except you."

Hayden can't agree with a mouthful of risotto in his mouth, but I know it's true. The fact that my best friend and business partner is now a married man surprises everyone, me most of all. He's a far cry from the sex-obsessed frat boy I befriended. Sometimes it's still hard for me to wrap my brain around the fact that he's a father. And a damn good one at that.

Hayden mumbles an affirmation and continues eating.

I lean back, sneaking another look. Why don't I take Giovanna's not-so-subtle invitation? I haven't been on a date in two months, though not for a lack of prospects.

The kind of money Hayden and I have accumulated these past few years tends to attract women. Lots of them. Just not the right types.

"No, thanks." The decision is an easy one. I enjoy her father's cooking too much.

"Your mom will be happy you're going home." Finally dropping G as a topic of conversation, Hayden smiles. "Tell her I'm sorry to miss it."

"You do know Tris is the one who's opening the restaurant, right?" I say, seeing the subject away from my mother. Though he's not wrong.

Mom was appalled to learn I didn't plan on attending the opening.

To her, family is everything. Work is, at best, a very distant second, multibillion-dollar business or not. Tristano's decision to follow in the footsteps of our father, a pizza shop owner, and open DeLuca's II Ristorante is a big deal.

"Congratulate him for me," Hayden says. "Don't forget to tell everyone I would have been there if I wasn't out of town. And be sure to mention I was the one who reminded you that work and success mean nothing without family and friends."

I roll my eyes, deciding not to explain that he had nothing to do with my decision. "Don't look at me like that.

I'm going. But seriously, you of all people should have been on my side. With the vodka problem and all, work is crazy right now."

"No business," Hayden reminds me.

It's been our one rule since we first started these weekly dinners. We talk business 24/7, but not on Wednesday nights.

I finish my wine and lift my chin to the waitress to bring another drink.

"No business," I agree, doing my best to shove thoughts of vodka and formulas out of my mind. "I'll tell them," I add, looking forward to seeing my family even though I already know I'm in for a tongue-lashing for having stayed away so long. "But if I don't come back, you know where to find me."

"At the bottom of Lake Shohola. You Italians scare me sometimes."

All jokes aside, while I might not be wearing concrete boots by the end of the weekend, there is zero chance I'll make it out of Bridgewater unscathed.

2

CHARI

"*C*heers."

Groaning at my brother's overly cheerful tone, I clink glasses with him anyway. A blast of cold air hits me from behind, and I curse for the millionth time this winter.

"I heard that," Devon says.

"I didn't say a word."

"Yes, you did."

"Who's winning?" the bartender asks my brother. Being one of Devon's good friends, he knows about our current bet, and probably the dozens that came before. It's something we do when we're bored, which apparently happens a lot.

"You seriously have to ask?" I quip.

Mike reaches for an empty beer glass on the bar.

"I don't know, Devon set himself up pretty good on this one."

I try, and fail, not to smile. It's totally true. I might complain about the winter weather every three seconds, but my brother is an infamous man-whore. This is one bet I could win, even if Devon keeps picking the closest seats to the door. Every time it opens, a blast of February air makes me bite my tongue.

My brother's a man-whore, and a sometimes asshole.

But he's also one of my best friends.

"So how exactly do you know Devon isn't having sex?"

That's the deal. I don't complain about the weather. Devon doesn't score a home run with one of his many dates. Whoever breaks first buys the loser a meal. Not very high stakes unless you count bragging rights, which, of course, we do. Of course, it's hilarious to think of Devon bragging about *not* getting laid.

"I trust him."

"Pfft." Mike clearly doesn't think that's such a good idea.

Devon glares at Mike across the bar. "Maybe have my back instead of stabbing it?"

"Maybe have mine and get me a date with your sister."

Mike makes comments like that pretty often, and given that he has an on-again, off-again girlfriend, I'm pretty sure he just does it to rile Devon up. My brother scowls as Mike takes the glass and heads to the tap.

"You are never dating my sister."

I'm not. Mike isn't my type. But that's beside the point. Devon doesn't speak for me, and I'm annoyed that he keeps trying.

"What if I suddenly decide I'm into edgy bartenders covered in tats?" I ask when Mike is out of earshot.

"Not funny."

Dammit. Another blast of cold air hits my back. I should have gone with my gut and stayed home to Netflix instead of dragging myself off the couch a few hours after crashing on it. I love my third graders dearly, but teaching them all week doesn't lend itself to late nights out on Friday.

"I wasn't kidding," I say and then take a sip of my beer.

Devon doesn't know yet, but it's going to be an early night for me. One and done. The only reason I agreed to let him drag me out was because he was coming to The Wheelhouse, which feels a lot like hanging out at home. My brother has already informed me this is just the first stop on this rodeo. He has a long night planned with his friends.

"Let's table that forever," he says. "New topic. Guess who's coming in this weekend?"

"Hmmm?" I try to think of any out-of-towner friends who might be visiting. "No idea. Tell me."

"Hey, Chari. Hey, Devon."

I spin on my stool. Our doctor, also an old family friend. And only two years older than me. Colleen has always been a prodigy. Homeschooled in high school, she was skipping grades and attending medical school when her classmates were still getting drunk every weekend in college.

"Hey, Coll."

I'm tempted to pull her aside and ask her about the smoke I've been smelling lately—Google suggests it might be a brain tumor—but I hesitate, trying to be mindful of the fact that Colleen has no more desire to work on a Friday night than I do.

"You want to ask her," Devon says under his breath. And maybe he doesn't outright laugh, but it's obvious he wants to.

"Seriously, I'm telling you it's true. It happened again last night."

Unlike my brother, I still live at home. But I've resisted the urge to tell my mom about the whole smoke thing. Like Devon, she thinks the only health problem I have is an incurable case of hypochondria. I caved and told him about the smell anyway, something I now regret.

"When I'm in the hospital having brain surgery, you can apologize then."

"Mmm-hmm."

Devon is too busy looking at Colleen's backside to listen.

"You know, she's single again," I taunt, mindful of our bet. Besides, Colleen has had a thing for Devon since, well, forever. It would be cool to see my brother date someone he actually likes.

"Not gonna work."

Ugh, would people stop opening the door? I really need to get out of the Northeast. Bridgewater might be adorable, especially in the fall, and lots of people would probably love to live in a small lakeside town, but every winter the weather seems to get colder and colder.

"I'm not going to say anything about the cold, but can we please move down there?" I point to the other end of the bar, turning my back to the door.

Devon ignores me, ordering yet another drink. If he weren't drinking Angel's Brew, I'd be giving him a lecture right about now, asking about his designated driver for the night. But not anymore. Not thanks to . . .

"Enzo's coming in."

Enzo?

I try not to react. Devon watches me like a hawk, as he always does when his BFF comes up in conversation. And it tends to happen often. The fact that Angel, Inc. was cofounded by someone from our tiny town is basically a daily discussion.

"Wow."

What else is there to say? I haven't seen my former crush in years. Except on the news. Or when I social media stalk him. At least I'm not alone. Pretty much everyone wants to know what Enzo DeLuca is up to.

"Yeah, I know. Cool, right? I haven't seen him since last summer."

"When he flew you to the Bahamas on his partner's family jet?" My brother was so impressed by that jet that he talked about nothing else for weeks afterward. Seemed a bit excessive to me, as if there weren't a million flights from New York to the Bahamas.

Whatever.

"I talked to him last night. He's coming in for the opening."

Which makes sense. His brother Tris is finally opening his restaurant after talking about it for as long as I can remember. Unlike my own family of three, the DeLucas are like their own little gang. Enzo is the only one who moved away permanently. His brothers, Gian and Tris, and his sister, Lusanne, all remain in Bridgewater, most of them working for the family business in some capacity.

How many meals had I eaten at their home, envying their big, joyful family? I'm more than grateful for our own little tribe of three, but there's just something about the DeLucas who have invited us, Mom included, to more meals than I can count.

Something about Enzo.

My brother is watching me closely.

"That'll be fun for you," I choke out. "When's he coming in?"

Another blast of cold, and I know the answer before Devon can say anything. I know it from the way his face lights up. He and Enzo have only seen each other a handful of times since graduating college. Mama DeLuca complains to anyone who asks about her son's fame that it comes with a price. Although Enzo only lives two hours away from Bridgewater, his visits are infrequent.

"Hey, Devon." The smooth, deep voice confirms what I already guessed. It's him.

I don't dare to turn around, preferring rudeness to the mortification of looking at the man I mooned over for most of my childhood. And early adulthood.

Holy hell.

Enzo DeLuca is here, in this bar. Right behind me.

"Is that Chari?" Enzo says, his voice deeper than I remember.

Nope. Not Chari.

Nothing to see here.

I suppose it's time to turn around.

3

ENZO

*C*hari.
Char like charbroiled, and e *like the* y *in baby.*

It might have happened years ago, but I still remember the way she told the new kid at school how to properly pronounce her name. I remember everything about Devon's sister, including the night we helped her celebrate her twenty-first birthday.

She's a hard woman to forget.

As Devon embraces me, I slap my old friend on the shoulder and wait for her to turn around. Her brown hair is longer than it was the last time I saw her. Admittedly, that was three years ago. Our paths didn't cross on my last several visits home, and before that, she was still in graduate school. Avoiding her when I have come home worked well until now. I casually asked Devon if she would be here tonight, and he said no. That she tends to stay home on Fridays.

But I've seen recent pictures of her. I don't have any reason to be caught off guard when she finally swivels on her stool. Doesn't matter—if the twenty-one-year-old Chari was hotter than she should have been for my best friend's little sister, the twenty-nine-year-old is guaranteed to get me into trouble.

She looks like a young Brooke Shields. Full lips, full brows.

Fuck.

Full breasts.

I force myself to appear completely unaffected. Devon, as always, is on high alert. Protecting his sister is one of his oldest habits, something he appears to have held on to despite the fact that Chari is now very much a woman.

"Hello, Enzo."

Standing from her stool, she approaches me with a smile. The kind you give an old friend, not someone you're attracted to. Which is perfect. That's exactly the response I need to get through this weekend.

"It's been ages," she breathes into my ear. As if that isn't enough to make me rock hard, her breasts press full-on against my chest.

"Too long," I admit, stepping back as quickly as humanly possible.

"Were your ears ringing? We were just talking about you."

I don't even get a chance to say anything else before we're completely surrounded. I always hope it will be different here, in my hometown, but in some ways it's worse. Here, the people who come up to me used to treat me like one of them. Now I'm *that guy*.

As graciously as possible, I shake hands and answer questions.

"Yes, it's great to be back home."

"No, Hayden isn't with me."

"Yes, we're still working on a line of liquor. Vodka should be available by the end of next year."

"The poor guy hasn't even made it to the bar," Devon points out finally. Bless him.

"All right, folks, leave him alone," someone shouts from behind the bar.

Pushing through the crowd, I reach out my hand to the bartender. Grasping it, Mike doesn't even ask what I'm drinking. He knows me well, even after so many years.

"On the house."

Moments later, Mike hands me a lager. When I take it, he waves a hand at the crowd behind me, telling them to back off. They know better than to screw with him, and they do as they're told. For now, at least, I can breathe again.

I begin to pull out a stool at the bar and then remember something.

Chari hates the cold.

"Should we move down there?" I point to some open seats at the other end. "Away from the door?"

I don't understand the look that passes between brother and sister, but when Chari bursts out laughing, I have a difficult time not staring. She's still so full of life. So vibrant.

But she's still Devon's younger sister.

"Sure, we can move down there," Devon says, not sounding particularly pleased about it. We head away from the door, and he sits between his sister and me, a calculated move, I'm sure. And probably a good thing. "So, Chari and I have this bet," he says. "She doesn't complain about winter. I don't have sex. Whoever caves first is the big loser."

"Well, unless things have drastically changed around here, I'd say Chari has this one in the bag."

I look at the future victor in question, and wish I hadn't.

She hasn't gotten any less compelling in the last sixty seconds.

"First Mike, now you. Where's the loyalty? Geez." Devon shakes his head. "No faith."

"In your ability to keep it in your pants? You're right. None at all."

Looking past Devon, I apologize belatedly to Chari. "Sorry for the crudeness."

Chari makes a face. "I can assure you, I've heard worse."

I change the subject anyway. "So Devon tells me you're at Bridgewater Elementary?" I know exactly what grade she teaches, but I pretend not to remember. "Fourth grade?"

"Third." And then the damn woman bites her bottom lip. I've seen her do it before, many times, in fact. But it feels different now.

Chari had a crush on me when we were younger, but by the time I realized it, I was already away at college. Then, a few years ago, I'd come home for the weekend on what happened to be Chari's twenty-first birthday. As the night wore on, the strong attraction I felt for her became harder and harder to deny and worried me enough to stay away from here these past few years.

Now here I am, eight years later, pretending I don't know what grade Chari teaches, trying to avoid Devon's eagle eyes.

"Third grade." I whistle. "A huge responsibility."

"Give me a sec." Devon stands up from his stool and steps away to talk to someone across the bar. Which gives me a full-access view of all the ways Chari has changed. She looks much the same, but the confidence that comes with age is evident in the way she sits, the way she holds my gaze. Right now she's dressed casually in jeans and a sweater, but I find myself imagining what she would look like in . . .

"How do you mean?" she asks.

Concentrate. "Third grade. A benchmark year for reading."

I can't help but laugh at her expression.

"Come on, Char, you know I'm not just a pretty face," I tease.

"I know, but still. I'm impressed you know about that."

I'm not eager to share *why* I know. Her brother knows, but I suspect it's one thing he hasn't told her. Before my family moved off the lake to be closer to the shop, we lived only four docks down from the Atwoods. Devon was like a third brother to me. Still is, even though we don't see each other often enough.

There are a lot of things you don't know about me that would impress you.

I don't say it, of course. "Do you like it?"

Taking a sip of beer, she nods. "I do. But it's frustrating too. I feel like I could be helping them more. Like I could have a bigger impact if . . . don't get me started. I'll be on this soapbox all night. And I'm not staying."

The hell she was leaving.

"Oh no. I haven't seen you in what . . ."

Eight years.

". . . in years. You're not going home."

Chari nods behind me. When I turn around, no less than ten people look away.

"You have enough of a fan club here," she says. "Not to mention Devon, who is pretty pumped to see you."

At the moment it looks as if Devon is pretty pumped to be in an entirely different conversation on the other side of the bar with a woman I don't recognize at first.

"Is that Colleen Karim? Isn't she a doctor now?"

"Yes. And yes."

"Looks like you might win that bet sooner than later. What did you bet, anyway?"

"Dinner." She smirks as she says it, but then something changes in her face and she looks down to her lap.

"That must seem silly to you. Someone with . . ." She stops.

I hate this part of my new life. Hate it. Of course I'm grateful for everything success has brought to me, but there's a flip side to the coin of fortune. I can't sit in my hometown bar without being stared at, my conversations overheard and analyzed. And a woman who was once a close friend now feels uncomfortable around me. But if I complained about any of that, I'd be laughed out of the bar.

"Please don't feel weird around me."

Chari looks toward the taps, her gaze narrowing on a familiar logo.

"But it's so strange. That's you. Your beer. I mean, it's crazy, Enzo."

It's the first time she's said my name tonight, and it sends a ripple through me.

"It's definitely a little bit crazy."

"A little? More than a little. You create an alcohol antidote that lets people sober up before they get behind the wheel. They say your company has saved something like a bazillion lives already. And it's just 'a little bit crazy'?"

How many times has someone asked how that makes me feel? Five hundred? A thousand? But this time, I give a real answer, not the kind of canned response favored by our PR team. Even though our success and the impact we've made *is* incredibly humbling, I'm sick of saying so.

"It's more than a bit crazy," I admit. "But there are days I wish I'd just graduated as a chemist and worked for a pharma company somewhere. Maybe back here."

She looks at me like I've lost it. People tend to think money and success negates a person's capability for self-doubt, but it's not true.

"And here I thought I was the only one who wondered about my career choice."

There is something dark behind Chari's laugh, an emotion she's trying to mask with humor. I shouldn't want to know what it is, but uncovering that mystery is suddenly the most important thing in the world. Unfortunately, unraveling it will have to wait.

"Sorry about that. I had to." Devon looks between Chari and me. "Talk to someone."

I can't resist ribbing him. "Ah," I say. "Is that what they call it these days in Bridgewater?"

"In fact, yes, they do," Chari says, her eyes sparkling. "What do they call it in New York?"

"They call it 'dipping the stinger in the honey.'"

Chari's laugh is worth the look Devon gives me. Some habits die hard, and apparently acting like a seventh grader is something I still do outside of Manhattan. Despite the looks and whispers around us, I feel comfortable here. Relaxed.

It's good to be home.

Or, more precisely, to be here in this bar, talking to Devon and Chari Atwood.

4

CHARI

"*T*ell me everything."

Lisa leans forward and looks at the other side of The Wheelhouse as if it's the scene of a crime. We're in what I call the daylight half. The ground floor is split into two—part bar, part bakery and deli. And it's always busy, especially in the spring and summer, once the old waterwheel next to us begins to turn again. On one end of Bridgewater lies a lake. The other, a river that cuts through the edge of the downtown. And while the huge wheel encased in wood just outside the window where we sit isn't actually used to produce power anymore, the owner of the building stills turns it on after the last thaw. Ambiance and all.

I was practically raised here. The husband and wife who own the building rent my mother the space upstairs for her souvenir shop. Usually, I'm as relaxed at this table overlooking the river as I am at home. But not today. Not after last night.

Bridgewater isn't a huge town. One main street. A handful of restaurants and bars, some closer to town and others along the nearby lake. But there's only one bakery. It's not far-fetched to think—to hope—Enzo might come by this morning, which is why I can't take my eyes from the door.

"I had no idea he was coming home," I tell my best friend since kindergarten.

Tall, blonde, and incredibly kind, Lisa is the one person in this town everyone, literally everyone, likes. Including me. And my brother, despite the fact that their brief hookup in high school didn't go swimmingly well.

I did warn her.

"Who would have guessed? I mean, how long has it been?"

"Years since I've seen him."

I reach for the ketchup, but Lisa pulls it away before I can grab it.

"Just try it without any. All I'm asking is for you to do it once. For me."

I grab the bottle back.

"Not even for you."

Squeezing a pool of red gold onto my plate, I prepare to dip my scrambled eggs, much to Lisa's chagrin. You'd think she would give up on trying to refine my food tastes. Eggs without ketchup? No, thank you. I might as well eat her broccoli and mushroom egg white omelette. Yuck.

"So? What happened?" she presses, looking away from my plate.

What happened, indeed? Just thinking of it gives me goose pimples from head to toe.

"You know, we talked a bit. He was swarmed by an adoring crowd. And then I left."

Lisa blinks rapidly, daring me to stop there.

"Okay. Long version. I nearly died when he said my

name. He sat two stools away from me and I could still smell him."

"You could *smell* him. Seriously?"

"He hugged me. And I may have breathed in too deeply. His scent never really left me."

A rich, sensual musk that I can smell even now if I close my eyes. I can see his face too. Dark hair, dark perfectly arched brows, deep brown eyes that seem to stare into your soul . . .

"You have a really weird look on your face," she muses.

I'm sure I do.

"Anyway, he asked about my job. We chatted for a bit and then Devon came back, so I left them alone to catch up."

"I see."

"How can I fall right back into crushing on him in one damn hour? Seriously. I'm much more worldly than I was back then."

She tilts her head. "Are you really?"

I think about the fact that I never left Bridgewater, even after promising myself I would not end up here. But Mom needs me, so here I stay.

"Yes, very much so," I lie.

"I'm not sure about that. But you are a total babe." Lisa shovels a mouthful of omelette before continuing. "Even if you won't get out of your own way when it comes to men."

Unlike Lisa, who is semi-attached at the moment, I am still single after more failed relationships than I'd care to admit. "Not this again."

She shrugs. "All I'm saying is there's no use pining for Enzo DeLuca unless you change your ways. Even if you guys did date, you'd break up with him just like all of the others."

Lisa accuses me of self-sabotage when it comes to my

love life. And maybe she's right. But it hardly matters when it comes to Enzo. He's so out of the question it's not even funny.

"Well, there's no need to worry. There's literally zero chance of that happening."

Lisa's eyes widen. "Oh?"

"Devon would kill me. Or him. He's only in town for the weekend, and he probably won't be back for another year. Let me see if there's anything else. Oh. Yeah. He's not interested me."

"You're sure?"

"Positive. He was exactly like you see him on the news. Cool. Collected. Polite. Not much evidence of the old Enzo."

"The old Enzo?"

Lisa has a way of making me talk a ton more than she does. Or maybe I'm just a blabbermouth. Yes, that's probably it.

"You know, the less stuffy, joking-around version. The non-bazillionaire Enzo."

The guy I knew from our childhood and the one I see in interviews are definitely two different people. I'm not sure how I feel about the new one, but it doesn't really matter. The last thing I should do is get hung up on either Enzo. Again.

"So that's it?" she says disbelievingly. "End of story?"

I finally dip my eggs into the red pool of yumminess and eat. "Mmm-hmm," I mumble.

"So, like, if he walked in here right now, no big deal? You wouldn't care at all?"

Washing down the eggs with my coffee, I don't even bother to answer. She can't goad me into saying more.

"The guy you had a major crush on for, like, most of your life, who you haven't seen in years, comes home in all his glorious, wealthy sexiness and no biggie? Is that what you're saying?"

"Yes, that's what I'm saying."

And, just like last night, I can tell from the look on Lisa's face that he's behind me. Only this is an entirely different expression from the one my brother had. Instead of *My buddy is here!* this one is more like *You're about to be proven wrong.*

I might have been staring at the door earlier, hoping he'd come in, but the truth is I'm not ready for it. Not again. This town is too damn small for a man like Enzo.

"He's here," I whisper frantically. "Isn't he?"

"Yep," she says, her smile firming up.

"What's he doing?"

The Wheelhouse Bakery & Deli is not a huge place. If he's standing across from her, she can probably see what he's doing.

"He's buying bagels, I think."

My heart pounds in my chest. Do I turn around? Pretend I don't know he's here? Just keep eating?

"So he's not staying?" I hiss in an undertone.

"No, I don't think so."

My internal freak-out kicks up a notch, and part of me wants to spring up from my chair and drag him over. To force him to stay.

Get a grip, Chari. Two days ago, Enzo DeLuca was as far from your mind as warm weather is from Bridgewater.

But now, after his sudden appearance last night . . .

"We meet again."

Lisa looks like she's going to spit out her coffee. But she doesn't, thank God. The last thing I need is for him to guess we've been talking about him. I remind myself to keep it cool in the face of . . . what? Enzo isn't a dating prospect. He's Devon's friend. A total big shot.

And he's standing beside our table.

"Morning, Enzo," I say, matching his cool tone.

"Still eating eggs with ketchup?"

Still breaking girls' hearts? I want to ask.

Literally every woman in the place—young, old, doesn't matter—is staring at him. Oh God, my view is exactly in line with the bulge in his jeans. Look up, Chari. I home in on his Steelers sweatshirt instead. I've seen plenty of televised interviews of Enzo, and he's always wearing a suit—the complete opposite of the casual attire he has on now. Both looks are equally as sexy, but this one doesn't mark him as a multi-bazillionaire. It makes him more approachable, somehow.

"Still waving that terrible towel? I'd have thought you'd be a Giants or Jets fan by now. New Yorker and all."

"Are you kidding?" he says with a grin. "A DeLuca never changes teams. Loyalty, girl."

I swallow.

"Sorry. Woman. You're certainly no longer a girl, Chari."

His words send a rush of heat through me, but he has already moved on to greeting Lisa, as polite and charming as if he'd taken etiquette classes his whole life. "Good morning, Lisa."

"Hi, Enzo. Good to see you."

"Same to you."

He glances back at me. "Gotta get these bagels back to the shop. You coming tonight?"

He means the soft opening of his brother's restaurant, DeLuca's II. Unlike the original shop that his dad owns, which only has three tables and does mostly takeout, DeLuca's II is a straight-up Italian restaurant. On the casual side, but very much an upgrade on the original. With prime real estate right on the lake.

Tristano DeLuca has been talking about it for years. It was rumored Enzo gave him the building for Christmas. But when I asked Devon if it were true, he responded with, "No comment." I had to wrest it from him later that Enzo did indeed buy Tris the building.

"I heard the guest list is small. A very private affair."

Enzo opens his mouth ever so slightly, making it impossible not to stare at his lips. "You heard correctly."

As a long-time family friend, I was invited, but my flirting skills are subpar at best, and I find myself saying, "But since you invited me . . ."

His brows rise in a perfect imitation of some old-time Hollywood actor. "Did I, now?"

"*You coming tonight?*" I repeat. "To some, that might sound like an invitation." I look at Lisa, who looks about ready to burst into laughter. "Did that sound like an invitation to you?"

Elbow on the table, chin in hand, she looks up at the most gorgeous man on this entire planet.

"Yeah, it kinda did. Sorry, Enzo."

Last night, aside from asking me, twice, to stay, he didn't seem fussed or flustered. I'd lain in bed hours after leaving the bar, picturing his expression, scrutinizing every word. And had come to the conclusion he thought of me the same way he always had, as Devon's little sister.

But the chill that shoots up my back now tells a different story. Still calm and cool as you please, despite the fact that everyone is staring. But with just a tinge of . . . something more.

"Nothing to be sorry for, Lisa. It was an invitation. And one I very much hope Chari will accept."

His eyes never stray from mine.

Good lord. He's so hot it should be a criminal offense.

"Of course I'll be there," I say. "Wouldn't miss it."

My words sound casual, if not my tone, which I'll take as a win. Because honestly, I'm finding it hard to put a coherent thought together.

"Good."

He winks.

Which isn't that unusual. Enzo DeLuca has winked at girls before. He even winked at me when we were younger. So why does this time feel different?

Because I'm losing it, that's why.

"See you tonight."

"Later, Lisa. Hope you can make it too," he calls over his shoulder as he heads out. People flock toward him, some bold enough to ask questions, others just there to watch. I even catch one person snapping a photo. I can't imagine living like that, under such constant scrutiny.

"What. The hell. Was that?" Lisa says.

Her words start to wake me from my stupor. I blink rapidly, then say, "Your omelette is getting cold."

"You're talking about my *omelette*?" She lowers her voice, perhaps remembering we're in a public restaurant, one Enzo might not have left yet. "As your best friend for life, I'm going to say one thing and then we can drop it."

This should be good.

"Either you totally lied or are so out of practice you really don't realize it, but Enzo DeLuca wants to fuck the ever-loving shit out of you."

I should not be excited by her words.

"And you are obviously not 'over' your crush," she whispers, "even if you did a decent job of hiding it."

"That was two things," I point out.

Lisa looks over my shoulder, presumably at the topic of our conversation, and then glances back at me. Was he gone? Or was he still surrounded by legions of hangover-less fans of Angel's Brew and Angel Pale Ale and Angel Red Wine and every other Angel product he'd put out over the past few years?

"One thing, two things. Whatever. Either way, you'd better figure your shit out by tonight, because I think you'll have a decision on your hands."

"Which is?"

"How ready are you to get back in the saddle?"

We both know my last breakup was harsh enough for me to swear off men for a long, long time. But this is different. This is Enzo.

"Doesn't matter," I say, and try to believe it. "He's leaving Sunday."

"But he's still around tonight," she suggests, wagging her eyebrows up and down.

"Yeah, and a one-night stand with one of my brother's best friends is a brilliant idea."

"Suit yourself. But I, for one, am looking forward to the opening tonight. Hey, are you eating those home fries?"

I shake my head, not able to think about home fries. Or food. Or anything except the man whose name I can still hear being whispered around us.

"An interesting night indeed," I finally agree.

5

ENZO

"Get out of the kitchen and go greet guests," my father demands of me. Demands, because my dad has never once *asked* for something in his life. And my brothers and I learned long ago never to question him.

I don't start now.

"Just making sure he doesn't screw up the sauce."

Tris glares at me, like I can help the fact that his sauce isn't as good as mine.

"Good thing Dad is back here to maintain quality control," I tease.

My brother ignores my parting shot. Our father did something tonight I can't ever remember him doing before —he closed the pizza shop. And to think I almost missed this . . .

"C'mon, pretty boy," our brother Gian says. "The place is filling up."

Gian's twenty-seven, the youngest of my brothers. Only Lusanne is younger than him. Being with my siblings feels right in a deep way, and it makes me regret being away from home for so long. I've seen them, of course, but we haven't all been together since the crazy family cruise I took them on in September. I was traveling for work over Thanksgiving and Christmas, but Lusanne and Tris visited me for New Year's weekend, and Gian came to see me last month. I like wining and dining my siblings when they visit New York, but there's something different about being home. About being together at the same time in the place we grew up.

Still, what choice do I have? Building a business empire is no easy task.

"What's wrong?" Gian asks as we step out of the kitchen.

"Nothing," I say. "Just happy to be here."

He nods as if he knew it, and he probably did. Gian, the only other member of the family who doesn't work for the family business, at least not exclusively, is also the best at reading my moods. Growing up I was closest with Lusanne, but Gian is the most sensitive of my siblings. He can read people like no one else.

The place really has filled up since I went into the kitchen. Mom and Lusanne stand by the door, greeting guests. They're like carbon copies of each other, one just younger than the other. I scan the room.

She's not here yet.

People start to notice me.

"Come on, let's hit the deck," I say to Gian.

It's a beautiful property, the enclosed deck opening to a full view of Lake Shohola. A temporary bar is set up along one side, big white lights dangling from the ceiling.

I lead the way to the bar.

"Shouldn't we greet guests?" Gian asks.

"They'll find us out here. Trust me." It's fairly empty at the moment, but I know it won't stay that way for long. I saw the stares, the whispers behind barely raised hands.

"I don't know how you can stand it."

Gian met us out the night before, plus he's witnessed me being mobbed in New York and even on the cruise last year. My life can hardly be described as normal anymore.

Angel, Inc. started with a sophomore discovery in college, something I managed tinkering around in the lab. A tasteless chemical is added at the very end of the brewing process. Later, a pill antidote reacts with this chemical to reverse the alcohol's effects on the body. Hayden pushed for us to patent and sell it, and his father gave us financing. Years of testing and licensing followed. FDA approval. Then finally, our first line of products, Angel's Brew, hit the market. We started in the Northeast, but it quickly spread nationwide. Now, we're going international. When we added wine to our offerings two years ago, things got even more out of control.

I could have never imagined Angel, Inc. the day that I first told my professor and Hayden about my findings. But here we are, and there's no going back.

"Celebrities have it much worse," I suggest.

Gian looks at me like I'm crazy.

"Two Angel lagers," I order, the bartender smiling at us.

"What if I want something else?"

It's a familiar joke—Gian always ribs me about drinking my own beer, but I just grin. "Are you driving home?"

Gian drove us here, so I know he has his car.

"Smug bastard."

I take the beers and hand one to my brother. "Just drink it, asshole."

Music floats out from inside. Tris hired musicians for the evening; it's a nice touch.

"I'm proud of all of you," I say, hit by an unexpected wave of nostalgia. Gian's marketing knowledge came in handy for the opening, and I'm glad he's still in Bridgewater so Dad and Tris have someone they can count on. I can imagine standing in the pizza shop, surrounded by my siblings, as this exact song blasted from the speaker near the ovens. We all worked before it was legal, but I never minded. Except on Fridays during Lent, when the line went out the door and going out with friends wasn't even remotely possible.

"Which is it? Are you proud of me, or am I an asshole?"

Gian and I walk toward the end of the deck. Normally there would be tables out here, but Tris put them in storage for the opening to give people room to mingle. They're sending around finger food, the soft opening more of a reception than a sit-down dinner.

"Both," I answer, wondering if she has arrived yet. Trying not to think about it. "He was smart to cover this," I say, tapping the temporary plexiglass coverings that serve as temporary walls lining the deck. Although not completely impervious to the elements, the deck boasts several space heaters, making it almost as warm as the restaurant inside.

"I still can't believe this is happening."

Neither can I. After three years of offering Tris money and being refused, I finally bought this place without his permission. He was pissed, of course. He'd been looking closer to town. This is a much more desirable location, though, and it'll definitely be more profitable. Something he knows, of course, but like the rest of my stubborn Italian family, Tris wanted to make it on his own. It was only after I explained that giving him this property was as much for me as it was for him that my brother finally agreed to take it.

If I can't always be there in person, at least I can do something important with the oodles of money I've earned and don't have time to enjoy.

"He's going to kill it," I say.

"There you are."

We turn, my gaze shooting to Devon before taking in the rest of the guests spilling onto the deck behind us.

"Hey, Dev," I say, sticking out my hand. "How's it going?"

Devon shakes Gian's hand too. If nothing else, I know how to pick my friends. Devon Atwood is a hell of a guy.

Did your sister come with you?

I want to ask, but he'll see right through me. And I'm trying not to flirt with Chari, right? If that's my objective, I'm not off to a great start after this morning.

How can I help it?

She's all at once as adorable as a ten-week-old kitten and so fucking sexy. So unassuming. So different from the women I meet these days.

"Earth to Enzo." Gian is watching me.

"Sounds like a TV show," Devon says.

And maybe it's crazy, but I have to know if she's here.

"Hold the fort out here, you guys. I'm going to check on Mom and Lus. I'll be right back."

I don't wait for a response. Greeting the gathering crowd on the deck as I walk by, I enter the main dining room and look around. Nothing. Loads of people, but no brown-haired beauties. At least, none that I want to talk to tonight. But I have no choice. So I make small talk. Answer questions. Ask Mom if she wants me to hang out by the door with her. Get shoved away by my sister, who says I'm too intimidating.

Whatever the hell that means.

I need another drink.

And then I finally see her near the kitchen door.

She's dressed in a long-sleeved cream dress. From here it looks like lace, but as she moves toward the crowd, I realize the dress just gives that appearance. I head to the bar and order two beers and head over to greet her. So much for playing it cool.

"Saved you the trouble." I hand her one of the beers. "Did you come alone?"

Since she didn't arrive with her brother, I assumed she would be with Lisa or her mom.

"Nope, I came with Devon. Just ran into the kitchen to congratulate Tris."

She's always been thoughtful like that.

"Why isn't he out here?" she asks, then takes a sip of the beer. My beer.

"You know him. Tris is more comfortable in the kitchen than out here greeting guests. I told him he'll have to come out every once in a while since he's the owner. Poor guy turned pale when I suggested he give a speech tonight."

I look toward the door. "Is your mom here?"

Chari and Devon are incredibly close to their mother, so I'm surprised not to see her.

"She sends her regrets. She woke up with a sore throat this morning and feels like crap. Looks like it too. I feel really bad for her."

"Sorry to hear it."

With the gentle buzz of conversation around us, music playing in the corner, there's an atmosphere of celebration. Chari is all smiles, and I'm pretty sure I am too. If we were still kids, that would be the end of the story—two friends enjoying a fun night out.

But we're not kids. Not anymore.

Chari is a full-grown woman, and I'm very much attracted to her.

And something has changed tonight. She's no longer

looking at me like her brother's friend. So last night's veil of indifference toward me was a front. Interesting.

We're at a stalemate.

If she were any other woman, I wouldn't hesitate. By the end of the night, her perfectly applied maroon lipstick would be a distant memory. Neither of us would have to wonder if our sexual tension was as off the charts as it felt at this moment.

That cream dress would sit in a heap on the floor, alongside every other piece of clothing we're both wearing.

"There you are."

Ah, there it is—the very reason I can't do or say what I want to Chari has come up behind me, breaking the spell.

"Found your sister," I say to Devon as if any other topic in the world were more interesting. Her expression, soft and inviting just a few seconds ago, morphs into confusion. I don't blame her. I'm confused as hell too.

"Cool. Hey, Char, how's Mom?"

I don't even excuse myself, knowing Devon will get suspicious soon if I keep dodging him. But who could have guessed how awkward this situation with his sister would be?

Maybe me. And I probably should have. Seeking out Chari will actively ruin one of my oldest friendships, and I knew it even as I walked toward her tonight. And in The Wheelhouse this morning.

There's no way this plays out well, and I can tell by Chari's face she knows it too. Looking forward all day to seeing her, stupid. Seeking her out tonight, just as stupid. I've been playing with fire, and this is the kind of fire that could get us both burned.

For the rest of the night, I'll talk to Chari as I would any other person in the room. Cordially. Sociably. Not like I want to jump her bones at any second. I'm not some kind of animal that I can't accomplish this. It's one night. Tomorrow, I'll be back in New York.

But first I need another drink.

6

CHARI

*T*his night is not turning out how I expected. But it's probably for the best.

"Hey, sorry I'm late." Lisa freezes when she sees my face. "Uh-oh. Come with me."

I follow her to the back of the restaurant, toward a set of stairs. We walk down a few steps and stop.

DeLuca's II is going to be a smashing success. All night people have been complimenting the decor, the food. The enclosed deck is beautiful, the whole place, packed. And everyone seems to be having a fantastic time. Everyone except me.

"This isn't necessary."

I can barely see Lisa's face. The stairs are dark, the only light from the bustling restaurant and half-closed door above us.

"Yes, it is. I know that look."

My eye roll is probably wasted on her on the dim stairs. Or maybe not, given what she says next.

"You can pretend to everyone else, but I was there when you tried on like ten dresses."

"Three," I correct her, still sipping the beer Enzo brought me.

"Okay, three. So what happened?"

"Exactly nothing. It must have been my imagination run wild this morning. He is exactly like I remember him. Nice. Funny. Easy to talk to. Incredibly sexy."

I can see enough of her face to detect a smile.

"OK, I guess the sexy one is new. I mean, he was always hot, but there's something about his confidence that really . . ."

"You're getting off topic."

"My point is that we were wrong."

Lisa shakes her head. "I don't think so. I know what flirting looks like, and Enzo was full-on flirting with you this morning."

Another sip.

"Maybe he changed his mind? Maybe he remembered he doesn't need to flirt with a country bumpkin. I'm sure he has legions of women who fall at his feet in New York."

"You are not a country bumpkin."

Except that I kind of am. And Lisa is too, but I don't tell her that.

"OK, I'm a sophisticated socialite who also happens to be a teacher from a small town in Pennsylvania. You're totally right."

"I thought you said you were worldly?"

I have to smile at that despite the pit in my stomach.

"I lied." And I'm about to do it again. I'm about to tell Lisa that I really don't need to be down here, huddled on the stairs, talking it out. I survived just fine without Enzo before this weekend, and can do so again when he leaves tomorrow.

"Everything all right down there?"

Even in the dark, I can see the whites of Lisa's eyes as they widen.

"It's him," she whispers.

As if it could be anyone else. I start to walk up the stairs, but I don't make it more than a couple of steps before Lisa tugs on my wrist, stopping me. Which is when she vaults ahead of me, racing up the stairs like it's the first day of spring and our annual *let's start running* phase, something that usually lasts no longer than four days before we decide to go get our nails done instead.

I start to follow her, but there's an exchange of hushed voices at the top of the steps, and suddenly a very clear new scent is heading toward me. Masculine hotness, otherwise known as Enzo, makes his way down the stairs.

"Uh, hi," I say. Because if I had any cool, it has long since burned away.

"I didn't mean to break up the party."

Did Enzo buy that new deep baritone voice with all his millions of dollars? I don't remember him sounding quite so . . .

"It's okay. Just a bit noisy up there. Lisa and I . . ." Are what? Spies? I have no good excuse to be down here. ". . . needed to talk privately."

He takes another step down toward me. And although it's still dark down here, my eyes have adjusted enough for me to see half of his face. And his eyes.

The glint in them has me waffling back to *I think he's flirting with me.*

He nods toward the basement below us. "The downstairs is for private catering. Wanna see it?"

There's a lot I'd like to see at the moment, but the

catering room isn't top on my list. Still, it will give us the chance to be alone together. For me to maybe figure out whether this is all in my head.

"Sure."

Enzo takes another step until he's directly next to me, so close our bodies nearly touch. The look he gives me practically sizzles, but I can't help but wonder if that's just wishful thinking. I have zero confidence in my ability to read him. The next thing I know, he's on the step below me, flipping a switch and illuminating half of the room.

"It's gorgeous."

Sliding glass doors lead out to a dock ending in the lake. The interior isn't fancy, but it's very comfortable. Exactly the opposite of what you'd expect from a characterless catering room. Old-time black and white family photos line the walls, and some of the furniture looks like it belongs in a living room instead of a catering space.

"You should see the view." He walks toward the glass doors, through the part of the space that's still dark.

"Is there another light back here?" I ask, joining him.

"Yes, but you can't see the lake very well when it's on."

We're at ground level now, lights from the deck above illuminating just enough of the patio for me to imagine how stunning this spot will be in the summer. More lights dot the area round the lake, though fewer than there'll be in a couple of months.

"How do you know?" I blurt before thinking better of it.

Enzo takes a sip of his beer. "Tris videoed me in for a tour when he bought the place."

Or when Enzo bought it for him.

"He's done an amazing job," he continues.

I agree. "Will your dad miss him at the shop?"

Enzo sighs, and I catch myself staring at his profile. I may have crap taste in boyfriends, but I'll give myself one thing. I know a good-looking man when I see one. All of the DeLuca boys are lady-killers, of course, but Enzo was always the one who held my eye . . .

"I'm sure he will. But things change. People grow up. Move on."

"Are you talking about Tris, or yourself?"

He turns toward me, and my attention narrows further, focusing on him. The line of his nose, his dark brows, and those eyes.

"Both."

The air crackles between us. This time, I know I'm not wrong. Friends do not look at each other like they'd prefer to be naked in bed together over socializing in an empty room of a restaurant.

"We should probably get back upstairs," he says, but I can tell he doesn't really want to do it.

So many possible responses come to mind.

Why?

Let's not.

How about we find a dark corner and make some bad decisions?

"Devon will be looking for us," he presses.

So that's it. My brother.

Fuck it. You don't get what you want by being a wallflower. Look at Enzo. He's a prime example of what a person can accomplish if they go after what they want and make it happen.

"You're worried about what he'll think?" I ask.

Enzo is standing too damn close for me to think straight.

"Nah. But you know Devon likes to be first at everything.

He'll be pissed if he finds out you saw the downstairs before him."

Which is totally true. I could never even get on the bus first without my brother pushing me behind him. The car, the stairs. Always Devon first.

But is he seriously worried about that? Is it possible I've read this wrong? A moment of panic steals over me before I notice his grin.

He's teasing me.

His shrug is an admission. "I'm not sure what he'll think. About showing you around, I mean."

Oh God.

Enzo moves toward me, and my entire body is aware of his proximity. I need to get a grip, but it's becoming increasingly difficult with every step he takes.

"When we were kids, you used to stick up for me," I say. And he did. He used to insist on the *ladies first* rule, not that Devon ever listened.

"We're not kids anymore, Chari."

No shit, Sherlock. "But that doesn't mean you can't still stick up for me."

My meaning is as clear as his: Enzo is worried about my brother's reaction to *us*; I'm not.

Their friendship is a totally different relationship than whatever is happening between us. I should say all of this, but my mouth refuses to open.

"I will always stick up for you." He takes another step, and now we're really, really close. "Always."

"Um, Chari," a voice calls. "Enzo?"

It's Lisa.

"Tris is about to give a speech."

The moment is over. And make no mistake, it was a

moment. I thought I wanted to kiss Enzo before, years ago. But now I want him to ravage me, the thought so over-whelming I can't even muster a response to Lisa.

"We're coming up," Enzo says. But then he leans in and whispers in my ear, "We aren't done here."

7

ENZO

*W*hen I'm at work, I'm thinking of work. End of story. Or at least that used to be the case. But this afternoon, as I wait for my five o'clock appointment to arrive, I find myself thinking of Chari. Of the look in her eyes on those stairs. Of her sweet mouth, opening ever so slightly. *We aren't done here*, I'd promised her. And I'd meant it, all the way. Only, Chari had called to check in with her mom after Tris's speech, and apparently Mrs. Atwood was burning up. Her new boyfriend was around—her new *doctor* boyfriend—but both Chari and Devon took off to see to her.

Apparently neither of them trust the guy. Based on what my brothers and sister knew, the boyfriend's reputation doesn't warrant their concern, but I didn't get a chance to talk to them about it.

"Excuse me, sir. Your five o'clock appointment is here."

I swivel my leather chair around as my executive assistant waits for a response.

"Send him in."

Standing to greet the visitor, I'm surprised when Hayden strolls into my office instead. He's rarely in the building. I've asked him more than once why we even pay for him to have an office. Being "stuck in here," despite having one of the best views in the city, is as painful to him as sitting through college classes. He enjoys roaming free, contributing to Angel, Inc. "out in the field." Which is fine by me. The guy gets it done.

"You're not my five o'clock."

"Nope, I'm not." Hayden heads for the refrigerator concealed in the wall behind me. "You can thank me later."

Grabbing a bottle of water, he closes the fridge and sits on one of the chairs overlooking Manhattan's West Side. There's a conversation area set up over there, with a few chairs and a coffee table, for more casual meetings.

"While you finished your call, I held your meeting in the waiting room."

"You're saying you met with the FDA's Associate Director of Regulatory Affairs, in the lobby, for all of"—I look at my watch—"five minutes. And he's already gone?"

"Until next year. Who sets up a meeting at five o'clock anyway?"

Looking more than a little pleased with himself, Hayden guzzles down the water. Water, at five o'clock. This despite the fact that we own an alcohol company and my business partner lives for happy hour. Or lived for happy hour, past tense.

This new Hayden—the family man—is hard to get used to. But I'll give him one thing. No one can sweet-talk a client or federal regulator like Hayden. Or Ada.

I smile at that particular memory, the first time he and his wife met. Until I look more closely at Hayden's expression. "So are you taking the rest of my meetings tomorrow too?"

"I'll take your meetings, sure. Tomorrow, and for the rest of the week."

Yep, I'm right. Hayden wants something.

"Spill it. What do you want?"

I can see he's looking for an angle, some way to spin this, so I cut him short. "Why don't you save both of us time and cut to the chase?"

"All right, then I'll just ask. Switzerland, later this month."

I know where this is going. "No. I can't go. Hayden, with the vodka giving us problems . . ."

Why doesn't he argue with me? It's as if he has an ace up his sleeve.

"If we're going to get it to market by next summer, I need to get the kinks in the formula worked out . . . Why do you look smug as shit?"

"My father-in-law needs a bypass, so we had to move the christening up. We tried for this weekend or next, but no dice."

Ah fuck. "Let me guess. You rescheduled for the weekend you're supposed to be in Switzerland?"

Hayden shrugs.

Ace in the hole. Family trumps my busy schedule, something we agreed to early on.

I heave a sigh. "What day is the meeting?"

"Friday the 26th. I'd planned to fly out to Zurich on a red-eye Wednesday night, stop over in Lucerne to take meetings, and then drive south for the launch."

Which would make it a five-day trip.

"You'll have to take all of my meetings," I say, having already given up.

"Done."

"Including MCM." The largest liquor distributor in the U.S. The owner's a total dickhead.

He scrunches his nose a little, as if smelling something foul, but he nods. "Done."

"You're killing me, you know that, right?"

He just comes over and claps me on the back. "Thanks, partner. By the way, how was PA? Sorry I was offline all weekend. I saw the pics—looks like DeLuca's II is off to a great start. Did you tell Mama DeLuca why I couldn't make it?"

"It went extremely well. And Mom says hi."

"So what's wrong?"

Most of the time I love that Hayden and I are like brothers. But at times it would be nice to have a little separation between business and personal life. In business, I'm known for my poker face. But it's never worked with Hayden.

What the hell? If I can't tell him, then who? If I'm being honest, I've wanted to tell someone.

"Chari Atwood is what's wrong."

He's never met Chari, but of course he knows about her, from Devon and also from me. From the role she inadvertently, and unknowingly, played in Angel, Inc.

"Talk to me."

I need a drink for this. Standing, I uncork a bottle of wine from the minibar and pour a glass, not even asking if Hayden wants one. He hates wine almost as much as he does asparagus.

"It was brutal."

"An interesting choice of words."

"She sent flowers to the restaurant. Was the only person to go into the kitchen to congratulate Tris before he came out. She teaches third graders, and my sister says no one does it better."

"So your former crush is basically Mother Teresa. How nice."

"I'm thirty-one years old," I growl. "I don't crush."

"Maybe you can convince everyone else you don't have a soft spot for Chari Atwood, but you can't lie to me."

"I'm not denying it, you ass," I say, bringing my wine over and sitting across from him at the window. "I'm telling you about the weekend, aren't I?"

Hayden leans forward. "So spit it out."

I shrug.

"She is so fucking hot it took every ounce of self-control not to beg the woman to let me fuck her brains out. Is that better?"

"A bit," he says, his lips tipping up. "Yes."

"And I think she felt the same way."

"Think? Man, you're losing your touch."

"She and Devon left the opening early. Their mom was sick."

"And?"

"And nothing," I say, wishing I had something more to tell him. "On Sunday, my family went to Mass and then breakfast. And then I drove back."

"Your mom must have loved that."

"The whole family going to Mass together? More than the fact that her son successfully opened his own restaurant." I smile, knowing it's not an exaggeration.

"So you didn't even talk to Chari?"

"Not really. We didn't get much past small talk. There was a moment when it seemed like something might happen, but it never got off the ground."

"Because?"

I roll my eyes. "Because Devon."

"You think he'd be pissed?"

I've thought of nothing else since walking into that bar on Friday night.

"If I screwed his little sister? I'm thinking yes."

Hayden goes quiet. And then, "So, what if you dated her?"

I was lifting my glass for a sip, and my hand freezes in midair. Hayden knows I don't date. Go on dates, yes. But relationships? Not since college. Not with a soon-to-be international business to run.

I lower my glass and say, "You know I don't have time for a relationship. At least one of us needs to actually be available at all times."

Hayden's hand flies to his chest, as if wounded. But my comment didn't shut him down. "Be real," he says. "You don't have time, or you won't make time?"

"Hayden," I warn.

"I'm just saying."

"Switzerland is our European test market," I remind him. "Something we've been after for two years. This is huge."

I don't finish the thought because it's not necessary. Hayden understands. If I had a family too, I wouldn't be able to cover for him in Switzerland. He's tied down, which is fine, but I'm not so sure the business can keep growing, keep expanding, if both of us had a family to put first. Not that I blame him or hold a grudge. We've been down this road before, and both of us are fully aware of my inability to delegate. Besides, my time may come too.

Someday, but not yet.

Hayden stands up. "Well, if that's the way you feel, appears you're stuck between a rock and a hard place."

"Yeah, no kidding."

"Glad I could be of assistance."

I stare at him incredulously as he saunters toward the door. "Are you serious? I'm going to Switzerland, and you gave me jack in the way of advice. Useless."

"As if you'd take my advice."

In matters of women? He's probably right.

He turns in the doorway, smirking. "There's always Wednesday. Thanks, Enz."

As the door shuts behind him, I figure out his meaning. Wednesday. Giovanna. Or someone like her, to take off the edge.

It's not terrible advice, but I hate the idea, which tells me I'm in even more trouble than I thought.

8

CHARI

"*M*om home?"

Devon plops onto the couch next to me.

"Nope. Out with *him* again."

While I haven't fully convinced Devon my concerns are valid, I'm not the only one who's slightly on edge about Mom's new boyfriend. Of course I want her to be happy, but she has a terrible track record with men.

Maybe I don't get to have an opinion on that—glass houses, and whatnot—but she did marry my dad, and he cheated on her and then up and left without ever sending Devon or me a birthday card, and we were still kids. Not even tweens yet. And this guy is just . . . so sweet.

A doctor. Divorced. Three grown kids. Nothing wrong with any of that, I guess, but he's so attentive to our mother, and always goes out of his way to be nice to Devon and me . . . Call me crazy, but it's suspicious. Or maybe I'm just over-protective.

"What exactly do you think he's after?" Devon asks. "It's not like he needs Mom's money."

We aren't Enzo rich, or even DeLuca rich, but Mom's

shop has always done pretty well. She inherited our house on the lake from her parents, and the property is worth a pretty penny now that Bridgewater is the latest "cute" small-town vacation spot. All the press around Enzo helped put us on the map.

Ugh. Can I not go three seconds without thinking about him?

"I don't know," I say, flicking through Netflix like a boss. "But have you ever met anyone that nice? He treats us like we're his own kids. Carries Mom's purse in public. Drives her to work with, like, two snowflakes on the ground. It's not natural."

Devon tries to take the remote from me. I pull back and shoot him a dirty look.

"He is nice. But so is Mom. And you're pretty nice. Most of the time."

"Thanks a lot. But you still can't have it."

Even though Devon doesn't live at home anymore, you'd never know it. When not at work, he's always either here or out with his friends. I'm not sure why he even pays for an apartment. Except as a place to take girls.

Which makes me think of Enzo. Again.

"There's obviously nothing catching your eye. Let me try."

"Don't you have somewhere else to be tonight?"

Thursday is the beginning of the weekend for Devon. Not for me. I have to get through one more day of chasing after eight-year-olds before I get to unwind. This is my typical bolstering routine for Thursday nights: TV and Chinese food. Which my brother is currently eating. He doesn't get to take over my TV selection too.

"Hey!" I say when he makes another grab for the remote.

Hurrying, I click on the first episode of a reliable mood booster. "There, see. Found something."

"You're kidding me. A fourth time. Seriously?"

I watch the bus hurtling down a country road, ignoring my brother.

Dr. Zoe Hart. That's my girl.

"Do you know how many good shows you've neglected by watching *Heart of Dixie* so much? It's not normal."

What's not normal is the number of times I've glanced at my phone since this weekend. Which makes absolutely zero sense because Enzo doesn't have my cell number. And even if he did, he wouldn't use it.

I thought for sure something would come of Saturday night—of that promise he made. But he didn't say a word when Devon and I left early, not that he would have propositioned me in front of my brother, and even though I dragged Lisa out to The Wheelhouse again for breakfast, he didn't show like I'd hoped he might.

Since then, precisely nothing has happened on the Enzo front. I'm back to an Enzo-less life. Which would be fine if I could get his chocolate-brown eyes out of my head.

"Give that to me. You're not even watching it. You've got that far-off look in your eyes."

Devon makes a grab for the control and succeeds in taking it from me. If I weren't so exhausted, I'd attempt to wrest it back. Instead, I lie back on the couch with my phone.

"Ass," I mutter as he flicks away from poor Zoe.

Texts messages. Still nothing. Social media. Whatever. And then, because I'm a glutton for punishment, I open my email. Unlike some of my colleagues, I do have my school mail integrated with my personal one. And I check it off-hours. I teach little ones, and their needs aren't always 9 to 4. Just last night a parent emailed me to ask for advice on getting her son tested for reading, something I had suggested at the last parent conference. The poor kid's been stuck in a no-man's land. Scores not low enough to be red-flagged, not high enough for me to feel comfortable with his progress. The mom wasn't ready at the time, and the dad pushed the idea aside. I'm glad she's changed her mind. It'll give poor Joey a chance to shine.

Emails like hers are the exact reason I like to keep communication open with parents. But a quick glance at my inbox tells me that no gold awaits me tonight. In fact, my email spam filter seems to be misfiring. Junk. More junk. An email from my principal that can wait until tomorrow morning.

And then . . .

To: Chari Atwood

From: Enzo DeLuca

Subject: How are you?

Hey, Chari. Sorry we didn't get to talk more this weekend. Devon said your mom is doing

better. Glad to hear it. I hope it's OK to email you. I didn't have your cell and wasn't sure Devon would appreciate me asking for it. Talk soon?

Enzo

My heart slams out of my chest. Or at least it feels that way. I put the phone down by my side, take a deep breath, and read it again. Yep. Same message.

From Enzo.

I hit reply but then stop. It's from an hour ago, and I don't want to look too eager. So I close my email and pretend to watch whatever cop show Devon found. He sits there without a care in the world, eating the rest of my chicken and broccoli with no idea one of his oldest friends just sent me an email. I know they still talk a lot, even given Enzo's crazy schedule. They've communicated since Saturday, obviously, since Enzo knows about Mom.

Would he care if Enzo emailed me?

Yes.

He would. And even though I'm a grown-ass woman, I can't ignore the fact that Enzo was Devon's friend before my ... whatever this is.

But plenty of people date their siblings' friends. Is it really such a crazy idea?

Reminding myself Enzo and I are not dating, that this is just one simple email, and an innocent one at that, I grab my phone. An hour and five minutes. Yep, enough time has passed.

To: Enzo DeLuca
From: Chari Atwood
Subject: Great!

Hi Enzo. Mom is doing better, thanks. So sorry we had to leave early Saturday night. The

restaurant is amazing. Tris got some great press on Sunday, so it looks like DeLuca's II will be a hit.

"You look pretty intent."

I glance up. Devon is watching me.

"Just a parent," I lie, hating it. I can't think of the last time I lied to my brother. We share just about everything. "You know how much I love cop shows." Which is true.

He turns back to the TV, but now I feel like crap. Thankfully, the feeling passes pretty quickly when I remember Enzo actually emailed me. I really didn't think he'd get back in touch.

And I agree, Devon would definitely wonder if you asked for my number. It's totally fine to email me, but feel free to text if you want. Number is 555-710-8314.

Chari

Probably an understatement, but I suspect Lisa was right, that Enzo didn't make a move because of my brother. No need to spook him.

"So," I say, shifting my attention to Devon. "What's the deal with Doctor Karim?" I try to sound casual, but he knows me too well.

Devon makes a rude sound. "Colleen? Nothing."

I'm not convinced.

"Didn't look like nothing the other night."

No answer.

"I hope it works out. I like her."

"There's nothing to work out. We're not a thing."

Of course they aren't. Devon doesn't do "things," otherwise known as relationships. "Too bad. She's smart and nice. She's sort of a friend, but I say go for it."

A not-so-subtle attempt to feel him out about the whole Enzo thing. I hold my breath and wait for his reply.

"You guys aren't exactly close."

I shrugged. "No, not really, but even if we were, you'd totally have my stamp of approval."

Another guttural male sound.

"To sleep with her? I highly doubt it."

I make a face. "No, ass. To date her."

Devon looks at me like I've lost my marbles. "This is why I don't date your friends."

"Because you're incapable of a real relationship? And only do one-night stands?"

I really shouldn't have asked the question because I already know the answer.

"Yes. Exactly," Devon confirms.

Which is when I toss a pillow at him. "And that's why they call them throw pillows."

Devon laughs and goes back to watching his show. "I'm pretty sure that's not why."

But I'm no longer interested in arguing with him. So much for feeling him out. Devon is utterly incapable of a serious conversation. But it does make me think. Based on the press I've seen, Enzo has never really gotten serious about anyone. What if he's a one-night-stand kind of guy? But if so, would he really risk coming on to me? He'd have to know Devon wouldn't appreciate his sister being used for sex.

Am I completely overthinking this? He didn't ask me on a date or anything. He just sent a simple email asking how I'm doing. That's it.

When my phone vibrates, I snatch it up like it's the hot potato and the song's winding down.

Enzo: And now I have your number ;)

That was quick. I love that he's not playing games. So I text right back.

Chari: And now I have yours. ;)

Enzo: Go out with me this weekend?

Oh my God! So much for text foreplay. But that's exactly Enzo. He goes for what he wants, no hesitation. Always has.

Does that mean he wants me?

Chari: That escalated quickly.

Enzo: A sign of things to come?

Holy shit on a stick. What does *that* mean?

Chari: Maybe?

Enzo: So is that a yes?

Chari: What night?

Me, playing coy. Because I literally have zero plans for the weekend.

Enzo: Sat. night into Sunday? I'll send a car. Come to NY.

Wait. Is he serious?

"Who you texting?" Devon asks.

Ugh. "No one."

I don't look up. Thankfully, he takes the hint, grunting and going back to his show.

Chari: For real?

Enzo: Yes, for real.

I have no idea how to take this. Most people start with dinner and a movie or something. Maybe drinks. But an overnight first date? With Enzo? I can't breathe.

Enzo: I have a spare bedroom. I hate to see you drive two hours back and forth.

So coming back to Bridgewater is not an option. Makes sense. I pretend to contemplate this, if only so I'll seem like less of a sure thing. But my decision was made the moment he asked. Short of a Nor'easter, I am going to New York this weekend.

Chari: What the hell. Yes.

Enzo: Be ready for a car to pick you up at four o'clock. Dress for dinner.

He really doesn't mess around. Kinda bossier than I remember too, and I'm surprised by how much I like it in this context.

Chari: OK

Enzo: You telling Dev?

Does he want me to?

Does it matter what he wants? This is my brother, my decision. And I don't want Devon to freak out over what might end up being just one date.

Chari: No

Enzo: K, see you Sat

Chari: :)

Welp. So that just happened.

9

ENZO

I'm aware of being a contradiction.

Anyone walking into my apartment at this moment would see the Enzo DeLuca I've become. They would take in the floor-to-ceiling windows in my penthouse apartment, the picture-perfect view of the Hudson and the city lights, the white oak herringbone floors, and the marble waterfall countertops the building's owner sold me on, going on about the famous designer as if I cared about such things.

I don't, for the record, and I care equally less that I'm apparently sporting a "tonal look"—a grey Donegal tweed waistcoat paired with a grey Prince of Wales shirt. Hiring the personal assistant who told me how to dress hip, yet classic, was the best decision I ever made. Unlike Hayden, I didn't grow up this way. Even now so much of it feels foreign. Fake. Like I'm a poser.

But walking the walk is as important as talking the talk, or so I'm told. And besides working out, which helps me think through problems, I don't have time for much else besides Angel, Inc., and certainly not for putting that much thought into my wardrobe.

Anyone walking into the apartment right now would probably have no idea I'm freaking out, because I've learned how to influence the way I'm perceived, yet my heart is hammering as quickly as it did the day we received FDA approval. Tonight may be completely different, but it's another make-or-break moment in my life. I'm fully aware of the implications of having invited Chari here this weekend.

But I couldn't help it.

Ignoring the bright white laptop computer screen in front of me, I watch the door from my living room. She texted an hour ago, and I know the Saturday evening traffic patterns. Which suggest she'll be here any minute now.

The fact that she chose not to mention this particular weekend to Devon is only a temporary reprieve. He'll find out soon enough, and I'll face an inquisition. If not for Devon, I would have contacted her sooner. Much sooner, in fact. But I waited, and waited some more, until Hayden called me out for it on Wednesday night.

"You usually have enough focus for me and your gnocchi," he said, which, yeah, he was right. I'd been staring into my plate like it was the Sistine Chapel. "Jesus, Enzo, just call her."

"I can't."

"Yes, you can. You won't be the first person in history to date his friend's sister. Devon's a good guy—he'll hear you out. You're being ridiculous."

"Really?" I shot back. "You don't think the first thing he'll ask me about are my intentions with Chari?"

"What exactly *are* your intentions?"

I just looked at him, at which point Hayden whistled. "You've got it bad, brother."

As if I didn't know that.

"You know I don't date."

"So? Make an exception?"

"Work comes first."

"Tell her that," he said with a grin. "Should go over pretty well."

I set down my fork. "I could be clear with her up front. Explain my situation. I mean, she knows as well as anyone how rarely I come home. I'll tell her what to expect and then see if she can handle it."

"And if she can't?"

"We part ways. No big deal."

Hayden snorted. For a rich guy, born and raised, he lacked the kind of refinement you'd expect. Boarding school, houses all over the world . . . none of it seemed to affect him, which is why we became friends. It took me a full year to figure out he came from money. Although he'd never lacked for anything at school, I hadn't either, and my parents owned a pizza shop.

Then Hayden's dad sent a car to pick us up one day, and a few hours later we pulled up to his house in Connecticut. No, not a house. A freaking mansion. Hayden merely shrugged when I asked him about it. And I knew that day we would be friends for life. How he managed to escape the pretentiousness of some of his childhood friends, I'm still not sure.

His parents aren't half as grounded as their only son. They look and act very much like the top one percent. And though Hayden's dad basically got us up and running with his loan, there were strings attached. I wouldn't trade my childhood with Hayden's in a million years, despite his family's wealth.

Our conversation about Chari didn't really ease all of my concerns, or even most of them, but I emailed her the next day anyway. Something I'm still half regretting. How could this possibly end well? Am I really ready to risk my friendship with Devon? The answer is no. If Hayden is a friend for life, Devon is even more so. We've been friends, brothers, since the second grade.

What the fuck are you doing, Enzo? Why did you email her, then?

There's a knock at the door. I call out for them to come in, and the door opens. I have my answer almost immediately.

It doesn't matter that she's wearing a long black coat. I catch the caring eyes of a woman I've known since childhood. I can see enough to know one hundred percent why I sent that email. I stand, thanking Mr. Jim, who escorted her up. One of the most expensive buildings in Tribeca comes with an attendant for just about everything, including the elevator.

He leaves, and from the way Chari's gripping her bag, and the fact that she didn't give it over to Mr. Jim, I can tell she's nervous. There are benefits to going on a date with someone you've known for years, I realize. Although there's a gap in my knowledge of her, I can tell the core of who she is hasn't changed.

I'm not sure whether the same is true of me.

"Let me take that."

I grab her small duffle bag and hold out a hand for her jacket.

"We have a few minutes before dinner."

I pretend to be totally unaffected as I help Chari remove

her coat, revealing a shimmering black cocktail dress. One side is off the shoulder. My eyes are immediately drawn to the exposed skin there, but I train them back to her face.

She's already looking past me, at the apartment.

"Go ahead, look around."

I put her bag and coat in the oversized coat closet as I make my way to the bar just off the kitchen.

"Can I get you a drink?"

I pour myself an Angel Red, in the mood for wine tonight, and pull out a glass for her.

"You know I'm a beer girl," she says, standing in front of the window across from me. "This view. Holy shit, Enzo. It's insane."

I do know that, and I reach into the refrigerator. "Angel Pale Ale or something else? I've got Premiere and Dogfish."

Chari turns toward me. "You have other brands?"

"Not usually. But I picked up some of the usual suspects. I know what you like."

That comes out more suggestive than intended, and I'm aware it's not entirely true. What I wouldn't give to know exactly what this woman likes, in every respect.

"I drink yours too," defending herself.

"Listen," I say, because I need to get this off my chest. "I tell everyone. You don't have to drink Angel just because it's mine. If you're driving, it makes sense. But you don't need to do it on my account. Plus we don't have the range of other beers."

If people like our product because they genuinely enjoy it, great. If not, it's up to our team to figure out how it could be better. But everyone likes to mix things up once in a while. I do too.

"I'm serious," I say in response to her skeptical look.

Chari smiles, running her finger along the windowpane.

What I wouldn't give to be that windowpane right about now.

"I'll have an Angel Pale, please."

I bring her the drink, trying to see the apartment, and the view, from her perspective. Trying to see it for the first time.

"When we first came to New York, it was only supposed to be for a long weekend. After two days of meetings, I stood over there." I gesture in the direction of Hayden's first apartment. "And thought to myself, I could never live here."

I glance at her, but the sight of Chari's mouth on the rim of that bottle is way too distracting, so I look back outside.

"And yet, here you are," she says softly.

"Yep, here I am."

"So do you like it now? Do you ever miss PA?"

That's a loaded question.

"I love it here. All of the things I thought I'd hate—the people, the noise, the constant comings and goings—they've grown on me. It's home now."

"And Bridgewater?"

I think about last weekend. My family. The pizza shop. The lake. My old friends.

"Also home. But one from a different life. I could never manage the business from there now. Every contact I've made is here." I gesture toward the bar. "Want to sit?"

She looks back out, and I get it. Even after all this time, it's a pretty spectacular view.

"I'm okay."

When I turned toward the bar, I intentionally moved a bit closer. I can smell her now, and it's an entirely different scent than last weekend. This one is vanilla. With a hint of coconut. And suddenly, an image of the two of us sitting on a beach sipping piña coladas makes me want a vacation.

With her. We could get away from it all, Devon included, and figure out this thing between us.

I glance back at my open laptop. "If you told me in college I'd be working every weekend, living in New York City, and . . ." I hesitate, not wanting to sound presumptuous.

"Sending cars for your . . ." She stops, not knowing what to call herself. And I can't help her. The word *date* sticks on the tip of my tongue too. "For your friends? I mean, Devon's told me the whole story, of course, but I'd love to hear it from you."

And even though I've told this story a million times, I'm happy she asked. Or at least happy because of the way she asked. It feels . . . intimate.

"I knew it was something big, almost immediately," I say, skipping over the part about the experiment that went wrong before I got it right. "When my professor confirmed my findings, he helped me set up trials. But it was Hayden who made the whole thing explode. If it weren't for his dad's backing, for the initial capital investment, I probably would have ended up selling the idea."

"Instead, you get to live like a king," she says, a corner of her mouth tipping up.

"A king who goes to sleep with that every night." I gesture toward my laptop. "But it doesn't feel like work to me. We've grown every year, and that feels like a new victory."

"Eye on the prize."

I turn fully toward her. "Exactly."

But the prize isn't more money. Or new products. Or new markets.

Not tonight.

I want to put down my glass, reach both hands behind

her neck, and pull her to me. Kiss her senseless until she begs for me. Until I give myself to her, completely.

But here's the thing: I know what it's like to joke around with Chari Atwood. To play kickball with her. To swim up to her in a murky lake, pretending to be a fish, and listen to her squeal in fright when I emerge from the water.

But I don't know what it's like to kiss Chari Atwood. To reach underneath her dress and run my hands up her thighs for proof that she's as turned on at this very moment as I am.

My usual confidence has abandoned me. If this were any other woman, I'd say fuck it, and pull her into my arms this very second. Dinner be damned.

But it's not.

So I don't.

"We should leave for dinner," I say. "Our reservation is for seven thirty."

Her face falls, and I can tell she's just as disappointed as I am. But I have every intention of making it up to her.

10

CHARI

*I*f I thought the ride to New York was nerve-wracking, having Enzo next to me in the back seat is at least ten times more so. From the moment I walked into his apartment, I've felt like a kid turning the crank on a jack-in-the-box, waiting for something to happen. Anticipating it. Fearing it. The tension is so thick between us, there's no doubt it needs to break soon.

With a kiss. With a conversation about Devon. With a discussion of what, exactly, is going on between us. I'm not sure what will happen, but I don't want to be the one to initiate it. I've decided to ignore all of my questions and worries for a change and try to enjoy myself.

How many times have Mom or Devon told me to stop planning, live for the moment? Lisa would take it one step further—she blames my need to control for sabotaging my last few relationships. I'm not a controlling person, or at least I don't think I am, but I do like to know what's coming next. Which is why this thing with Enzo is putting me so on edge.

Not to mention I've never wanted to touch someone

more in my entire life. Lying at home in my bed, imagining him kissing me, touching me . . . that's one thing. But it's a whole new ball game now that I'm sitting here next to him. When it could actually happen.

This is the big leagues, and I'm way out of practice.

"Here it is."

It's close enough that we probably could have walked, but there's no denying the elegance of pulling up to the restaurant and having the driver come around to open our door. I sometimes imagined myself living in the city after college, but places like this intimidate me.

Enzo gets out first, but only so he can reach for my hand and help me out. I forget my purse and have to make a not-so-elegant grab for it at the last second. Then I put my hand in his and all of the white noise starts to float away.

Breathe. Like a normal person.

His grasp is so firm and confident, pulling me out of the car. Before I can register anything else, he lets it go, the brief touch ending way too soon. But our eyes meet, and at least I know I'm not the only one affected here. To think, a little over a week ago things were humming along just fine. Teaching the little ones. Having dinner with Mom. Happy hour with friends. Cursing the cold. Waiting for summer.

Life was good, or at least good-ish.

Now here I am, entering the most luxurious restaurant I've ever seen in my life. I didn't catch the name because I was too busy staring at Enzo as he took my coat and handed it to the attendant. I try to look nonchalant, but it's not easy.

"They are custom Bernardaud chandeliers," Enzo says when he catches me looking up to the ceiling. "I only know that because Hayden told me the last time we were here." Other than the chairs, everything in here is white—the column, walls, tablecloths. And yeah, those chandeliers. Wow. Though I have no idea what, or who, Bernardaud is.

"I see."

Enzo winks as if to say he didn't know who, or what, Bernardaud was either.

"This way, Mr. DeLuca," says the attendant.

The net worth of the people in this room is probably greater than that of most small countries. The guests all ooze wealth and importance. Which makes it feel even weirder that they're watching Enzo walk by like he's some kind of god. Some murmur their hellos. Others nudge their companions. I know he's like a celebrity, especially after the Senate hearings and the other beer companies trying to get Angel, Inc. shut down. But to be stared at, by people who probably see celebrities all the time. It's so completely out of the realm of my life experience.

"The Skybox is ready for you and your companion, sir. There will not be two more?"

The skybox?

"No, just us. Thank you."

I want to ask why we're leaving the main dining room, heading toward the kitchen. But I don't need to—the corridor opens to reveal the most beautifully set table I've ever seen. Glass and silver and white ceramic dishes match the rest of the decor. It's kind of like a booth, closed in on three sides. The third is a silver curtain that matches the silver velvet cushions. And the kitchen's directly to the right of our booth.

I sit, watching through the glass as the head chef winks at me. At least, I suppose he's the head chef. He looks like he's in charge. I don't notice until the maître d' closes us in, drowning out the noise from the kitchen, but we are completely encased in glass. How did I not see that before?

"Enzo, this is incredible."

He's watching me, waiting for my reaction.

"You like it?"

He might be part businessman, part celebrity billionaire, but this is the Enzo I grew up with. He's hopeful and boyish, with almost a hint of shyness.

"I love it."

My eyes roam from the pictures on the wall toward the kitchen. "I can't believe we can't hear a thing. This is incredible."

"It's called the Skybox. Hayden's dad took us here to celebrate when we were approved by the FDA. We all knew it was the start of something big."

His words kindle something inside of me. Does that mean he thinks this thing between us is the start of something big? But there's no chance to ask, if I even would—the glass door opens, admitting a man clad in a crisp white shirt and fancy vest.

"Good evening, Mr. DeLuca. Ms. Atwood."

How does the waiter know my name?

"I would normally invite you to look at the wine list . . ." He smiles at Enzo as he lets the comment trail off.

"The wine list will be fine." He takes it from the waiter. "Thank you. And sparkling water, please."

"Very good, sir."

The waiter leaves us to our glass box. I look down. Shit. I really should have refreshed my memory on utensils. You won't find more than three—a fork, spoon, and knife—at any restaurant in Bridgewater. Maybe I could handle one extra utensil. But there's as much silverware on our table as is probably lost in my couch at this very moment.

"It takes some getting used to."

I look up. Caught.

"And really, most of them aren't even necessary."

Enzo's mouth lifts in this special smile of his that has a way of making the beholder feel comfortable, and noticed, and valued, and I want to reach over all the fancy place settings and pull his handsome face toward me.

"When you look at me like that, Chari—"

"Pardon me." The waiter opened the door to speak to us, and the full force of the bustling kitchen sounds reach us. It's so strange. From silence to a sneak peek behind the scenes. I wonder what Enzo was about to say.

"Moscato d'Asti maybe?"

I realize the man standing with our waiter is talking to me.

"I know you don't typically drink wine, but do you want to try something light?" Enzo asks.

I can't actually imagine ordering a beer here. I could drink vodka, but what the hell? "Sure, I'll try it."

"May I suggest Ca' d'Gal Vigna Vecchia for Ms. Atwood?"

It's still freaking me out that everyone knows my name. This must be the sommelier. I nod, and Enzo orders a drink for himself too. The minute the door closes, I wait anxiously for Enzo to finish. But he seems to have forgotten what he was going to say.

"How exactly was I looking at you?" I prod, knowing the answer full well.

Enzo sits up straight and leans forward. Something about him has shifted. This isn't the man I knew in childhood anymore. This is the confident billionaire who feels comfortable in a restaurant like this. And weirdly enough, he's no less sexy or desirable. I'm not even sure which one I like better.

"You were looking at me the same way, I imagine, that I've been looking at you since last Friday."

I swallow, unable to respond to him.

"And when you look at me like that, Chari, I forget for a second that you're Devon's little sister."

Here we go.

"And is that such a bad thing?"

Our conversation staggers to a halt again when the sommelier brings our wine. He shows me the bottle. I nod, realizing he's waiting for a response. And when he pours a bit in the glass, I take the hint and sip it. It's really good, actually. Another nod and he fills my glass.

Enzo goes through the same dance, and when the sommelier leaves, Enzo raises his glass. So I do the same.

"Maybe it's not such a bad thing. To a night in New York with . . . not my friend's sister, but the kind, beautiful woman whom I've wanted to get alone since we were reacquainted last week."

Each of his words stirs something in me, and I meet his eyes as I clink my glass to his, then drink.

Is it me or does this not taste like wine? I don't like wine, and this is delicious. Though not as delicious as what he said, and what it promised. He's waiting for a response, so I give one.

"That makes two of us, Enzo." I lift my glass again for a second toast. "Cheers."

11

ENZO

"I'll take that."

Closing the door behind us, I lay our jackets down and make my way behind the bar.

"Nightcap?"

Chari reaches down to peel off one heel, and then the second. Two sets of perfectly manicured toes wiggle around, and for the millionth time in my life, I thank the fashion gods I don't have to wear those things.

"Are they that bad?"

Her shoulders sag in answer.

"Ugh, yes."

Placing her black heels next to the couch, she steps onto my cream floor rug, and I know what she's feeling. It's cozy, almost as much so as the couch. When I moved into this apartment last year and had it decorated, comfort was as important to me as design. I knew I'd spend plenty of late nights sitting on that couch.

"Sorry, I don't have moscato here."

She puts her hands on her hips and turns to me. So fucking hot. At the restaurant, I wanted to reach across the table and kiss her. In the car and then the elevator, I nearly did. But something stopped me.

We'll undoubtedly cross the line from friends into something more—we've been dancing around it all night. But like I told Hayden, dipping my toes into this pool means I'll get drenched.

I respect Chari, and her brother, too much for anything else. And yet, I know it probably won't work in the long run. No one can keep up with my lifestyle. Am I a fool for wanting to try?

"That's fine," she says, reminding me of my quest to get her a drink. "Surprise me." She turns toward the wall of windows, looking out again.

"I've got you," I say, pulling out a bottle and filling two glasses with my brother's homemade limoncello, not sure how much longer this will stay platonic.

"Should I sit over here?" she asks, gesturing toward the couch.

"Sure." I cap the bottle, flick off the kitchen lights, and switch on the fireplace. It roars to life.

"Oh!"

"Better?" The skyline lights up even more now that the interior's dark save for the fire. I hand her the glass and sit, effectively answering Chari's question. Which is safer than what I wanted to say. Sitting on my lap is probably not the best idea if we're going to take this slow.

Chari smells inside the glass. "Tris's limoncello?"

"Mmm-hmm."

She sips, and I watch her face pucker up. Adorable. I've seen that face before, and it brings back a cascade of memories.

"Remember the night of your twenty-first birthday?"

She looks at me like she wants to kill me. Though we're

sitting too far away to touch, the heat between us renders the fire I turned on mostly pointless.

"Parts of it."

Laughing, I say, "If you'll remember, someone tried to tell you twenty-one shots of cinnamon liquor was not a good idea."

"Yeah, well, I wouldn't pat yourself on the back too hard. You're the one who took me to your dad's pizza place at three in the morning to give me a nightcap of"—she lifted her glass—"this."

Time to start fessing up. I have a lot to tell her, might as well start dropping a few truth bombs now.

"If you recall, we opened the pizza joint just so you could fill your stomach before you went to bed. And I believe Tris asked me, and not the drunk birthday girl, to try the limoncello, when you snatched the glass out of my hand."

She takes another sip. This time, her taste buds are ready, so no sour face.

"Also, you didn't actually do twenty-one shots."

Chari makes a face, not unlike the one she pulled after her first taste of limoncello. "Yes, I did."

People pay millions for the view in front of us. But it's nothing compared to what I'm looking at. Legs crossed, hair tossed back, she looks like she belongs there, sipping limoncello on my couch.

Maybe she does.

"No—" an endearment is at the end of my tongue, but our situation is confusing enough, and I settle for her name, "—Chari, you didn't."

I sip my own drink, silently thanking my brother. This stuff is top-notch.

"You had, I don't know, maybe ten. And that's when your brother and I started filling your shot glass with beer."

Her eyes widen.

"No, you did not."

I want to move closer, but I know that'll be it. Just one inch, and it's all over. I want that, but I'm also wary of changing things so absolutely.

"Yes, we did. The bartenders were in on it. You were so drunk you had no idea." She's still scowling at me in a way that suggests she's not convinced I'm telling the truth. "Do you remember asking if we switched to tequila?"

She squints her eyes. "Vaguely."

"Yeah, well. That was beer."

When she bites her lower lip, I'm lost. Standing, I take a deep breath and fetch another drink. This is going down way too smooth.

"Are you teasing me?" she asks.

I return to the couch with my refill, settling in next to her.

"I'm not. Ask Devon. I'm surprised he never told you."

That's all it takes.

During dinner, we carefully avoided the subject. We played catch-up with each other's lives, talking about the company and Chari's job. How much she loves her students, something I'm particularly grateful for. Everything I learned confirmed that Chari is the same amazing girl I knew, now a fucking gorgeous woman.

But neither of us mentioned Devon's name after that first moment in the Skybox.

Until now.

"I think I'll pass. But speaking of . . ."

Chari finishes her drink, putting the empty cup on the glass table in front of us. "Oh, sorry. Do I need a coaster or something?"

I put my drink next to hers to show her that, no, a

coaster isn't necessary. The move brought me closer to her, and I catch a whiff of vanilla coconut.

"We should talk about that."

I don't need to ask what she means—we both know. And while I'm no more eager to discuss it now than I was earlier, she's right.

I nod, and she says, "I know you're worried about Devon, but you shouldn't be."

"No?" I ask, surprised by her response. Based on what I've seen, she's nervous about him too.

"No."

"How do you figure?" I inch just a little bit closer.

"I know you guys are besties . . ."

I laugh. "You say it like we're two seventh-grade girls."

Chari's smile reaches her eyes. Hazel. Like her brother's.

"But we are our own people. And you're more like a brother to him than a friend. No matter what happens with us . . ." She shrugs.

I edge closer again, until her knee touches mine. I've got to control myself here. Although I get why she's acting like we can take a casual approach, this is not just any date. Or just any woman.

"Us?" I say, feeling the pull to tease her a little, if only to calm her nerves. And mine. "So we're not just two old friends, catching up?"

The idea is preposterous. Every single time we've been in each other's presence recently, the rest of the world falls away, leaving only the two of us behind. We both know it. We both feel it.

"Do you invite many of your friends over for weekend visits?" She says it with a hint of attitude, but her sassiness drops away and her hands start fidgeting. "Actually. Don't answer that."

I finally let myself touch her again, sliding my hand onto her lap, over hers. Reaching between each finger, I hold on, steadying her. I feel steadier while touching her too, I'm surprised to discover, but the touch ignites us both.

"No. I don't make a habit of inviting 'friends' to stay the night." My other hand moves behind her neck. "Not female ones, anyway."

She swallows and bites that damn lip again.

Chari's hair is as soft as I'd imagined. I let my fingers roam a bit before resting them on her neck, pulling her closer.

"And I suppose you don't treat them to a two-thousand-dollar dinner either."

I laughed in the car when she looked up our restaurant and found the price of the table online. She chastised me for not inviting two more people since the cost is the same for two or four. As if I would have shared her with anyone tonight.

"Sixteen hundred dollars," I correct her.

Just a few more inches. It's like we're moving in slow motion, each movement charged with anticipation. With desire.

"Can I kiss you, Chari?" I ask out of respect.

I ask, praying for the answer I need.

I ask because I know this kiss will change everything.

"Please do."

12

CHARI

*T*his entire night has been like something out of a movie. It can't be my real life. Just a temporary fake one, culminating with the most gorgeous man on the planet asking to kiss me. Is he serious right now?

I can't believe this is happening.

As he pulls me the remaining distance toward him, I find myself wondering if I'll remember how to kiss properly. I can't seem to do anything else right tonight, stumbling along in this borrowed life. In this dream world. But when his lips finally touch mine, I'm no longer worried.

Passion takes over, my lips parting, my head slanting for better access. I barely have time to get accustomed to the feel of him when his tongue touches mine, gently at first. I can't help but groan at the feel of him.

Enzo DeLuca knows how to kiss.

Because of course he does.

Before long, his touch is no longer gentle. No longer exploratory. It's more insistent now, and I'm ready to give as well as take. Neither of his hands have moved, but I want them to. I want him to touch me everywhere at once.

It's taken exactly ten seconds for this kiss to spiral out of control.

"Chari," he whispers, his voice molten lava against my ear. Kissing that too, Enzo pushes hair back from my shoulder. "I've wanted to do this since I first walked into that bar last weekend."

He trails kisses down my neck and onto my shoulder, leaving me a puddle on his couch. I knew he would be a good kisser. But not this good. Part of me wants to take this slowly so I can remember everything about it, about him, but the rest of me just wants more.

With my free hand, I reach around to grab a handful of hair, to push him . . . where? He can't be everywhere at once.

"You taste like coconut," he murmurs. "So fucking perfect."

His words send a bolt of longing through me, and I run my hands through his thick black hair the way I've wanted to do since, well, forever. Pulling back just slightly, I think I'm regaining control of myself, of my senses, when he takes the hint and kisses me again.

Hard.

His mouth covers mine until I can't breathe. And I don't want to if it means this kiss has to end. If it could go on forever, I'd welcome it. But now I'm too distracted by his other hand, which has let go of mine and is currently sliding up my leg.

Oh. My God.

I can't see his fingers, but I can feel them on my skin. I stared at them all through dinner, long and slender. Back in the day, I used to watch him spin pizza dough in his dad's shop. They moved so quickly, so expertly. Like now.

"Jesus, Chari."

I smile against his kiss, knowing exactly what he's reacting to.

"Are you kidding me?"

He pulls back to see my reaction. I can't help but smile.

All night I've been off-balance in a world that isn't mine. But now, for the first time tonight, Enzo is too. Even if it's just for a second, until the shock of me not wearing panties wears off.

"I would never kid you," I say as his hand pushes my legs apart. I don't hesitate for a second.

"I can't stop myself," he says, his voice hoarse.

"Why would you?"

Thankfully, he doesn't. But as his fingers inch closer to their goal, he says, "Lots of reasons. But none of them seem important right now."

With that, Enzo leans forward and kisses me again just as his fingers enter me. I gasp against his lips. From the pleasure. And also from the fact that this is Enzo, finally, and we're together, and he's touching me, and oh my God, where did he learn to do that?

With his palm pressing against me, he moves his hand. His fingers. His tongue mimics the same movements, and I swear, I will never be the same. I find myself pressing upward, wanting more. Wanting him.

"Mmmm."

That low sound in his throat is my undoing. Clenching and convulsing against his hand, I moan into his mouth, pulling him even closer. I literally came apart at his touch.

But I don't have any time to think about it, or to come down from my high. Just like that, I find myself lying on the couch, Enzo poised above me. And I want it. I want *him*, more than I've ever wanted anyone or maybe anything.

Enzo doesn't move, though. He stares at me, and I stare back.

When he finally reaches down to kiss me, I meet him halfway. And just like before, it spirals out of control so quickly that we might as well be having sex. Except we're both still fully clothed. Other than the whole panties thing.

Enzo breaks away, supporting his weight above me.

"Chari."

I can tell he's going to say something serious, something that ends this moment, and I don't like it one bit. Despite the fact that I'm literally lying under him after experiencing one hell of an orgasm, from his fingers mind you, I can feel us cooling off.

"I didn't ask you to stay here for sex."

Too bad.

"I just"—he groans, and oh, what a sound—"I just had to see you again."

His words, coupled with the sight of him above me . . . it's all so surreal.

"I'm glad you emailed me."

Something glimmers in his eyes. "I am too." Then he jumps up, pulling me with him. "I have an idea."

If his idea has anything to do with continuing where we just left off, I'm all in. Tugging me forward, he walks to the door and grabs my bag.

"I'm not sure I like your idea if it involves kicking me out of your apartment," I quip. Or at least I'm mostly kidding. I'm still curious about how we went from being horizontal to . . . this.

"I'll take you to your room. Why don't you change, and I'll do the same. Meet you in the kitchen for another nightcap?"

For real?

"I'm not sure I can handle another of Tris's limoncellos."

"Fair enough. See you in a few minutes," he says, stopping next to the first door we reach in a hallway that I know most New Yorkers would find absurd. This place is huge. Does he own the whole floor?

I say, "OK," mostly because I'm not sure what else to say. He clearly doesn't want to go any further—at least not yet—so *get into my bed* probably wouldn't be appropriate. Enzo flips on the light and leaves me in the room. Elegant, just like the rest of the place. Actually, it reminds me of the restaurant we went to tonight. All whites and brown. Impeccably decorated, but obviously not used much.

I change, grateful I took a pair of leggings and a sweatshirt in addition to the brand-new negligee. Might as well freshen up too. A few minutes later, I head back down the hall. He's back in the kitchen already, somehow more handsome than before.

I've seen Enzo in sweats a million times in my life. But for some reason, the abrupt change from the put-together billionaire who strode through that restaurant tonight like he was right at home and the comfortable PA boy that I grew up with is super hot.

"Hey," he says, the smell of heaven just now reaching my nose.

"Is that coffee?"

"It is. Figured since you were done with the limoncello, I would be too. Besides, I don't know many other people who can drink coffee after midnight and still go to sleep no problem."

I laugh, sitting on one of the stools at the kitchen island.

"You remembered."

And it's true. Enzo and I have that same strange affliction. Caffeine hardly affects us. Although I still feel the lack of it, it doesn't make me jittery or sleepless. Devon was always jealous of us for that.

"I remember a lot of things," Enzo says as he hands me a cup of heaven.

"Such as?"

He leans back against the counter opposite the bar where I'm sitting and looks at me so intently I begin to squirm. It should be illegal to look that hot in a hoodie.

"I remember the night you turned twenty-one," he says.

"Yeah, you said so." But we both know he's talking about something other than beer shots now.

"I remember the way you looked at me after a half-dozen shots."

I take a sip of the coffee, avoiding his gaze. It's exactly how I like it.

"I didn't think you noticed."

"Oh, I did."

When I look up at him, he's smiling. And my perception of that night slips a little more. I decide to push him a bit.

"So what changed?"

"I was scared then."

Those words, coming from this supremely confident, successful man, just don't add up. Or maybe it's that they don't compute.

"Scared? Of what?"

"Of screwing up my relationship with Devon. Of hurting you."

"You'd never hurt me." The words come out reflexively, before I can think them through, but I know it's true, like I know one plus one equals two. He just wouldn't—it's that simple.

"Not intentionally, no. But you're not exactly a one-night-stand kind of woman, Char."

I laugh, and thank him for that.

"Seriously. If you were, I would have taken your hint that night and run with it."

His words remind me of what happened, or almost happened, on his couch.

"And last weekend?" I take another sip, the surreal haze of the last few hours wearing off. This is actually . . . comfortable. Enzo and I sitting in his kitchen, chatting like old friends.

"I'd have learned in the basement of Tris's new restaurant that you like to go commando."

Holy shit, this guy.

"So you're saying you'd have asked me out sooner?"

"Do you honestly think I would have stopped myself back there"—he nods to the couch—"with any other woman?"

Ah, so that's it.

"I told you. You don't have to treat me with kid gloves. I'm not a young girl anymore."

He makes a sound that forces a smile from me. "No kidding."

I wanted more. Still do. But now I'm kind of glad he stopped. Sitting here with him, drinking coffee at midnight as the fire roars behind us, the New York skyline spread out in front of us . . .

This just might be my new favorite part of the night.

Well, with one exception.

"I had a good time tonight," I admit.

"So did I."

Good. So we aren't playing games.

"And I'm serious, Char. You have no idea how difficult it was for me not to take you on that couch tonight. How hard it will be not to invite you into my bedroom."

My core clenches a bit.

"I can't believe I'm saying this," he adds, "but we should probably take it slow."

I'm not one hundred percent on board with his plan, but I suppose there's some merit to it. If only I knew exactly what it meant. But my pride won't allow me to ask, and to be honest, I'm nervous about what he might say. What he might reveal.

"Sounds good to me," I lie. "Nice sweatshirt, by the way."

Cornell, his undergrad alma mater. "Luckily we're in two different conferences."

I realize, belatedly, the joke makes it sound like we'll be together come football season. Which is ridiculous. This is a first date. An epic first date, sure, but nothing more.

Suddenly, Enzo's reasoning makes sense to me. His desire to take it slow. We aren't two strangers with no stake in this thing. I might not know Enzo the billionaire, but I know the guy standing in his kitchen in sweats. And there's little to dislike about this guy. Given our chemistry, and how this date is going, he's probably right, maddening as it is.

How can I possibly keep myself from falling for him, hard and fast?

Deep inside, I know it's already too late.

"*E*arth to Enzo."

We're about to head into a meeting with our marketing team, but I can't concentrate—something I've been struggling with all week.

"Yeah." I grab my laptop and start to follow Hayden from my office. Normally he wouldn't be at this meeting, but since we're considering firing our marketing liaison, he's graced us with his presence.

"Hold up," he says at the last second, coming to a sudden stop.

I all but run into him.

"I need more than 'It went well' if you're going to turn into a zombie on me. I can take the lead in there, but only if you give me more intel."

I really picked a doozy of a business partner.

"Are you serious? Right now?"

"Deadly."

I laugh at his sober expression. He really should have been an actor. Hayden doesn't even crack a smile.

"We're going to be late," I remind him, looking at my watch.

"No." He shoves me back into my office. "Because of your chronic insistence on being early for everything, we are not. Sit."

He's right—it's early—but I still stare him down.

"I'm serious, Enz. You're a space cadet. We have fifteen minutes. Sit, tell me about your girl. And then we'll go in. Maybe you'll be more focused if you get it off your chest."

For about the millionth time, I find myself thinking there are pluses and minuses to working with someone who knows you so well. Only, maybe I'm more transparent than I thought. Gian called last night, and after five minutes, he asked me what was wrong.

"Fine."

I sit, reluctantly. But only because he's right. The last thing I'm thinking about at the moment is the botched social media campaign that led us to question the competence of our chief marketing officer.

"Talk to me."

"Not much to tell."

Hayden rolls his eyes.

"Seriously. I took her to dinner. Eight courses later, we went back to my apartment."

"Eight courses? Where did you take her? Holy shit, did you eat in the Skybox?"

I nod.

Hayden whistles. "Trying to impress her?"

There's no use denying it. "Maybe."

"And then?"

"And then we had a pleasant evening. She went home after breakfast on Sunday. I had to get to the lab."

"On a Sunday?"

I leave most of the chemistry to my team these days, but we have a new product in development, and I like over-seeing that process myself. Our lab is in Jersey, so just an hour away without traffic, which is why I went on Sunday. I hate wasting time in traffic.

"Yes. On a Sunday."

"I feel like you're skipping a bunch. Did you have a good time?"

Of course, but it was so much more than that.

"Yeah," I downplay it. "We were up until almost four o'clock." Hayden's already grinning, so I stop him right there. "Talking."

"Uh-huh."

"Seriously."

His eyes widen.

"I told you, she's different."

Hayden whistles. "Apparently." He crosses his arms. "So no sex," he surmises.

I think about our first kiss. And my hand, gliding up her thigh to find she wasn't wearing any underwear. And how wet Chari was for me . . .

"You're doing it again."

"Sorry."

"If you didn't have sex," he says with a snicker, as if he doesn't quite believe me, "what exactly did you do until four in the morning?"

I look out at the skyline, so dreary today. Unlike Satur-day, when it was filled with promise. I know what's missing, and it doesn't bode well after one damn date.

"I told you. We talked."

And we never once ran out of things to say, even though we'd already spent hours catching up over dinner.

"Now what?"

I stand. "Now we go into that meeting and probably find a new marketing firm."

Hayden shakes his head, though he stands too.

"No, dumbass. Now what with you and Chari?"

I actually like the way that sounds. Me and Chari. *Us.* But it still feels like a pipe dream, like something that can't happen, or maybe something I can't let happen.

"Good question," I admit. "We have a virtual date Saturday night."

"A what?" Hayden looks at me like I'm crazy.

"I can't take a whole weekend off again. We're too close to our launch in Europe."

Something that's been two years in the making. It hasn't taken this long because of a lack of interest—rather, there's plenty of red tape and regulations to consider. The antidote, or the "Angel pill" as it is commonly known, threw a huge monkey wrench into the equation. Despite the fact that it only works with our brand, and if taken alone, has no more effect than a placebo, a drug was a drug. We knew from the start it wouldn't be easy. But Angel is finally ready for its European debut.

"So you're having a virtual date? What does that even mean?"

"It means the fifteen minutes are up and we have to go. Ready to play good cop, bad cop?"

It's a routine we do well by now. Me, always the bad cop. Hayden, the charmer, Mr. Nice Guy. I'm used to being underestimated. When I was younger, none of my teachers ever thought I would amount to much, but I've proven them wrong and then some. If the marketing firm thinks Hayden and I are a college frat boy duo who stumbled upon a cool discovery without two licks of sense, well, we'll show them otherwise.

For the moment, I force Chari to the back of my mind. Time to do business. Angel, Inc. is just getting started.

I PICK up my phone for the first time in hours.

She texted, just after four o'clock.

Still on for Saturday?

Screw Saturday. I had a shit day. No lunch, or dinner. Sitting in the back of my car, I watch as the buildings whiz by. It's after seven, and I'm starving.

But there's something I want even more than food. So I text back.

Plans in an hour? I had meetings all day. I'd like to see your face.

I wait, glad neither of us has the patience to pull the kind of juvenile back-and-forth I typically deal with. If she's not busy, she'll respond. It's nice knowing that.

One hour. See you then.

You'd swear I'm a fifteen-year-old boy with his first real girlfriend. The thought of seeing Chari, actually talking to her after texting all week . . . I told her we should take it slow, but every part of me wants just the opposite.

I have no clue how I let her out of my apartment on Sunday without more than a few kisses. With the exception of what happened between us on the couch the night before. The fact that I nearly came just by touching her . . . that was my first clue. We're too connected for something casual. By the time she walked out, her backside in a pair of jeans that made it look even sweeter than it had cradled in that little black dress, it took all of three minutes for me to have my hand wrapped around my cock. Even then, the speed of my release was slightly terrifying.

Just the fact that I'm sitting here texting Chari like a teenager instead of looking for a new CMO says a lot.

He had to go.

I can tolerate a botched campaign or two. Everyone makes mistakes, but he took no responsibility for his, and worse, he deflected the blame onto members of his team. That kind of disloyalty is unforgivable, and it's not a quality I want in any of our staff.

But getting rid of him also means adding more work to my own pile. Now, on top of the vodka development issues and our big launch in Europe, we need to search for a new marketing exec and firm. Maybe we should pull it in-house as Hayden suggested. We'll sit down tomorrow to crunch the numbers.

The black Mercedes pulls up to my apartment building, and I head inside. I still have almost an hour to kill before my call with Chari, so I take a quick swim downstairs and call next door for takeout. My personal assistant doesn't come home with me. Hayden thinks I'm nuts, but the idea of having someone in my apartment, finding me food . . . nope. I don't care if I can afford it. Never going to happen.

I look at my watch.

Three minutes early.

You calling me?

I flip on the fireplace, set the wine I've poured on the coffee table, and text back.

Yep.

Flipping my laptop open, I balance it on my lap and open a video screen. As it rings, I feel myself relaxing for the first time that day.

"Hey, you." She's in her bedroom.

"Looks familiar."

"Me or this room?" She turns her own computer around so I can see her bedroom.

"Both." Although she's redecorated her bedroom since we were kids. I remember all pink and white where now it's mostly grey and white.

And then she's back. Smiling, a bright spot in my day.

I like my job. Love it, actually. Because I believe in what we do, and every decision I make brings us closer to the top. But on days like this, I wish I could leave work at the office like some people.

"How was your day?" I ask. "Smell any smoke lately?"

She's dressed casually. A Penn State sweatshirt, maybe a nod to the fact that I wore my college sweatshirt the other night? I almost say something about going to a game together. Chari bleeds blue and white, and I haven't been to a PSU game in years. But that's months away.

"Oh my God, I forgot to tell you. I actually don't have a brain tumor. A neighbor was burning trash in their back-yard. The one behind my bedroom. Though I have no idea how Mom couldn't smell it."

I try not to laugh.

"You also don't have an esophageal disorder. That was one of your more interesting ailments."

"Stop it!" She's smiling. "Who the hell has a burn barrel in the middle of winter?"

"You're in Bridgewater, you know. Stranger things have happened." But I move on quickly, not wanting to focus on the fact that we're in two different cities. "Sounds like you're having a good day, then?"

"Eh. One of my kids sneezed on a classmate. So I got a call from the mother asking if I could please give them a lesson on proper sanitization protocols. My principal—"

"The douche canoe?"

She smiles. Her words, not mine.

"Yeah, him. Somehow he got wind of it, and he also wants to know why we don't teach kids to sneeze in their elbows instead of all over their classmates."

"What did you say?" I grab my wine, deciding I like Chari with a ponytail. A lot.

"I told him to pound sand."

I nearly spit out the sip I took. "Seriously?"

"No. But I wanted to. I mean, we do teach that. But just the day before he had zero time to talk to me about a new reading program. So frustrating."

Getting kids to read. One thing I'm not ready to talk to her about yet.

"How about you?" she asks. "Sounds like it was a hard day."

"You don't want to know. But," I cut her off, "I have something to ask you."

I've been thinking about it all day. All week, really. The idea is a bit insane, but you only live once. I've been working so hard all these years, and Hayden always tells me I need to work hard and play harder. This will be fun. Beyond fun.

If she says yes.

"You look so serious."

Maybe because this *is* a bit serious.

"Remember I talked about taking this slow?"

She pretends to think. When she shifts to the side, I get a clear view of the sheen of her lip gloss and wish I was there to lick it off her lips.

"Um, let me think. Take it slow. Oh that's right, I believe you told me that while you were lying on top of me."

And just like that, I'm as hard as a rock.

"Easy, tiger," I say, my voice strained, "or this is going to become a very different kind of call."

She laughs. Not a delicate, girly laugh but a deep one that makes me forget every single thing in the world except that sound.

"Oh yeah?" she says. "And there's something wrong with that?"

"Not at all." I swallow, imagining the possibilities. "But aren't you the least bit curious about my question?"

To be honest, I've almost forgotten what I was about to ask her. All I can think about is Chari stripping off her clothes, one item at a time. No, I want to be there for that. Live and in person.

"I am curious. Hit me."

"Well, the next two weeks are going to be nuts."

"Yep, you said that on Saturday."

"But the weekend after that, I'm actually going away for work. Do you remember me telling you about our European launch? How we're test-marketing in southern Switzerland?"

"Of course. You're looking at it as a microcosm of how Angel might perform in the surrounding countries."

The fact that she was listening so closely makes me oddly happy.

"Exactly."

Chari shifts, crossing her legs and giving me a brief peek at her whole body.

"Hayden was supposed to go, but he had a family emergency. So I'm taking his place."

I can see she doesn't understand yet.

"I'm going to Switzerland on the 23rd for a long week-end. I want you to come with me."

I've never wanted anything so badly as I want her to say yes. I know the area well. Hayden's parents have a house there. The thought of showing her around, of sharing this experience with her . . .

"I'll have meetings, of course. But there'll be plenty of downtime too."

"How many days?"

"Five. Thursday to Monday."

She presses her lips together.

"That'll be all three of my personal days. But it's far enough away that I can probably get them off."

When my stomach does a flip as she inches toward saying yes, I should be terrified. This is the opposite of slow.

"So what do you say?" I tried for a casual tone, but I can tell I didn't quite achieve it. My voice sounded strained to my own ears.

"I'll put in for them tomorrow."

I can't help but smile.

"Great."

More than great. Fucking awesome. Just last week, I was dreading this trip—now it's all I can think about.

"Holy crap. Are we really going to Switzerland? I've never been there before."

She looks happy. I know I am—a deep kind of happiness and satisfaction I haven't felt for a while. It's a huge turn-around from how I was feeling an hour ago.

"You'll love it."

"I'm sure I will." She pauses, then adds, "I'd also love to finish our conversation from last night."

Something else I learned about Chari Atwood, third grade teacher, that I wouldn't have expected.

She likes to talk dirty.

Luckily, so do I.

"Remind me, tiger, where did we leave off?"

14

CHARI

"*Happy birthday to you.*"

The entire bar finishes singing with a flourish. My brother, never one to shy away from attention, lifts his beer in salute as cheers go up across the room.

Saturday night at The Wheelhouse in Bridgewater. Nothing quite like it.

I feel like I'm in an episode of *Cheers*. Everyone in this bar does know each other, with a couple of exceptions, and most of us have lived here our whole lives. There's a special comfort in it. Snow blankets the streets outside, but in here it's cozy. Joyful.

And I'm trying to live in the moment. Celebrate my brother's birthday, which is actually tomorrow. Attempt not to look at my phone.

Enzo, as usual, is working at home after sending my brother two tickets to some professional golf tournament for this summer. Devon nearly lost his mind.

Lisa nudges me. "At least pretend you're having a good time."

"I am having a good time. I was just thinking of how cool

it is that everyone here knows Devon. It's probably not like this everywhere."

"If by everywhere you mean New York City," she says with a slight smirk, "you're probably right."

It's getting harder and harder to pretend life is completely normal. Three weeks ago, I was sitting at this bar, happy as a clam other than the constant cold drafts of air hitting my back. Totally unsuspecting of the freight train that would barrel into my life in the form of Enzo DeLuca.

I can't stop smiling.

Mom knows about Enzo, and she keeps begging me to tell Devon. Which I totally plan to do, at some point.

"You have that faraway, dreamy look on your face again. As usual."

I smile into my glass. "I can't help it."

"Are you drinking wine?"

I lift up my glass as if to toast her. "Nope."

"Smart-ass. Since when are you a wine drinker?"

Since Enzo.

"I tried it that night at dinner."

"You mean the two-thousand-dollar one?"

"Yeah, that one."

Lisa shakes her head, shoving a drunk guy who stumbles toward us. "I still can't imagine. Two thousand dollars. For one dinner. It's insane."

"Anyway, I really liked the wine I had that night." I lower my voice even though Devon is too far away to hear, surrounded by friends. "Enzo says the quality matters. I've been trying out different kinds, and I really like Riesling. The white wine his company makes is a bit too dry for me. Not sure I'm ready for that yet."

"Let me taste."

Lisa doesn't really drink wine either. She takes a sip and shrugs. "Not terrible."

Since she's drinking Angel's Brew, Lisa is the designated driver, freeing me up to go non-Angel. "Can you imagine? A few years ago, we'd have had to get a ride home."

Angel keeps adding more products, and people have begun to make it a big part of their party plans. Who's drinking what? Non-Angel, you aren't driving. It's hard to imagine going back to life before the Angel pill.

"Yeah, your boyfriend changed that," Lisa says.

I snort, a pretty unladylike sound, to be honest.

"He's *not* my boyfriend."

"Really?" Lisa's brows rise. "Have you or have you not talked to him every day since New York?"

I think back to the last two weeks. "I didn't talk to him the first few days after. We were just texting at first."

Lisa rolls her eyes. "Since then?"

And yes, it's become a routine. During the day, we set a time, usually based on Enzo's crazy work schedule. And then we video chat before bed. Sometimes just talking, other times . . .

"And you're going to freaking Switzerland with him."

"Shhh."

"You really have to tell Devon."

"I know, I know. I'm waiting until after his birthday."

Lisa looks at me like I'm crazy. "What the hell does that have to do with it?"

Well, when she puts it that way . . . still, I persist. "Devon loves his birthday. Mom makes a big deal of it for like two weeks."

"Yeah, I know. Always wished I could be adopted by her."

I almost say, *But at least you have two parents*, and then

realize how quickly that will kill the mood. I rarely feel the urge to talk about my nonexistent father, and this is no exception.

"Say the word and she'll have a month-long birthday celebration for you too."

Lisa looks pleased by the idea.

"Speaking of your mom, what's going on with her new boy toy?"

I give her a scathing look.

"Sorry," she says with a laugh. "I kinda like him."

She met him last weekend. And sure, I haven't found any evidence to dispel his image of the ultimate nice guy, but I'm still watching for any missteps.

"Uh-huh," I murmur.

Lisa stares at me. Hard. I already know I won't like what comes out of her mouth next.

"I think you may be jaded."

Here we go.

"Lisa, I'm not jaded. I've just never met anyone that nice. There must be something wrong with him."

"Or not."

"Yeah, and he's divorced because he's the next Mr. Rogers."

"Geez." Lisa takes a drink and glances over at one of Devon's friends. Aaron is a good guy, but he's not really relationship material. If I had to guess, I'd say Lisa's on-again, off-again boyfriend is moving toward off-again. I honestly can't keep up. "You're tough. But I get it."

I shoot her a *not now* look.

"In other news, your phone just buzzed."

How did I completely forget to look? The thing's been attached to me for weeks. I snatch it off the bar just as my brother sidles up next to us.

"Whatcha doing?"

He's more than a little tipsy. Thankfully, Devon is one of those drunks who turns into the life of the party.

"Just talking about how I wish I was in your family and still got big birthday bashes and Easter baskets well into my twenties," Lisa quips, thankfully taking Devon's eyes off my phone. If he'd looked down just a second earlier, he would have seen Enzo's message pop up.

A close call.

I want to text him back, but Devon is hovering over us. It's not going to happen right now.

"Hey, Aaron," he calls to his friend as he puts his arms around us. "Did I ever tell you I have two sisters? Aren't they awesome?"

Aaron looks squarely at Lisa. Yep, something's going on between them for sure. Or if it hasn't happened yet, it will.

"Yeah, pretty awesome," he says.

My brother looks between Aaron and Lisa. "Ooooh, I saw that look. Better be careful with her, bro. I don't want to have to school you."

Lisa swats him.

"Can you please play overprotective brother with your real sister?"

Devon places his hand on his heart, as if wounded. "Me? Overprotective? Never."

If that were true, I wouldn't have had to put Enzo in my back pocket. A vibration tells me he texted again, and my fingers are itching to check it, to text him back.

But tonight is about Devon.

"Chari, am I overprotective?" he asks.

As if he could reasonably expect me to deny it. I grab my wine and take a sip in answer.

"Hey, come on. Stick up for your big brother here?"

Lisa clears her throat, and guilt rushes through me. I feel bad she has to hide my secret from him. I really do need to tell Devon about Enzo. Not that we're officially dating or anything, but I am going on an international trip with him next week. Devon is sure to notice that. Despite Enzo's worry, I just can't keep a secret from my brother. Though I do wonder how Devon will react.

I guess we'll find out in two days. It probably is silly to wait until after his birthday, but what will two days matter?

Another text.

"Holy shit, are you kidding me?"

Devon drops his arms and looks at someone near the door. I can't see who it is, but at least I can text Enzo back.

But first I turn around to see who Devon is looking at.

"Two times in a month. What the hell are you doing here?"

I try to lift myself up from the barstool to see, but it's crowded and I can't get the angle right. "Who is it?"

"And thanks for those tickets. That's one hell of a birthday present."

No. It can't be . . .

I grab my phone from my jeans and look at it before I can actually see him.

Are you still at The Wheelhouse? Have a surprise.

It's Enzo.

15

ENZO

I must be crazy. But it's not like I was accomplishing anything anyway. After an hour of staring at my laptop—or more accurately, staring at the spot on my couch where Chari came apart in my hands two weeks ago—I made a decision. It was late enough that it wouldn't take my driver long to get out of the city. I figured I could see her, celebrate with Devon, check on Tris's restaurant, and head straight to the lab first thing in the morning. Plus I could get some work done on the way there and back.

I called my mother from the car to let her know what I was planning. Or at least to tell her I'd probably be staying at the house tonight. She, of course, suspects something.

"You couldn't come home for Christmas, but now you're here twice in one month?"

I stretched my legs out as far as they'd go in front of me. One Christmas, and I'll never live it down.

"I realized how much I miss everyone." Which was true, but not necessarily the reason for my visit.

"Bullshit."

My mother never minces words. And she's always had a special radar for lies.

"Devon is at The Wheelhouse. It's his birthday weekend." Everyone in town knows the Atwood birthdays are legendary. Devon and Chari's mom makes a bigger deal about them than my own parents do, which is saying something. "I'll be home late and have to head back in the morning. Maybe we can all get breakfast at Mignon's?"

The lakefront restaurant is known for their Sunday breakfast and brunches.

"My treat."

Silence.

"Who is she?" my mother asked.

I'm not sure how she guessed—it certainly wasn't anything I said—but she did. Maybe she just knows me. I didn't answer her, not wanting to lie. Instead, I made an excuse to end the call and told her I'd see her in the morning.

I'm not here to tell Devon that I'm dating his sister—I know she wants to wait until after his birthday, which I get. And I intend to honor her wishes.

The almost panicked, deer-in-the-headlights look on Chari's face says she doesn't know if we're still on the same page. She glances from me to Devon, eyes wide, and I shake my head ever so slightly to allay her fears.

"Happy birthday," I say to Devon. "Long time no see."

"I can't believe you're back. Did you text me?" Devon pulls out his phone.

"Nah, figured I'd surprise you." I let myself glance at her again. "Hey, Chari."

The tension between us is palpable. Can't Devon tell?

"Twice in a month? To what do we owe the pleasure?" she asks, already knowing the answer.

When Chari jumps off the barstool, I hold my breath. The need to touch her is part of the reason I'm here. But I can't greet her the way I want to, the way I need to—a hug will have to do. When she wraps her arms around me, I inhale the scent of her hair—vanilla and coconut—hugging her back. Just as I'm getting used to the idea of her in my arms, she pulls away.

"Hey, Enzo," Lisa calls as the country music from the jukebox blares around us.

I'm definitely not in Manhattan anymore.

"Hey, yourself," I say, trying not to stare at Chari.

"How long are you in for?" Devon asks.

"Just the night. Heading back in the morning."

I see a few people staring at me, some edging in closer, but I'm not in the mood to talk shop—or to make nice with anyone other than my friends.

"I talked to Tris earlier," I say. "He offered to host after-hours drinks at the bar as soon as we're done here."

DeLuca's II stops serving at ten and closes the bar when everyone is gone. But there are perks to being the owner's brother.

"Cool," Devon says. "I'm ready for a change of scenery. Who's driving? Time to take your pills."

I look at Chari, who sends some special signal to Lisa.

"Got mine." She holds up the white packet and opens it. "And my car."

"I have a car too," I say. "And a driver."

As she pops her Angel pill, Lisa meets my gaze. Some sort of understanding passes between us, and I know she's going to help us before she says anything.

"Cool, I'll come with you," Devon says, but Lisa grabs him before he can finish his sentence. "I got you, birthday boy. Who else?"

The pill will take at least ten minutes to work, depending on how much Lisa drank. In the meantime, I hang back, trying not to draw suspicion. By the time rides are arranged for the people moving on to DeLuca's II, Chari and I have had a full-on silent discussion.

She will be driving with me. Alone.

After an agonizing fifteen minutes, we finally leave the bar. No one seems to notice us hanging back, except for Lisa, of course. She winks at us and then jumps into the driver's seat of her car.

Not for the first time in the past few years, my chest swells with pride from the knowledge that she's totally sober. This is why we can't stop now. Angel needs to be in every bar in the world.

"After you," I say, climbing into the back seat of my car after Chari. Although she's dressed more casually tonight, in jeans and a hunter green puffer jacket, she's every bit as stunning as she was on our date. As soon as the door shuts behind me, I tell the driver where we're headed and shut the privacy screen. I have no desire to waste even a half second of the ten-minute drive.

Thank God for the privacy screen.

Pulling Chari nearly onto my lap, I kiss her, hard. She opens for me, our tongues tangling. My hand finds the bottom of her sweater, takes advantage of the opening there, and meanders upward. I need to feel her skin. Pressing my palm to her rib cage, I frantically pull down the lace of her bra. But just feeling isn't enough.

I need a taste.

I lift her sweater and lower my head to her breasts, flicking my tongue over one of her nipples before gently biting down. Chari pulls my head closer, my name falling from her lips over and over. And I swear I've never been so hard.

Lifting my head up, knowing we don't have a lot of time, I replace her bra.

"It's not enough," I say, looking deep into her eyes.

"I can't believe you're here."

I kiss her, the first of a million kisses, I hope.

"I texted you." My hands are everywhere at once. I want to memorize the shape of her, the feel of her, to carry me through the bleak, lonely hours without her.

"I got it"—she smiles—"after I saw you walk through the door."

I can tell she's pleased.

"Happy to see me?"

She nods. "Beyond happy."

"Maybe we should just tell him tonight," I venture. While I don't want to ruin the mood, I also don't want to keep pretending Chari's not important to me, that she's just Devon's little sister. Although I'm not at all looking forward to his reaction.

She frowns. "No, please. Not yet."

The words sting, even though she already told me she wants to wait. And a part of me does too. But it feels like she's rejecting me. Like she's saying I'm not good enough.

"Are you embarrassed of me?"

The moment the words leave my mouth, I wish I could bring them back. That's the grade-school Enzo talking, the one who was laughed at because he couldn't read. The middle schooler who was told not to bother applying to a prep school. The high school Enzo whose guidance counselor told him flat out that he would never get into Cornell.

That Enzo is dead and buried. At least, I thought so.

"Oh my God, are you serious?"

I wish I weren't. But honestly, I get her reluctance. If it weren't for Switzerland, I'd not be in a rush either. Devon won't be thrilled at first, but maybe he'll be happy to see us together once he realizes how much we care about each other.

"Well," I say, hating how vulnerable I sound, how weak, "you know we have to tell him soon anyway. Why wait?"

"Because he might be upset at first . . . and I don't want that to happen on his birthday. But I do want to tell him. I'm proud of you, Enzo. More proud than you know."

She takes my face in her hands then, and all I want to do is kiss her.

So I do.

Willing her mouth open, I silently apologize for being ridiculous. For pushing her. Even for coming back home unannounced. I love her lips and can't get enough. But unfortunately, the car stops in front of Tris's restaurant.

"Promise me you won't say anything tonight?" she says softly.

I don't like lying to Devon, but I'm the one who put us in this position by showing up unannounced.

"Promise. But—"

"I'll tell him everything on Monday. Before Switzerland."

I can't help but smile at that. "We're leaving on Thursday, so you're not going to have much of a choice."

"I know. And I'm going to do it. But for tonight"—she backs away from me as the driver opens the door for us—"we're just friends. Old friends."

"With benefits," I add, sliding out. "Ones I intend to take full advantage of somehow."

Although I'm not quite sure how. She lives at home. I can either stay with Mom, Dad, and Lusanne, or Tris and Gian, who live together. Either way, there won't be much privacy. I thought about getting a hotel room, but I didn't want Chari to think I came here just for sex.

But now that I see her . . .

"I'm sure you will," she says as I reach out my hand and then quickly pull it back. I glance ahead at the other two cars, which are emptying, but thankfully no one seemed to notice.

16

CHARI

*B*eing this close to him, pretending we're nothing more than friends . . .

It's impossible.

Maybe Enzo's right, and I should tell Devon the truth? We're sitting around the new bar, and Tris and Enzo are slinging drinks and joking around with each other. Every so often, Enzo sneaks a glance at me. My body responds to each one. First, a flush. And then, as his chocolate brown eyes linger just a bit longer than is probably safe, my heart speeds up.

Enzo takes his phone out, and when my pocket vibrates a few second later, I know I can't reach for it too soon. Besides, maybe it won't kill me to play it cool for a few seconds.

"So I hear you're heading overseas this week?" Gian asks Enzo.

Oh boy.

"Yeah, Switzerland. Mom tell you?"

All eyes turn to the youngest male DeLuca. "Yeah, she said she talked to you on your way here. I still can't believe you came in again so soon after your last visit, and for less than twenty-four hours."

Enzo looks at me, nodding ever so slightly downward. A nudge to check my phone. Which I was just about to do. But now I think it might be fun to play with him a bit.

Casual in jeans and a button-down, he's still a bit of a standout in our crowd. If a stranger were asked to pick which of us is worth billions of dollars, they'd have it in one.

"Must be pretty exciting, the idea of Angel making its way to Europe," says my brother, who's standing next to me.

"Exciting, yeah," Enzo says, patting his pocket—his phone—as he answers. I try not to laugh. "But it's stressful. Just two days ago, we thought the whole thing might fall apart."

I almost blurt out, *You didn't mention that*, but restrain myself.

OK, time to check his text.

Your lips were made to be kissed

I laugh. That's the urgent message? I was hoping it might be an invitation to meet him in the basement or something.

"What's so funny?" Devon asks next to me.

I quickly tuck the phone back in my pocket. "Nothing."

I really do hate lying to him. But every time I open my mouth to say the words, they get stuck. What if Devon's so upset it ruins their friendship? I'd never forgive myself.

But that's just silly. Devon thinks the world of Enzo, and once he gets over his big-brother-protectiveness thing and realizes Enzo and I are . . . well, not serious maybe, but seriously interested in each other, he'll be thrilled for us.

Won't he?

"I'm glad it's back on track," Tris says. "When do you leave?"

Enzo stares straight at me. I know what he's thinking. But this is not the way to do it.

"Thursday."

"Must be cold over there now, huh?"

Enzo takes a swig of his beer and avoids eye contact. This is clearly hard for him too. So what was he thinking, showing up tonight? He knew I planned on telling Devon this week.

I pull my phone back out to ask him.

Unlike me, he doesn't pause. His answer buzzes in my hand a few seconds later.

Wasn't thinking.

Needed to see you.

Now I feel all warm and fuzzy—he hopped in his car for a two-hour drive just because he *needed to see* me. No guy's ever done that for me before. And in return, I'm pretending we aren't three seconds away from throwing ourselves at each other.

I make a decision.

I'll tell him tonight, I text.

Which is when I notice Devon peering over my shoulder.

"Chari, what the hell?" he says.

"Why are you looking at my phone?" I shoot back.

Everyone stares at us. Most of our friends look confused, but Lisa has an *oh shit* look. She, at least, knows what's about to go down.

"Because you've been acting super weird. And now I know why."

The room stays painfully silent, Devon's eyes boring holes into me.

"Excuse us," I say, pulling him away from the bar and out onto the covered patio.

Devon crosses his arms, beer and all. "Care to explain?"

Part of me wants to continue to bemoan his breach of privacy. An old argument with us. But it would be childish to deflect the blame—I know this is my fault for not being honest.

"We were going to tell you."

He doesn't make it easy. "Uh-huh? And what, exactly, were you going to tell me? Why is Enzo texting you from three feet away?"

Like tearing off a Band-Aid, I say, "We're dating."

Oh my God. Are we dating?

Enzo comes out of nowhere, like an archangel swooping in out of the dark to rescue me.

"Seriously?" Devon says, his eyes bugging out. I can't tell if he's pissed or not.

"It hasn't been for long," I rush to add. "Just since he was here last time."

Devon shifts his attention to Enzo.

"You're here for Chari?" he asks, deadpan.

Enzo doesn't hesitate. "Yes. And your birthday."

"Details?"

It's like they're speaking their own guy language now, and I'm just a bystander to the conversation.

"We started talking after that weekend. And then she came out to New York for a night."

Devon turns back to me. "How did I not notice you were gone?"

I shrug. "I just went for dinner and came back early. You're not my keeper," I say, starting to get defensive.

Enzo continues in a much calmer tone. "We've been talking since then. And Chari agreed to accompany me to Switzerland next week."

Geez, when he tells the truth, he goes all in. No sugarcoating. I would have tried easing Devon in a little first, but what the hell. Now he knows everything.

"I see," Devon says. He doesn't really sound upset. But you never can tell with him.

"When did you plan on telling me?"

I jump in. "On Monday."

Devon makes a face.

"After your birthday. Just in case you were pissed."

He rolls his eyes. "You're so much like Mom it's scary."

He says it like it's a bad thing, or at least an annoying thing.

"I wish you'd told me sooner," he says. "But you don't have to look at me like that, Char. I only care that you're happy. You should know that. I know I can be an overprotective asshole, but Enzo isn't just any guy."

I let out a deep breath and give Enzo an *I told you so* look.

"I know but . . . I'm sorry I didn't tell you sooner."

Devon wraps his arms around me, and I feel like I can finally breathe normally again. He knows, and it's okay. I haven't ruined anything, and now Enzo and I don't have to keep things secret anymore.

"It's fine. Let's get back to the party," he says, and I could not be more relieved.

"Sounds good to me." I glance at Enzo, but he's not moving. Instead, he and my brother are looking at each other. Which makes me think there's several layers of subtext I'm missing here. Maybe things aren't so okay after all.

"I'll catch up with you in a sec," Enzo says.

Without any other choice, I walk back to the bar wishing I could stay to . . . what? Protect Enzo? I was just caught lying to my brother, and yet I'm worried about him. Which is silly. He's a big boy and can take care of himself.

What could possibly go wrong?

17

ENZO

"What the hell, Enz?"

Devon is extremely pissed. Rightly so.

"I'm sorry."

The words seem so inadequate, but I don't know what else to say. Keeping this from him was a shitty thing to do, and I especially shouldn't have come here tonight knowing Chari didn't want to tell him yet. But I wasn't lying to Chari: I really didn't put much thought into it. I couldn't concentrate. Pacing my apartment did no good. Looking at my couch only made me think of Chari spread across it. So I acted on impulse. Uncharacteristically, as so many people have commented on tonight.

"So? What are your intentions?"

This is the question I've been waiting for.

"I'd never hurt her," I say honestly. Devon knows that. I think. But it still bears saying.

"Not intentionally. But come on, Enzo. I know you better than anyone."

A round of laughter reaches us from the bar, which only seems to underscore the serious mood between us.

"What's that supposed to mean?" Although I'm pretty sure I already know.

"If you don't have time for a Yankees game . . ."

My family got Devon and I to root for them at a young age, and we both became lifelong fans. So when I got Dev tickets to a playoff game and told him to take a friend, that I was too busy with work, he blasted me. Told me point-blank that he respected everything I'd done but my money was no good to me if I couldn't enjoy life.

Of course, my mother has been saying the same for years. But they just don't understand. I'm building something, and that requires sacrifice.

"We're just dating," I say in a futile attempt to pacify him. "Listen, Dev, no one is more surprised by this than me. We talked a bit when I came here for the opening. And things just progressed from there."

"An awful quick progression," he huffed. "Switzerland?"

I wince. "Yeah, I know."

And I do. It's not like me at all. But that's the point.

"I'd never fuck around with Chari. You know that."

Devon still has his arms crossed, closed-down body language if I've ever seen it. He's always been this protective of Chari, only now it's directed at me. I hate being at odds with him. It's like fighting with one of my siblings. But worse. They have no choice but to stay related to me.

"I do. But I also know you're a workaholic. And that you co-own an international business. Something that's not exactly conducive to a long-term relationship."

Tell me something I don't know.

"And the second thing?" Because I can tell there's something he's not saying, something he needs to say in order to clear the air between us.

He hesitates.

"Dev?"

"I can't. She'll kill me."

The hair on the back of my neck rises.

"What do you mean?" I ask.

Devon frowns. "Chari had a . . . thing for you."

"I know that. What does some schoolgirl crush have to do with this?"

"Schoolgirl crush?" he says, brows rising. "I think it was more than that."

My heart races at the possibility that Chari might have had a thing for me for longer than I'd realized. "Like in high school?"

Devon makes a face.

"Middle school?"

That, I wasn't aware of.

"Try again."

"Grade school?" I say incredulously. "You're kidding me."

But he isn't. I can tell by his expression.

"She got better at hiding it, even from me. But I'm pretty sure my sister has had a crush on you for basically forever."

"That doesn't change anything."

And it doesn't. Except I kind of like it and look forward to teasing her about it.

"The hell it doesn't. She's been half in love with you her whole life. And now you swoop in with all of this." He waves his arms at me.

"I'm not sure what that's supposed to mean."

"Most guys don't take their girlfriends to Switzerland on a second date."

I smile, unable to help it. "We haven't firmed up that status yet. And third date. I'm counting this as our second."

Devon gives me a look. "I suggest you firm up your status fairly quickly. I know you wouldn't intentionally hurt her, Enzo. But you guys have history. And that matters. Don't break her fucking heart."

"If I do, you have my permission to beat me to a bloody pulp."

I mean that, and Devon could certainly do it. He's been boxing since before he could ride a bike. It didn't matter that I worked out five days a week or grew up with two brothers who liked to wrestle. But I have no intention of breaking Chari's heart. I might not have a clear idea of where this is going, but I'm in it, all the way.

"We should have told you sooner," I continue. "I'm glad you know now, Dev. I would have stayed away if I could've, but I couldn't get her out of my head. There's just something about you Atwoods . . ."

Devon knows I'm being serious. Finally, still unsmiling, he sticks out his hand.

"You have my blessing, but I'm also serious about what I said. Don't think I'm above taking you up on your offer."

"I know you're not," I say, deadly serious, and shake his hand. I'm glad this is over—that he knows—but I feel even more unsettled than before. Because I'm asking myself if I deserve the blessing my friend hesitantly gave me.

I'm not so sure that I do.

18
___

CHARI

"*You* look like you're about to jump out of your skin," Mom says.

She's right. I feel like it too.

"Maybe a little."

Enzo invited me to come to breakfast with his family this morning, but I know he doesn't get to spend much time with them. I didn't want to interfere, so I skipped breakfast with the DeLucas. But he promised to stop by on his way to the lab, and I can't sit still while I wait for him to show.

Mom took the day off to go skiing with the new beau. Which is weird in that we're not much of a skiing family. We tried a few times at a local ski resort when Devon and I were kids, but neither of us took to it. I hated the cold, and Devon broke his arm on, like, his third run, so that was pretty much that. Mom told me that she used to ski, before us, and apparently she wants to take it up again.

I'm glad she found people she can trust to work in the shop. She deserves a day off. But I'm still a bit unsettled about the new guy.

I pick a piece of bacon off a serving plate in the kitchen. It's sat there for a while, but I'm full of nervous energy.

"You missed Devon earlier," Mom says, loading the dishwasher. "While you were in the shower."

I finish the bacon, moving to help my mom.

"Yeah, he texted after he left to tell me he'd stopped by." I pause. "Did he say anything else? About Enzo?"

Mom shakes her head. "Not really. But you know him."

Devon isn't always the most forthcoming when it comes to things like feelings.

"He seemed OK with it," I press.

She takes out a dish I loaded and rerinses it.

"I think so too. Maybe just a little worried."

"About?" I say, my tone a little harsh.

Mom continues to load up the dishwasher, as if we're discussing something as inconsequential as the weather.

"Enzo always was kind of . . ." She hesitates.

Please don't say something bad about him, Mom.

". . . intense."

"Meaning?"

"Just seems unlikely he'll be ready to settle down anytime soon. With all he has going on."

"He kind of owns a multibillion-dollar company that's about to go worldwide. So yeah, I'd agree with that."

Then comes the look.

"Mom, we're not getting married. I don't even know if we're, like, boyfriend and girlfriend."

"I would say going to Europe on a date qualifies you as boyfriend and girlfriend."

Maybe.

"I like him," she says, "Always have. But I'm not sure if he makes good boyfriend material, that's all."

She closes the dishwasher and blows out the candle in

the center of the table. Mom loves her scented candles and goes through like two a week.

"But you're a big girl and can handle yourself. Of that I have no doubt."

My shoulders straighten. "Thanks, Mom."

There's something else I've been meaning to talk to her about, and I figure now's as good a time as any.

"So, speaking of boyfriends . . ."

I let that linger. We haven't talked much about Jeff, but I've asked pretty much everyone in town about him, and no one has a bad word to say. Of course, I suspect his ex-wife might have a different story.

My mirror image, twenty-five years older, looks back at me, quirking her brow. Suddenly I'm not so sure what to say, or how to say it. I settle on, "I realize I've been kind of strange about Jeff."

"Chari, I told you to talk to me about him when you're ready."

"I guess I'm ready. And I really want you to be happy. It's just . . ." I swallow. There's no nice way to say this. "Your track record isn't great."

My mom laughs, but I'm serious.

"Dad is a total jerk. That engineer guy was horrible. You do really well, with the business and everything . . ."

She sits down at the table, so I do the same.

"You're as protective of me as Devon is of both of us," she says. "And I appreciate that. But Jeff is not your father. Not even close."

"Obviously. But if he's such a catch, why has he been single for so long?"

She gives me a look as if to ask, *Really?*

"You are the exception."

Mom smiles from one side of her mouth.

"So maybe I've been slightly . . . closed off to him," I admit, and I can't help but grin as I add, "But you're a big girl and can handle yourself."

I love my mother's laugh.

"Thank you, Char." She reaches across the table for my hand. "I also know why you still live at home. Why you invite me out with your friends so much."

I try to argue, but she won't have it.

"You don't need to do that, you know. I'm fine. Even without Jeff, I am fine."

I can tell she wants to say something more.

"What?" I press.

Mom sighs, hesitating.

"What is it?"

"You don't need to stay here for me."

She's totally right. I should have my own place by now. But the thought of her living alone . . .

"I kind of like not having rent payments," I say, knowing it's a weak argument.

"I don't mean in this house."

"In Bridgewater?" I ask, genuinely shocked. "Why would I want to leave? I have a good job. You're here. Devon is here."

She squeezes my hand and stands.

"A good job. Yes. But one you love? You've complained about this small town for as long as I can remember. I honestly never thought you'd come back after college."

I stand too.

"I like Bridgewater," I say, without passion. "And I love my kids."

Which is true. I'm not exactly fond of dealing with all the red tape and state assessments and stupid crap that

doesn't actually teach kids how to read. But the kids them-
selves? I love them.

And Bridgewater is . . . fine. It's comfortable.

"All I'm saying is, you don't have to worry about me. I'm
fine. Truly."

What started off as a talk about Jeff has suddenly
become something bigger. My mom's right. I did consider
moving away after college, preferably to somewhere with a
warmer climate. But I didn't consider it for very long. My
mother isn't the type of person who should live alone—she's
too warm, too nurturing, too Mom. And maybe this Jeff guy
isn't that bad after all, but I'm not willing to adios on a
maybe.

"OK, Mom," I say, anxious to find a new topic of discussion. "What time is Jeff picking you up?"

She looks down at her phone sitting on the table. "In an
hour. I better get—"

Mom is cut off by the doorbell. We look at each other,
and she shoos me toward the door. I try to walk at a
normal pace, as if I haven't been looking out the window
for the past hour. My heart pounds as I open the front
door.

He looks even better than he did last night. I love him in
a sweater.

"Morning," he says, smiling. "Have time for a coffee
before I head back?"

"Of course." I step back to let him inside. "Let me grab
my jacket."

He closes the door behind him just as my mom appears
in the hallway.

"Hi, Enzo," she says warmly, giving him a hug.

"Hi, Mrs. Atwood."

She's told him a million times to call her by her first

name, but he'd never do it. Would he change his mind if she was his mother-in-law?

Stop it, Chari. Way ahead of yourself there.

If Lisa knew I was thinking like that, she'd give me a look, and probably a talking-to.

"Where are you guys headed?" she asks as I open the coat closet.

"I was thinking Ledges for coffee," he says, looking at me for my nod. I give it. "I have to head back soon."

She asks about the business. He asks about her shop. Their familiarity is so strange, but it's a good strange. Most of the guys I bring home haven't known my mom their whole lives.

"Ready," I say, shrugging into my coat. "Have fun, Mom. And be careful." I turn to Enzo. "She's going skiing."

"Nice. Didn't know you skied. Is Devon coming with you?" he says, laughter trailing his voice. Everyone remembers his broken arm.

"Definitely not." She smiles at us both. "Have fun, kids."

It's something she's always said to Devon and I, and to Enzo too, come to think of it, and there's something charming about hearing it now, even though we're obviously not kids anymore.

"Same to you," he says with a grin, standing off to the side so I can walk past him.

"Later, Mom," I say.

His car is waiting for us, and I'm pretty sure I'll never get over the novelty of having a driver cart me around. Still, I won't deny it's a welcome opportunity to be alone with Enzo. He pulls me to him as soon as I close the door behind us, and I don't protest in the least.

Before I can even process how close he is, or the warmth of his touch, he's kissing me. I open for him immediately, the touch of his tongue becoming more familiar. But it's not enough. Last night was even more frustrating than New York.

Fact is, I want him like I've never wanted another human being, and I know he feels the same. Moaning against my lips, he pulls away.

"Six days," he says, looking deep into my eyes.

I make a mental calculation, confused.

"We'll be in Switzerland in four," I counter.

We haven't actually talked about sex explicitly. As in, when we might go for it. But his meaning is abundantly clear. And I'm one hundred percent on board . . . only I don't want to wait quite that long.

"I know," he says, taking a strand of my hair between his fingers, "but Thursday is a travel day."

Now I'm thoroughly baffled.

"And?"

Twisting my hair through his fingers, which I kind of like, he smiles as if he knows something I don't.

"When we get in, I have to meet a few people at the bar where Angel's launching. It's going to be a long day. And I have meetings all Friday morning. But I've kept my afternoon clear."

"Still confused." And hot. It feels like it's a thousand degrees in this back seat. And I'm never hot in February.

"I may have made some plans for us on Friday."

He's more serious now than before, but he's still playing with my hair in a way that's both sexy and faintly mesmerizing. I don't want him to stop.

"I see."

But I really don't.

He hesitates. "I want it to be special."

It. Sex. Us.

My heart melts.

"Think you can wait that long?"

I reach up, cupping his cheeks with my hands. They're just a little rough, the perfect amount of stubble.

"Devon admitted he spilled his guts to you last night," I say. "So you already know the answer to that one."

It's hard to tell him that, but he made himself vulnerable to me, and it would seem like almost a betrayal not to do the same.

"I've waited this long, haven't I?" I finish.

19

ENZO

"I don't think I can wait," Chari's voice pipes through the phone.

We've had a crazy week getting ready for our launch in Europe. Hayden told me last night he's never seen me like this, and I know exactly what he's talking about. It's concerning, actually.

I'm distracted. Losing focus. Before Chari, most of my excitement was reserved for the company. For weekly reports and lab results. Now I'm staring at my phone and counting the hours until she and I video chat every night. Never mind thinking about this weekend. I should be planning for the launch, but the promise of finally having Chari in my bed preoccupies me.

Pushing those thoughts aside, I look at my screen. She's wearing a fuzzy sweater wrap thing that makes me want to crawl through there and feel it. And her. "Did you look at the weather? It's unseasonably warm this week."

Chari nods. "I packed layers."

"Don't forget your passport."

"Already packed."

I hate to get off with her, but I still need to pack too.

"You're one step ahead of me. It was crazy today at the office. I just got home when you called."

She scrunches her nose. "At nine o'clock?"

Chari is home by four o'clock every day. Even though she knows my hours by now, they're a constant source of amazement to her.

"Yeah," I tease. "Early night."

She can't tell if I'm kidding or not.

I'm not.

"The car will pick you up at three a.m. Get some rest. You're going to need it. See you at the airport?"

She gets this dubious look on her face—the same expression I get from my family members every time I tell them I've sent a car for them.

"Don't look at me like that. There's no reason you should drive to the airport in the middle of the night."

"Except that I have a car. And know how to drive. I've been doing it for twenty-nine years."

I bite back a laugh. I love it when Chari responds impetuously to something. It's part of her charm. She immediately realizes her mistake. "I mean, hold on . . ."

"Thirteen years," I provide.

"Exactly. That's what I meant. I've been driving for thirteen years. See, that's why I teach reading and not math."

"Don't shortchange yourself. There's no such thing as being inherently good at math."

"I know, I know. A math teacher friend of mine reminds me all the time not to trash-talk her subject. Says the kids are listening, and they need to know they can all be good at it."

"Exactly."

"But I still hate it."

I smile. "What I hate is the thought of lying next to you tomorrow night and not being inside you."

An abrupt change in subject, but one she rolls with easily. It's been like this all week. The promise of what might happen—*will* happen—two nights from now is nearly killing us both.

"Easy to fix."

It really did sound like a good plan in my head. Make Friday afternoon the best date Chari has ever had in her life. An unforgettable day, and night. But I forgot the part about sleeping in the same bed with her the night before.

Making it to Friday is a challenge at this point, one she seems set on making me lose.

Chari should know me better than that. I don't lose.

Ever.

"Think how amazing Friday night will be," I counter. "And on that note, I'm off to pack."

"I'm off to attempt to sleep."

I never get much sleep the night before a flight either. But I wish her luck, and after we hang up, I quickly pack my bag.

I can't sleep, of course, the anticipation keeping me awake. It's hard to imagine that a few weeks ago I was cursing Hayden for making me take this trip. Now, I can't remember the last time I looked forward to something this much. When the alarm rings, I'm surprised. I honestly didn't think I'd ever nod off.

We agreed to meet at the gate, knowing we'd be separated in security anyway. Chari doesn't travel as much, doesn't have PreCheck, and will likely be held up for a while. Thursday tends to be one of the busier days at JFK, even at this time in the morning. So when I sail through security and walk toward the gate, I'm surprised to see her sitting alone, earbuds in her ears, looking my way.

She spots me.

My heart races, knowing this is the beginning of . . . something. This weekend may be a business trip, but it's a hell of a lot more than that.

We haven't talked about the status of our relationship yet, but it's inevitable it'll happen this weekend. I worry how Chari will take the whole work-life balance speech I know I have to give her. Either we'll come out of this a couple or . . .

"Hey, handsome."

"Morning, tiger," I whisper as she stands to greet me. She's stuck with the name at this point. And then I become something I hate.

A public-display-of-affection person.

But I can't help leaning down for a slow, deep kiss. One not entirely appropriate for an airport. I hate to break away. Getting lost in Chari is my new favorite pastime.

"Ready for an adventure?" I say.

"Signs point to yes."

That's when I notice two coffees in a carrier on the seat next to her.

"You are a gem," I say, picking up the unopened one.

"How do you know it's for you?" But she grins and takes the other, throwing the carrier away.

By the time we board, my nervous energy from earlier has dissipated a bit, and I'm ready to settle in for a long travel day. Typically, I would take a red-eye to Europe, but there were no open seats on the flight Hayden was supposed to take, so I had to reschedule us to a morning flight when I added Chari's seat. But I don't mind, not with her by my side.

"I'm trying to play it cool, but holy shit," she says,

looking at our seats. Since I had to rebook, anyway, I made sure to have my assistant choose an airline with some of the best first-class service available.

"Nice, right?"

We settle in, Chari looking exactly like I did the first time I flew first class. Hayden considers it downsizing since his dad owns a private jet. We could afford to keep our own planes now, but neither of us do. I don't travel enough to justify it, and Hayden uses his dad's.

"What would you like to drink, Mr. DeLuca? Ms. Atwood?"

Chari stares at the flight attendant while I jump in.

"Two mimosas, please."

I'm loving the look on Chari's face.

"People are still boarding," she says in one of those whispers everyone can hear. "We haven't even left the runway, and she's getting us drinks?"

I can't resist. Leaning over, I kiss her, enjoying the lingering taste of coffee on her lips.

Enjoying her.

"This is actually comfortable," she says, shimmying into her seat after I lean back. "I could get used to this."

"Good," I say before I can think better of it, "I hope you do."

Chari gives me exactly the kind of sidelong glance I'd expect after dropping that kind of bomb. But I meant it. And I tell her as much by not in any way hinting it might have been a joke.

Because it wasn't.

I want her to like this. Me. All of it. Today is just the very beginning.

Wait until she sees what I have planned for tomorrow.

20

CHARI

A knock on the door wakes me up, so of course the first thing I do is look for Enzo. But the other side of the bed is empty, and for a moment, the sight of it sends a jolt of something through me. Then my better sense kicks in, and I remember he told me he'd be gone before I woke up.

Another knock.

I jump out of bed and fish a sweatshirt out of my bag, pulling it over my head. Fixing my hair in a topknot, I walk to the door, opening it.

"Good morning, Ms. Atwood."

Room service.

"May I bring this into your room?"

"Of course," I mutter, stepping to the side. Watching as he unloads platter after platter onto the table, I wonder how much Enzo thinks I eat. Three separate dishes of food. An individual coffee pot and . . . flowers? Is that normal?

"Mr. DeLuca asked that I give you this"—he hands me a notecard—"and mention that my tip has already been arranged."

With a quick bow, he bids me a good day and leaves.

I wasn't even thinking of a tip. Thank goodness Enzo took care of it. My brain is barely functioning yet. I put the card on the table, looking forward to reading it with coffee, and brush my teeth. I still haven't gotten over how big the bathroom is—it's larger than my kitchen at home. Everything about this hotel is luxurious, even the name: Victoria Le Montreux.

Deciding I'm too impatient to wait, I snatch up the card and open it, thinking of the previous day. Everything about it was absolutely perfect. Aside from Enzo working during a lot of the flight, which was fine because I had plenty to read and watch, he could not have been more attentive. And kind. And sexy.

Every time he looked at me—on the plane, during the car ride from Zurich to Berne, at the restaurant where we met the launch team—everything else faded away. At dinner, I stayed mostly quiet, enjoying the opportunity to see Enzo in his element, wining and dining his business associates. After that, we rode here, to Montreux.

The official launch is tomorrow, but after his meetings this morning, Enzo will be mine for the rest of the day. A good thing too because he was totally serious when he said we'd be exhausted by the time we checked into the hotel. We didn't get here until midnight—five a.m. for us considering the time difference. Given my interrupted sleep the night before and the fact that we'd been traveling all day . . . I didn't have the energy to test Enzo's willpower. I barely managed to change, brush my teeth, and lie down before I zonked out.

I woke once, when Enzo did, my limbs wrapped around his. In a haze, I felt him kiss my forehead, but sleep pulled me back under.

I pull the notecard out from its envelope.

Chari,

Good morning, tiger. I hope you like breakfast. I wasn't sure what you'd want, so I ordered one of each. Enjoy your morning exploring the town. See you by 1:00.

Enzo

P.S. Before you eat, make sure to open all the curtains.

He could have texted me, but the handwritten note is a nice touch. I wander over to the first set of curtains and open them, gasping. They are everywhere, so I open the ones in front of me and to my left. We're in a corner room, and the view surrounding me is breathtaking.

I hurry onto the balcony, not caring for once whether it's cold. But like the day before, no blast of February air hits me. Instead, a fresh, balmy breeze envelops me as I stare in front of me in awe. I'm no stranger to lakefront properties, or even mountains. But those pancakes in Pennsylvania are nothing compared to this.

On the drive yesterday, I was surprised to see more fields than mountain peaks. I'd always thought of Switzerland and the Swiss Alps as one and the same. But apparently we were just traveling through the valley regions while it was still light.

Not anymore.

Rising high into the sky all around me are snowcapped mountains, taller than any I've ever seen. And as if the mountains weren't stunning enough, there's a sun-touched lake in front of me.

I look down on a promenade filled with people. Some walking, others running. None bundled up like I would be back home, which makes sense. It was almost sixty degrees yesterday, and it feels like today will be the same. Why did I think Switzerland would be colder than PA? I mean, I saw the forecast but . . .

My stomach reminds me to go back inside, but I keep the balcony door open. Pouring a coffee and selecting a little something from each of the dishes—a croissant from one plate, ham from another—I eat, staring out at the most beautiful view I've ever seen.

Finished, I look at my phone. It's two in the afternoon back home. I video call my mom, sipping my coffee while I wait for her to answer. Wondering if I died and went to heaven.

"Hello?"

"Hi, Mom."

"Hi, sweetie. What's going on over there?"

How can I possibly describe this?

"There's no way I can put what I'm seeing into words."

"You're in Montreux?"

"Yep, just woke up. Enzo said I'd probably be up early with jet lag, but yesterday was such a long day that I actually slept in a little."

"So what exactly are you seeing?"

I take a sip of coffee and prop my legs up on the chair across from me.

"It's unbelievable. Like if we took our lake, made it bigger and bluer and surrounded it with snowcapped mountains. And French-looking buildings. Look." I turn my phone around so she can see it.

"Oh wow, that's beautiful. So they speak French where you are now?"

I turn the phone back to face me, remembering everything Enzo told me about Switzerland on the plane.

"Actually, they speak four different languages. I'm in a French-speaking canton now, but in other areas they speak

German. And most also know English. The fourth is Romansh, but apparently that's dying out. It's incredible, but I feel so . . . ignorant. Just knowing English."

"You can learn French, or any other language you want."

"But who would I talk to?"

"Hold on a sec."

A muffled sound reminds me she's at the shop. When she comes back, I tell her about yesterday—the amazing flight I didn't want to leave, the dinner with Enzo's business partners, the hotel.

"So what's on the agenda today?"

"Honestly, I'm not sure. Enzo says Montreux is a great walking town with lots of shops, so I'll probably wander around a little. He'll be done with his meetings by lunch, and then I guess he has some big things planned."

Mom sighs. And I get it. This really is like a fairy tale or a TV show or something that should be happening to someone else, but it's happening to me, and I plan on enjoying every minute.

"Will that be all?"

She's talking to a customer.

"You go ahead," I say. "I just wanted to check in."

"OK, have fun today. Love you."

"Love you too," I say, hanging up. I mess around on my phone for a few minutes, checking email and social media, but that view calls to me. Coffee in hand, I step back out onto the balcony to savor it some more, and to maybe take a few pictures for Lisa and Devon.

Unbelievable.

So this is how the other half live? It's exciting—exhilarating, even—but it's also a bit intimidating. I've been hanging so far, but there are definitely times I feel way out of my league. At the restaurant in New York. In first class on the plane. Last night at dinner with all the suits.

I feel like an elementary school teacher playing grown-up. Can I really hang with Enzo's crowd tomorrow? Or in general? His new life is so different from my own, and I'm not sure I can achieve the same equanimity with which he approaches it.

But I decide it's time to stop agonizing and start exploring. Before long, Enzo will be back. And tonight . . .

It's finally time.

21

ENZO

hough the meeting with our supplier went longer than I anticipated, everything seems to be in order for tomorrow's official launch. Thankfully, this isn't my first rodeo. I've been to Switzerland a handful of times. The house Hayden's parents own is in Lugano, just a few hours south of Montreux, and they're actually dual citizens. Naturally, when we started discussing our plan for rolling out Angel in Europe, Switzerland made the top of our list.

I walk into the lobby of the hotel, anticipation growing with every step.

There's no doubt I was a little distracted this morning, but I managed to compartmentalize, somewhat, and keep thoughts of Chari at bay. Hayden called in, and we hammered out the final details for the launch with our distributors, the bar owners, and the marketing team in charge of getting word out. It took a little longer than antici-pated, but I'm confident in our plan.

I wanted to get both Angel's Brew and Angel Wine launched at the same time, but Hayden and the Swiss team convinced me it would be prudent to start with just one product. If the U.S. market is any indication, demand will grow naturally because of the nature of the product. Multiple countries have already expressed interest, and the sales team is confident our biggest issue by the end of the third quarter will be meeting supply.

I look at my watch in the hotel elevator. Two o'clock. Our reservation at the vineyard is for three, and it's a half hour drive from the hotel. I was hoping for more time in the room first, but this is probably just as well.

I made a vow that our first time together will be special, and I intend to keep it. If I managed to keep my hands off her this morning after waking up with her legs tangled through mine, then what's another few hours?

Tonight.

My hand is almost shaking as I swipe the key card. I've never been this out of control in my life, and the reason for it is standing on the balcony, not having heard me come in. I want to join her, but I have to change, and I know the whole waiting thing is going to be a hell of a lot harder if I have to change in front of her. Or even if I have to see that glint of attraction in her eyes before I bring my clothes to the bathroom. So I change before going out there, ditching the suit for a pair of jeans and a sweater.

I won't even need a jacket. The mild, sunny weather couldn't be more perfect.

"Hello there," I say, spotting a coffee cup in her hands.

Chari turns.

She looks me up and down. "You already changed. I didn't even hear you come in."

I join her at the railing, the view no less spectacular because I've seen it before.

"I'm stealthy."

I lean in to kiss her, and she weaves a hand into my hair,

bringing me closer as our tongues tangle. It takes less than a minute for me to become hard as a rock. Knowing we're alone, with a bed just a few steps away . . .

I pull back.

"Unfortunately, we have to head out already. Sorry I'm a bit late."

"It's fine. How did it go?"

It shocks me more than a little to realize the last thing I want to talk about is work.

"Good. We're all set for tomorrow." I take her hand. "Ready to go?"

She's wearing jeans, brown boots, and a chunky salmon-colored sweater, the loose turtleneck making me long to pull it down and devour her neck, kissing my way up behind her ear and making her beg for us to stay here, in this room.

I groan as she brushes past me, not sure I can make it all day.

Tonight, I tell myself again. It's quickly becoming a mantra.

On the drive up the mountain to Coteau Vineyards, Chari clutches my hand, squeezing it hard enough to hurt whenever a car brushes past us on the narrow, winding road.

"We're going to die."

I try not to laugh.

"We'll be fine. But maybe don't look." Even as I say it, she glances at the side of the road as it plunges into what could reasonably be considered a cliff.

"Holy shit, are they serious?"

I'm not sure who "they" are, but Chari's response to everything on this trip makes me smile inside. There's still so much that I want to show her, do for her. I'm not as flashy as Hayden, but I don't shy away from some of the nice things our hard work has earned for us.

"There it is." I point to the fields above us. Even brown and divested of grapes, they are beautiful. Rolling hills of vines that hint at the lush greens of spring to come.

"A vineyard!"

Our car comes to a stop. Getting out, I speak to the driver, arranging for our pickup.

"I know you've been liking some varietals," I tell her. "I thought this would be a good place to test more out. And I think you'll like the scenery."

"Have you been here before?"

Chari and I walk hand in hand down a hill the car couldn't navigate, and given my usual reluctance to show that kind of affection, I'm surprised by how natural it feels. Like she belongs by my side.

"Not this one, but another across the lake. Did you know"—I point to the mountains on the other side of Lake Geneva as it comes into view below us—"that France is just over there?"

"Seriously? When I'm looking out from our balcony, I'm looking at France?"

"Straight ahead and to the right, yes. To the left you're looking at the Swiss Alps."

A man, probably in his late sixties, comes out of the building to greet us on the cobblestone street.

"Bonjour, Monsieur DeLuca. Mademoiselle Atwood."

My lips twitch at Chari's expression. She's already admitted it freaks her out that everyone knows our names before they meet us. She thinks it's magic.

I know otherwise. We're paying handsomely for the courtesy.

"Bonjour, Monsieur LeSeurre." I tell Chari, "He is the owner of Coteau Vineyards."

"Alexandre, please."

A round of handshakes follows.

"Thank you again for opening for us this afternoon."

Many businesses in Montreux are shuttered during the week in the winter. Tourists flock to the ski resorts, leaving other attractions around town relatively quiet. But Hayden's father has more connections than anyone I know.

"It's my pleasure. This way."

He leads us around to the back, Chari's gasp of pleasure exactly what I'd hoped for. Under a trellis covered in twisting vines waits a table set for two with platters of bread, meats, and cheese. But the real beauty of the patio is a 360-degree view of Lake Geneva, surrounded by vineyards to our left and right with snowcapped mountains all around us.

"It's beautiful."

"You should see it in the summer," Alexandre says. "With everything in bloom, colors explode in every direction."

"If only I could be so lucky," Chari answers with a smile, charming him as she does everyone she meets. He pulls out a chair for her, and she sits.

"I'd like to introduce you to Louis, our vigneron," he says. "He will be taking care of you today."

We say goodbye to Alexandre and greet the newcomer.

"Please help yourself"—Louis points to the table —"while I start the service. As you may know, our vineyards benefit from three sources of heat and light: direct sunlight, reflected rays from the lake, and heat absorbed by our extensive network of stone walls, which return their warmth to the vineyards during the night. You'll not taste wines anywhere else in the world quite like them. Today I'll be serving eight wines, starting with our Chasselas blanc, which takes its personality from the soil."

He pours a tasting into both our glasses before excusing himself.

Chari lifts her wine glass, looking a bit stunned.

"I don't know what to say. This feels like a dream."

I lift my own glass. "A good dream, I hope?"

Although I'd hoped to sneak a smile out of her, her expression stays serious as she says, "The kind I never want to end."

Something passes between us then. Not the unchecked lust that has hung over us since the moment I greeted her in the airport. This is different. Deeper.

"To never-ending dreams," I say, clinking my glass to hers.

"To never-ending dreams," she repeats, her words filling my chest, flooding me with something like hope.

22

CHARI

*O*ne month ago, I didn't drink wine. And now I've graduated all the way to red.

One month ago, I had forgotten that Enzo DeLuca existed. And now, as he makes his way back to the table, my insides vibrate.

One month ago, I thought I'd been in love before, and now I'm not so sure. No one has ever made me feel their loss so keenly. And it's only been five minutes.

"Miss me?"

If only he knew how much.

"Hardly noticed you were gone," I lie. "Just taking in the view."

The restaurant isn't huge, but it's extremely elegant. Waiters and waitresses dressed to the nines, sparkling crystal and extra shiny silverware everywhere. Our table is one of four arranged next to the floor-to-ceiling window. Though we can't see the lake now that it's dark out, lights twinkle from across it. Thanks to Enzo, I know those lights are actually in France. For some reason, that still amazes me, to be sitting in one country with a view of another.

"Really?" he asks, sitting. "It seemed to me you were looking my way."

I was, of course.

"You were watching me," I deflect. More than five hours of drinking, on and off, have had their effect. We were careful not to imbibe too much at the winery, Enzo telling me it was just the beginning of our night. After that, we took a pause for a drive through the countryside of Montreux and a stop at a delightful chocolatier. But we've sat in this restaurant for nearly the past two hours. Eating the most delicious Italian food I've ever had. Talking. Drinking. Laughing.

"Always," he says, and the intensity in his eyes deepens, if possible.

When Enzo looks at me this way, I'm just glad I don't need to answer any difficult questions. Like, *What's your name?*

"Can I show you the dessert menu?" the waiter seemingly comes from nowhere.

We exchange a glance.

"Do you want dessert?" Enzo asks.

I shake my head and the waiter leaves us.

"The only thing more I want to taste tonight," Enzo whispers across the table, "is you."

And oh God, how am I supposed to make it back to the hotel?

The anticipation has grown more unbearable with each stop on this incredible date. The best part of all is that his focus has been totally on me, other than one call he had to take at the winery.

On the way to the restaurant, I asked him how he'd managed to arrange all of this. Did his assistant do it?

Enzo insisted it was all him, with Hayden's help. Which makes it even more special.

But it's finally, blessedly time to leave. As we walk through the elegant Michelin-starred restaurant, I wonder how I ended up here. Nothing about it feels real. Except for Enzo's lips on mine the minute we slide into the back seat of the car.

I love kissing Enzo, but I want more. To feel his skin next to mine. To know him as intimately as two people can know each other. By the time we get to the elevator in the hotel, something snaps between us.

As soon as the door slides closed, Enzo claims me, his tongue tangling with mine. I can't wait any longer to feel him. I pull the shirt under his sweater out, needing to feel skin. Needing an anchor. I groan as I find the ridges attesting to his hours in the gym.

Enzo's hands cup both of my ass cheeks, squeezing and pressing me toward him, trapping my hand in his sweater. The ding of the elevator door barely penetrates the cloud of pleasure surrounding us. I jump back, realizing we could easily be caught. But no one is there.

I don't even know how we make it to the door of our room, but we do. I'm about to pull him back to me when I see it out of the corner of my eye.

"Enzo!"

There are flower petals everywhere. The light from one lamp is enough to show me what he's done to the room. A champagne stand and two glasses. Hundreds of rose petals. The curtains, all open, and the flickering lights across the lake visible from the restaurant are now outside our room on all sides.

I have no words.

"I wanted it to be perfect."

I shiver. Enzo notices, and he comes to me. It looks like he's about to say something more, but I'll never find out what. Because I'm the one who kisses him this time. Hard.

And Enzo responds.

My sweater is off so quickly, I'm surprised by the rush of cold air, but then Enzo's hands are everywhere, and I no longer care. I can't seem to strip his clothing as quickly. After what seems like a year and a half, his sweater and undershirt are off. His sculpted chest and shoulders are on full display. Different than when we were young.

This is a man's body.

"Chari," he breathes, his mouth on my neck. I tilt my head to the side, giving him better access as my hands explore. "I've waited forever for this."

Not as long as I have.

While my pace is still frantic, he's slowed down. Not like he wants to stop, but like he wants to take his time. I grab, but Enzo caresses, his tongue trailing a path up toward my ear. He knows I like that, and it's so much better now that we're naked. Or half naked.

Which reminds me.

I reach down with what faculties still function and attempt to unzip his jeans. But Enzo stops me.

"You first. If you touch me right now, this won't go like I planned."

His voice is thick with desire, and I'm here for it. And I can't help but feel a hint of wonder that he feels like that because of me.

He reaches behind my back and unclasps my bra with the deftness of someone who's done it many times before. One bedside lamp is enough for me to see his expression, his parted lips. Dear lord, my insides are breaking apart.

One second he lays his hands over both breasts, cupping

and teasing the nipples as he watches my reaction. The next, he does to me exactly what I'd intended to do to him. Jeans, unzipped. Pulled down. And of course I'm not wearing underwear.

Never do.

"Holy shit."

Something snaps in him. Enzo doesn't even bother to take off his jeans before he pushes me onto the bed. On top of me, gloriously dominating me like I've wanted him to do since forever.

I kiss him back as Enzo's fingers both part and enter me at the same time.

"Screw slow," he says, his lips back on my neck, which is totally fine because now I can grab ahold of that tousled black hair of his and hold on for dear life.

"What," I gasp, "are you doing?"

I mean, I know what he's doing, but it's like the first time, on steroids. How can it possibly be even better than before?

"I am finger-fucking you, Chari," he whispers in my ear, his tongue in rhythm with his two fingers inside me. "And then I plan to fuck you for real."

"When?"

I tug at his jeans, needing more of him. All of him.

"When I hear my name coming from your lips."

He pulls away to watch me as his hand continues its magic.

"Enzo," I say, eager and ready.

"Hmm," he actually chuckles at me, his thumb now entering the fray. "Not quite like that."

"Enzo," I pant, trying again.

Still, he holds himself over me, his shoulder flexing as his arm moves rhythmically. I can't hold on much longer.

"Enzo." I'm breathing heavier now, so close. Closing my

eyes, I let the moment take over. I'm done trying to convince him to give me more. I'm ready to just *feel*.

My hands now grip the pure-white duvet cover beneath me. The unbelievable fact that I'm in bed with Enzo DeLuca, in Switzerland, as his fingers drive me expertly to the edge, is so stunning that my eyes fly open just as I begin to pulse into his hand, Enzo's palm pressing over me.

"Enzo!"

That one was no kitten call. It was from the chest of the tiger he accuses me of being.

"That's it," he says, jumping from the bed as I revel in the aftereffects. "That's what I've been waiting for."

He didn't just want to hear me say his name, he wanted me to scream it. I wish he'd just said that in the first place. But I'm too distracted to say so. Enzo's jeans now lie in a heap on the floor, and he's pulling down the very last barrier between us, and oh my.

"You're huge," I blurt before I get control of my mouth. I blame the orgasm.

The right corner of his lip curls up, but Enzo doesn't respond. Why am I suddenly so nervous? This is crazy.

I notice the small package in his hand then. Enzo proceeds to roll a condom over his cock like a boss. When he moves back over me, I have no idea what to do or say as he looks into my eyes. That look . . .

Like he knows me, inside and out.

Like he wants me, more than I've ever been wanted.

Like he knows we're both going to enjoy this. Tremendously.

I swallow hard.

His hand on my inner thigh jolts me back into conscious thinking. He's pushing his fingers into me again, feeling to be sure I'm still wet, which, of course, I am.

I grab on for dear life.

He's right there, poised to enter me.

"Yes?"

I love that he's asking me that, even now.

But I answer anyway. "Hell yes."

Before he's fully inside me, the gravity of this moment makes it hard to actually breathe like a normal person. Seeing him on top of me like this, feeling him fully . . . and then he moves.

"You're perfect," he says, "so beautiful, Chari."

"Kiss me," I answer.

He does. And a splash becomes a tidal wave. Just like that, we go from slow and sweet to hot and frantic. His tongue plunges into my mouth as he mimics the movements down below, pumping harder and harder every time.

He slides a hand between us, but I don't need him to stimulate me any further tonight—in fact, it would be painful if he did. So I pull his hand up and wrap my fingers through his. In response, Enzo pins my hand above my head and circles his hips.

I thrust up to meet him.

Again and again until my muscles tense everywhere. When he pulls away and looks down at me again, it's the final straw. I can't look into his smoldering eyes and feel his cock so deep inside me and keep it together.

So I don't.

"Come with me," I demand, knowing he can.

With a roar more medieval than modern, he does. I lose all sense of reality for a minute as everything tenses and squeezes, and I don't even know my own name.

"Chari."

I almost thank him for the reminder.

Enzo pulls himself up, no need for words as we stare at

each other. I know that wasn't normal. I don't need him to say so. Honestly, anything he says now will lessen this moment. So I put my finger to his lips, content just to revel in whatever that was together.

The perfect ending to the best date in the history of dates. I'm almost afraid to imagine what's next, because nothing could possibly top that.

23

ENZO

I won't wait until we're back at the hotel.

I can't wait. Not for this woman.

Even though we're at the European launch for Angel, and I should absolutely not be this distracted.

"Chari," I say. And when she turns from one of my business associates to look at me, I add, "Can I talk to you for a minute?"

My sudden desire to get her away, to myself, has nothing to do with the fact that this guy is better looking than most. Or that Chari has already hinted at her affinity for French accents. I'm not a jealous person.

Correction.

I've never been a jealous person before now.

"Sure," she says. And when I nod to the back of the bar, she hops off the barstool. I try not to stare at her ass. I'm in work mode, or at least I'm trying to be. Hayden just texted to ask me how it's going, and I'm not quite sure what to say.

Professionally?

Perfect. The English-themed pub is packed, Angel signs and press everywhere. The ball has been pushed off the proverbial European mountain, and now it just needs some time to get rolling. Tonight marks the beginning of a new chapter for us. Within a year, Angel will be in three countries.

Personally?

It's out of control.

I don't just want to be with Chari every second of the day —I crave her. We were apart for exactly three hours earlier, and it felt like three days. Now I can't stop watching her, wanting to be the one she's smiling and laughing with, even though I know it's my job to work the room.

And Chari is just being Chari. Friendly, maybe a bit flirty because that's her personality. She's charming the asses off everyone, and that's more than fine.

But I need a taste for myself. And I refuse to wait.

"What's wrong?"

Rather than answer, I pull her out of the side door that spills into a narrow cobblestone alley. Though unseasonably warm, even though the sun has gone down, it'll get cold quickly out here. But I don't need that long.

"Nothing," I assure her. As the door slams closed, I reach for her, my hand fisting her hair. Gently pulling her toward me, I make my intentions clear.

Chari's eyes soften as she realizes what I want.

Our kiss isn't a gentle one.

I spin her around, pressing her back against the wall of the bar. I just wanted a quick kiss, but now that I've had one, it's not enough.

Part of me wants to unbutton the pale-blue shirt that's been taunting me all night, the buttons begging for my fingers to pop them open one by one.

But just in case we're caught . . .

"Enzo," she protests as my hand works the button and

then the zipper of her black pants. "What if someone saw us leave?"

I really don't give a shit if anyone saw us, which is, needless to say, not like me. But instead of saying that, I just watch her eyes widen as my hand slips lower, finding its goal.

"Thank you," I say, cupping her.

Chari's lips part. "For?"

I slip a finger inside, positioning myself between her and the door, just in case.

"Being so fucking awesome."

Her chest rises and falls, the buttons across her breasts taunting me as I flick my thumb across her clit the best I can in this position.

"Do you need that shirt after tonight?"

Her face is becoming flushed.

"Why?"

I'm relentless, and I make no apologies for it.

"Because when we get back to the hotel, I can't guarantee you'll have any working buttons left on it."

My little tiger likes when I talk dirty, so I don't let up, knowing we have to get back inside soon.

"And I don't plan to be gentle. Not with your shirt"—I flick my thumb again and work her pussy as if my life depends on it—"or with you."

That does the trick. Chari comes apart in my hand. I wait long enough for her to catch her breath and then bring my other hand around, the napkin I grabbed on the way out replacing the hand in her pants.

"You come prepared." The smile in her voice lifts me as high as the mountain peaks around us.

"I'm getting the hang of dating a girl who likes to go

commando," I tease her, carefully zipping her pants back up. I kiss her one last time, knowing we have to go back in.

"I like the sound of that," she says, pulling away slightly.

"Going commando?" I deliberately misunderstand, earning a swat from her. I know what she means, of course, and I like the sound of it too.

"No."

"Well, we are dating, are we not?"

She nods as if it's a no-brainer. But it's not. We haven't really had a discussion about it yet. And we need to. Work. Expectations. Long-distance.

But those matters can wait.

I think of the good-looking French financier. One thing can't wait.

"Do you still want to date other people, Chari?"

I can't believe how the words stick in my throat. If she says yes, it will kill me.

Her reply is instant, thank God. "No, Enzo. I don't."

I let out a breath.

"Good." I start to open the door, my eyes on her, and she clears her throat. I laugh, having done it deliberately.

"Um, did you forget something?"

I look up, trying to remember. "Oh yes, I think I did."

Chari grins in response.

"I forgot to introduce you to—"

Another swat. I give in, turning serious. More serious than I probably should be, only a few weeks into this. But it's too late for regrets. I'm already in deep.

"I don't want to date anyone else either, Char."

Not tonight. Probably not ever. But that really is another discussion for another time.

"Shall we go back in?" I say in my best French accent.

Instead of swooning with undiluted desire, she grips her stomach and giggles.

"Figured it was worth a shot."

"There you are."

I turn from my laptop to see Chari in my new favorite outfit. A sexy satin chemise with my grey Cornell sweatshirt over it.

"Nice top."

Chari shivers. It is warmer than you'd expect in February, but it's still cool out here on the balcony.

"I spilled tea on mine. Hope you don't mind."

Her hair sits on top of her head in a messy bun. No makeup. Cute as hell. Yep, this is my favorite look so far.

"Not at all." I reach for her, grabbing the sweatshirt and reeling her toward me. When she leans down, I kiss her slowly, sweetly. Trying not to let it get out of hand. I've been up since 4:30 this morning, but I still have to take care of a few things before we pack for the airport.

"This is how I'd like to start the day every morning," I say as Chari stands. "I'll be inside soon. Just finishing up out here."

She looks down at the screen. "Launch stuff?"

I shake my head. "Chemistry stuff. This is for the vodka."

"You don't skip a beat, do you?" she says, shaking her head slightly. "The launch was amazing last night, and now you're on to bigger and better things already."

"Always," I say. And in a work sense it's true. Part of me worries what will happen when Chari realizes how true that is. How driven I am. "I already placed an order for room service. Just call down and tell them we're ready. I'll be in when it comes."

She hesitates, looking up at the mountains. It really is a spectacular view.

"I'll miss it too," she says. Then she dramatically shivers again. "Aren't you cold out here?"

"I didn't want to wake you. But yes, to answer your question. A bit."

She reaches down to feel my hands. "Come inside and work."

I nod toward the room. "You go ahead. I'll be right in."

"OK."

I resist the urge to swat her backside as she walks away. This really has to get finished. By the time we're in the air, the development team will already be in the lab. What feels like five minutes later, I stand up and join Chari.

Her half-eaten breakfast tells me it was more than five minutes.

"Sorry, I got caught up a bit."

Chari pours me coffee. I really could get used to waking up with her by my side.

"No problem," she says, and seems to mean it. "Here you go."

I reach for a plate, pile on the scrambled eggs and bacon —a totally American breakfast but I don't care.

"I really do love bacon."

Chari laughs. "I can tell. And thanks for asking them to bring ketchup. I know that's not standard here."

When I finish eating, I shift in my chair a bit. "Better."

Now I have a view of the lake, the mountains, and my girlfriend.

Girlfriend. It feels natural to think of her as that, to call her that, but a part of me wonders what the hell I'm doing.

"I can't imagine anyone coming here and actually leaving," she says dreamily.

"Like us?" I remind her.

"OK, leaving and not coming back."

"So I take it you'll approve of me taking the European market lead from Hayden?"

Chari's eyes widen. "Are you serious?"

"Deadly serious," I manage without a smile.

"But you're already so busy."

I can't argue with her on that front.

"We shifted some things around this morning. With his baby and all"—I shrug—"it makes sense. Besides, I told him there's no chance you'll miss out on the next Montreux trip."

"So we'll be back?" The excitement in her eyes will make the added workload worth it. I really shouldn't have suggested it. Hayden thinks I'm nuts. But I can tell this place has burrowed its way into Chari's soul. And sure, we'll have to work around her school schedule for trips, but we can do it. I think.

"We will," I say.

Chari and I exchange a look. It's time.

"I'm not a hundred percent positive how this is going to work," I admit. "With you in PA. I work a ton, Chari."

She takes a sip of coffee, looking out toward the balcony where I just spent three hours on my laptop. "I can see that."

"In some ways, we're still a start-up. Between my involvement in the development side of things and my inability to give up control, it's a lot."

Chari laughs. "At least you can admit to your faults."

"Some of us actually have them," I tease.

"Are you kidding me? I have a ton of them."

I try to think of one. "Such as?"

"Well, there's the whole eggs with ketchup thing. Lisa would definitely count that as one of my faults."

"So your palate isn't totally refined. What else?"

Chari cocks her head to the side. "I'm too optimistic."

"That's one of those non-fault faults," I say with a laugh. "And you know it."

"And I've been told I'm a hypochondriac."

"That I won't argue with." Chari has a long history of being convinced she has one ailment or another. Personally, I think it has something to do with her father. I can't remember when she last brought him up in conversation, which I'm sure can't be a good thing.

Though I'm no psychologist. If I were, I'd have fixed myself years ago.

"So that's it? You like ketchup with eggs, and I'll need to keep your doctor on speed dial? I think I can handle that."

A shadow passes quickly across her face, and it's obvious from her expression that her mood has turned more serious.

"What is it?"

Chari pretends to be nonchalant, but I can tell she's anything but.

"I hope I can hang with all of this."

"All of what?"

"This." She waves a hand around the room. "The luxuries. The protocols. There are times I feel"—she frowns—"like a country bumpkin."

I remember that feeling well.

"It's a lot," I admit. "But I had Hayden to show me the ropes. And you have me."

I lean forward to make sure she understands this point is important. "More importantly, it doesn't matter. If you use the wrong fork, say the wrong thing . . . I don't give a shit. And neither should you."

I can tell she's not convinced, so I try a different tactic. Reaching for my phone, I press the screen to check the time and mumble, "Plenty of time."

Her brows furrow. "For?"

I put down my coffee mug. "You have to ask?"

Chari realizes my intentions pretty quickly. I grab her as she stands from her chair, my hands not waiting until we reach the bed.

"If you ever decide to start wearing underwear," I manage, "we're done."

Her laugh echoes in my ear just before it turns into the sweetest sharp gasp as I plunge my fingers into her wet warmth.

No, I don't want to leave Switzerland. Or Chari.

But unfortunately, I have to do both today. Just not before I make sure this is one long weekend she won't forget anytime soon.

24

CHARI

"Oh my God, it's Enzo."

Lisa and I are on her couch, a pizza box on the table in front of us. From DeLuca's, of course. I can't help but think how different this Friday night is from the one I had a week ago.

Lisa was about to stream *French Kiss,* an old movie, but she has an unhealthy love affair with Kevin Kline. No one gets it, including me. But the news caught her attention. Our attention. Sure enough, there he is.

"Turn it up." I lean forward to listen.

"A successful European launch of Angel, Inc. begins to raise some of the same questions as it has in the States. With the success of a unique alcohol and its accompanying antidote, will DeLuca and Tanner, owners of a now-global brand, be faced with mounting pressure from brewers and wine-makers alike to partner with them?"

I try to place the setting and realize this must have been filmed last Friday morning, when Enzo left the hotel early for his meetings. He didn't even mention being interviewed.

"As always, we're going to keep our focus on what our

brand offers, which is a safer way to consume alcohol, whether it's here in Europe or anywhere else in the world."

"Holy shit, Char. He's so freaking hot. When did that happen?"

I roll my eyes. "Ages ago. How did you not notice?"

Lisa grabs a slice of pizza. "I mean, it's hard not to notice the DeLuca brothers. But you know I've always thought Tris was the cute one."

I'm only half listening as the interview with Enzo wraps up.

"Did you hear anything I just said?"

I look at her, guilty. "Something about Tris?"

Lisa finishes chewing her pizza. "If I were to date a DeLuca, it would be Tris. But I do get Enzo's appeal."

I stare at her openmouthed. "You *get* his *appeal*?" There are no words really. "The guy is drop-dead gorgeous. He's super nice. A good friend. Hardworking. Smart. A true romantic. And don't get me started on how good he is in bed. Seriously, I can't close my eyes without remembering—"

She waved me off. "Like I said, I get it. No need to sell me on him."

"I'm just saying, how could you compare him to Tris?"

Lisa shrugs. "Maybe because I'm not in love with him?"

I blink, pretending I haven't already turned the thought around in my mind. It's not some big revelation, really. I've sort of been in love with Enzo for most of my life. But now that we're actually together . . .

"Look at you. You're a million miles away."

She's right. My poor kiddos. It's been impossible to concentrate at work.

"So. What are you gonna do?"

I need another beer. Jumping up from Lisa's couch, I

head into her apartment kitchen and grab one from the fridge. There's no Angel's Brew in there.

Everything, literally everything, reminds me of Enzo now.

"Want one?" I call into the living room.

"Sure."

When I come back, Lisa doesn't relent. "We're going to talk about this, you know. No saved-by-the-bell nonsense for you."

Crap.

"You're madly in love with Enzo DeLuca. A man who was on our TV screen five minutes ago. Who lives in New York. And you live here. So," she asks again, "what are you gonna do?"

"We've been dating a few weeks and just became exclusive. Don't you think it's a bit too early for me to start thinking about what happens long term?"

Or at least it's too early for me to talk about it. Because I've been doing plenty of thinking about it.

"I suppose," she relents, grabbing the second beer I brought her. "Has Devon said anything about it since you came back?"

"Oddly, no."

My phone vibrates on the coffee table.

Lisa smirks a little as she says, "Go ahead, it's fine."

We have a strict no cell rule for movie night, but technically we haven't started it yet.

It's Enzo. I told him what I was doing tonight, which makes it a surprise, though not an unpleasant one, that he's calling now.

"Hello?"

"Hey, tiger," he says, his deep, raspy voice quickening my pulse. "Sorry to interrupt movie night."

I look at Lisa and try not to laugh. She's making kissy faces and totally attempting to sabotage my call.

"It's no problem. We didn't start the movie yet."

"What are you watching?"

"*French Kiss*," I admit.

"Seriously? Still?"

It's one of many reminders that this isn't just any guy. It's Enzo, who's known me for years. Enzo, who was around when I learned to ride my bike.

"It's been . . ." I ask Lisa, "How long has it been since we've seen this?"

She thinks. "At least a year."

"At least a year," I repeat.

Enzo's soft chuckle makes me wish he were here, in PA, and not more than two hours away.

"I won't keep you from Kevin Kline, but I just wanted to let you know I have to cancel Sunday."

My heart drops into my stomach. Enzo was going to drive down for the day. Maybe I can go to New York instead?

"Something came up with the vodka formula. Looks like I'll be in the lab most of the weekend."

So much for me visiting him.

"No problem," I say, because it doesn't sound like there's much of a choice. "Hope everything is OK?"

He sighs. "I hope so too. We're having some trouble with the peak effects—" He cuts himself off, just like he always does when he starts talking chemistry. As if I might find it boring. Which I wouldn't. "Anyway, I need to get into the lab to see what the hell is going on. I'm thinking I'll be there at least a few days."

When Enzo's in the lab, time becomes a foreign concept to him. Which means we probably won't talk much until he gets it worked out.

"I'm sorry, Char." I can tell he's sincere. And the fact that he's as sad to miss Sunday as I am . . . that's what matters.

"We'll have more Sundays," I say, and Lisa pouts in sympathy for my obviously cancelled plans. "Go work your magic. Give me a call when you can."

After last weekend, it feels like there should be something more. But no way I'm going to use the big L word first. And when it does happen, I'd rather be with him.

"Will do. Tell Lisa, and Kevin, I said hello."

I smile into the phone. "OK. Talk soon."

Ending the call, I look up. "Enzo says hello."

"So no Sunday?"

"Nope." I grab another slice of pizza. So much for stopping at two. "Work."

We talked about this on the flight back, Enzo's relentless work schedule. And I told him I get it, that building an empire is a full-time gig. Of course, truth be told, I *don't* one hundred percent get it. It's just one more way in which his life is foreign to me. But I'm trying to understand.

"What are you going to do?" I ask as if it's no big deal.

Lisa picks the remote back up, and I nod, ready to get lost in the film. Although I felt a little readier to get swept away before Enzo's call. Now I wonder how Kate and Luc made out after they fell in love. Did they stay together or did the realities of their actual lives interfere?

Reminding myself the answer is neither, that it's just a movie—one filmed years and years ago—I sit back to watch.

Last weekend my life felt like a movie too. Too bad we couldn't have stayed in Switzerland, because real-life long-distance dating totally sucks.

25

ENZO

"*Y*ou look like shit."

I shovel a bite of lasagna in my mouth, ignoring Hayden's comment. It's only now that we're here at Faustini's that I realize I completely forgot to eat all day.

"Hey, those are the Angel guys."

I try to pretend I didn't hear that either. This is the first time I've been away from the lab, or my office, since Saturday. The last thing I want to do is talk about the business. Or answer for the millionth time, "How do you feel about having so many enemies, from brewers to wine makers and powerful liquor companies? All coming at you 24/7?"

Hayden and I knew we were going to piss off a lot of people. As we've said in interviews, while we're making our own beer, and wine, and spirits, partnerships with existing alcohol companies could be in our future.

But that's not how it played out.

"You look like you're ready to kill someone." Hayden leans back, giving me a glimpse of the cocky rich boy I met.

He's different now, mostly, but every once in a while an expression or tone reminds me of the old Hayden.

"I'm just tired."

Hayden's brows rise.

"I was thinking about yesterday's call with the Brewers Association." But I still don't feel like talking about work, and one of the rules of our Faustini's dinners is to keep it off the table. So I add, "But that's water under the bridge. Talk to me about something else."

"How about Cornell winning another game? I think they could actually win the Ivy League."

"They won?" I ask.

His eyes go all bug-eyed. "Seriously? You missed the big game?"

Hayden shakes his head a little as he takes a bite of his linguine. Honestly, he needs to learn to order something else. Every Wednesday, aglio e olio. Like clockwork.

"I was in the lab," I say, although he probably figures as much. I sent him an updated timeline for the vodka just this morning.

"Yeah, but seriously. You're really burning the candle at both ends."

"As if I have another choice."

Hayden uses the napkin on his lap to wipe the oil from his chin.

"You do, and you know it."

Here we go. "No work talk."

"This isn't work. It's me trying to make sure I still have a business partner in five years. If you keel over dead, then what?"

"First of all, I don't think people keel over at thirty-one because they work too hard. Second of all, if I *did* keel over, you'd be just fine."

"No, I wouldn't."

"Yes," I argue, "you would."

Hayden leans forward in his seat. "Enzo, you *are* Angel. You came up with the formula. You continue to help the team discover ways to expand our offerings."

I look at him wryly. "I'm pretty sure if you stopped now and only sold beer and wine you'd be just fine."

He quirks his brow and nods slightly.

Fuck. He's a wily bastard. I realize belatedly he's trapped me.

"Fine. You got me."

"Enzo," he says, his tone losing some of the bite, "we've done more in the past few years than we ever imagined was possible. We have a lifetime to expand, to get Angel in every bar and restaurant in the world."

"I wish I ordered meatballs," I say, because I don't want to talk about this. Not again.

"You *are* a meatball. How's Chari dealing with your need to take over the world?"

I give him a warning look.

"Ah, a sore point?"

"She's fine," I argue.

"Mmm-hmm."

"She gets it."

"Does she?" Hayden sounds more than a little skeptical. Then he waves a hand. "You're in the honeymoon phase. Of course she gets it."

"What's that supposed to mean?"

Hayden puts down his fork with a clank just as our waiter checks on us. Thankfully, there's no sign of Giovanna, but there does seem to be fewer regulars in here tonight. More than a few people are looking at us.

"Exactly what you think it means."

I fold my napkin and place it on the table. For being so hungry a few minutes ago, I can't fit another bite in my stomach.

"She's coming up on Saturday," I say, in an attempt to mollify him.

"I thought you were having dinner with the Virginia distributors Saturday."

"I am."

"With Chari?"

"I had to cancel last weekend"—I shrug—"so yeah."

I can't go much longer without seeing her. A business dinner isn't ideal, but at least it's something.

"Sounds romantic."

"You would know." Hayden once prided himself on being the king of romance. But his wife sees through all his bullshit, always has.

"I'm just saying . . . Sorry I can't go for you. In-laws are coming in for the weekend."

"It's fine," I say, waving my hand in the air for the check. "She'll be up late afternoon. And I probably can spare a few hours Sunday morning too."

"Pfft. Lucky girl. A whole twenty-four hours."

I give him an *I'm done with this conversation* look, and Hayden lifts up his hands, signaling he'll back off.

"Talk to me about the playoffs," I say. "You seriously think we have a shot?"

The conversation moves on, but a part of my mind lingers on what he said. Devon called me after Chari came back from our trip. He said Chari's been walking on air and reminded me not to fuck it up.

Part of me worries it's already happening.

26

CHARI

*W*here the heck did Mom find this?

I pick up a small glass frog from the shelf, thinking about Enzo, and how he spent his childhood catching frogs, keeping them as pets. Naming them. Talking to them, both his own and ones in the wild. Pretty much everyone knew he had an obsession with them for years.

He's given me so much, maybe I'll give him a little gift too.

I'm filling in for Mom this Saturday morning at the shop so she can attend an antique show to pick up more eclectic finds. It's a slow month. Tourism in Bridgewater doesn't really pick up until April, and some years not until May. But Mom is smart about her finances and plans for the downtime.

She's a savvy business owner, and I know it's slightly disappointing to her that I don't want to take over the shop. But it's just never called to me.

I turn the glass piece over in my hands.

Does teaching call to me? I thought so. In college, after three majors, I finally landed in elementary education after working as a camp counselor for two summers. Everyone said I had a "knack" for working with kids. And I've always loved children. Their curiosity. Their imagination.

But the deeper I get in the education system, the more I realize how broken it is. Some days I feel like I'm just spinning my wheels, not really getting anywhere.

"Chari?"

I take the frog, intending to give it to Enzo, and head back to the register. I don't recognize the voice, but as I turn the corner, I freeze.

Lusanne DeLuca.

She was a year behind me in school. And I know her, of course, because Devon and I spent a lot of time at their house as kids. Lusanne and I have always liked each other, but hanging out at the DeLuca house never translated to hanging out anywhere else, and we don't really travel in the same circles.

"Hey, Lusanne," I say, sliding behind the counter. "How's it going?"

She's definitely looking at me a bit more intently than usual, but then again, I haven't seen her since Enzo and I started dating.

"Good. I'm heading to a birthday party out of town tonight, and I figured it might be fun to bring something unique, something local."

"Is it for an adult?"

She nods, her long, glossy hair so pitch-black against her cream coat that I can't stop staring. The DeLucas have better genes than any other family in Bridgewater. Or PA. Maybe the East Coast.

"My college roommate."

Like Enzo and Gian, Lusanne left home for college. Enzo is the only one who never came back to Bridgewater.

Aside from the frog and a few other new glass figurines, I don't think there's anything new in the stock, but I do have an idea.

"Take a look at these," I say, walking around the counter and navigating shelves toward the back of the shop.

"Something smells so good."

It always does. The shop smells like a combination of the vanilla wax melts Mom loves, plus a very slight musky bookstore scent. If only we could capture that scent and bottle it.

"Right?" I say, arriving at a jewelry line that Mom discovered a few months ago at the Penn State Arts Festival. "What do you think?"

"Oooh." Lusanne picks up a silver bracelet. "These are so pretty."

Remembering the glass figurine in my hand, I open it slightly to look at the delicate piece. Lusanne notices it as she puts the bracelet back and picks up a necklace.

"A frog," she says, catching my eye. She knows about her brother's childhood obsession as well as I do.

"Yeah, I just found it this morning. Mom must have just gotten them in."

"For Enzo?"

I nod as she looks back at the jewelry. "Yeah. I thought he might like it."

"He will. I swear he'd keep a live one in that fancy apartment of his if they let him."

She says it like she knows I've been there, which almost certainly does. Should I say anything about Enzo and me?

What actually comes out of my mouth is less than inspired.

"He can't have pets?"

She replaces the necklace.

"No, not even a frog." She nods toward my hand. "Though maybe that one."

The bell rings over the door. Another customer. Now or never.

"I'm sure he's mentioned us?"

She picks up the original silver bracelet.

"He has. And we're so thrilled, Chari," she says, seemingly genuine. "Mom still can't believe he came home two weekends in a row." She walks back to the register with me. "I'm sure you know how rare that is."

Unfortunately, I'm learning exactly why that's the case.

"Yeah, he works a lot."

Lusanne laughs. "That's an understatement."

The new customer isn't someone I know. They explore the shop in the same way most of our newcomers do, meandering slowly through the shelves of eclectic souvenirs.

"We're hoping"—I slide behind the counter and Lusanne hands me the bracelet—"maybe you'll knock some sense into him."

I begin to gift wrap it, realizing belatedly I never asked if she wanted it wrapped. I hold up the box.

"Oh sure, go ahead. Thanks."

"How do you mean?" I ask.

"He . . ." She stops, so I glance up. Something about the look on her face freaks me out a bit. Part of me wants to tell her to forget the whole thing—that we don't need to talk about this at all. I look down again and finish wrapping the box, adding a big purple tulle bow.

"How do I say this? We're all so proud of him. Beyond proud, actually. But . . ."

"But?" I gently prod as I hand her the box and ring her up. Now I really do want to know what she's thinking.

"I can't pretend to know what it's like. His business. That lifestyle. Ah, screw it."

That sounds just like him. It makes me smile despite the warning in her tone.

"It consumes him. Sometimes, like when he came in to see you before Devon's birthday, we see glimpses of the old Enzo."

She takes out a credit card and swipes it in the machine.

The old Enzo. I feel like I've seen a lot of him. Of course, I've also seen a lot of the suave billionaire who's comfortable eating with endless forks and spoons and whatnots. Who travels first class and plans an impossible five-day date in Switzerland.

"But more often . . ." She signs the receipt I lay in front of her. "He's like a machine. We hardly see him." I can hear the sadness in her voice, and I totally get it. His family is the kind I've always wished for. Big. Loud. People everywhere. A Sunday dinner can turn easily into a thirty-person, extended-family event.

Family is everything to the DeLucas. To Enzo.

At least it was, precollege. Pre-Angel, Inc.

"I am surprised I hadn't seen him in so long before . . . this. I was away too, but . . ."

But I've been back in Bridgewater for years.

"I'm sorry," she says, taking her package. "The *last* thing I want to do is discourage you. Seriously. We are beyond thrilled, and we just hope Enzo is smart enough to realize what he's got." She smiles. "It's like you're already a part of the family."

The idea warms me all over. I won't deny, at least not to myself, that I want that. But I also don't want to get too far ahead of myself. Of us.

"Thanks, Lusanne," I say. "You know I love you all."

And I do. Devon couldn't have picked a better best friend, and Enzo's character isn't a fluke. Everyone loves the DeLucas.

"We love you too." She takes out her keys. "If you need anything at all, give me a shout."

I don't actually have her number, but the sentiment is appreciated, and I can reach her easily enough on social media.

"Will do. Thanks, Lusanne. And have fun at your party."

"Have fun in New York," she says slyly. I'm not surprised she knows about our plans. For as little as he sees them, I know Enzo talks to at least one of his family members every day.

"I will."

She leaves, and despite her well-intended words of warning, I can't help but feel a bubble of excitement. In just a few hours, I'm going to be able to touch Enzo again. To taste him. Video chatting is great for keeping in touch, but it doesn't come close to the real thing.

And more than that. His promise from last night comes back to me.

"Tomorrow after dinner, you'll be glad I had to cancel last weekend," he said.

"Really?" I asked him. "And why is that?"

"Because I plan to make it up to you . . . with my tongue."

And he calls *me* a tiger.

27

ENZO

*M*arc Walden, owner of SouthBev, the largest wholesale beer distributor in the Southeast, is kind of a dick. But I'm stuck with him for the time being. His team apparently came down with something on the flight, and both of them are upstairs in their rooms, sick as dogs. Chari's not here either—not yet. She texted half an hour ago to say she was stuck in traffic. I tried to send a car, but she insisted on driving into the city.

At least Marc and I have had a chance to talk business, which we dispensed with fairly quickly. In truth, this is an entirely unnecessary meeting—something that could have been done remotely—and I suspect the new owner of SouthBev, who inherited the position from his recently deceased father, came here to play. He strikes me as the type who's more interested in a weekend out on the town than business meetings. Which is fine. Marc just agreed to extend our contract for five years, and given his company's reach, that means our foothold in the Southeast is secure.

"Pardon," the waitress says, coming up to our table for

the third time. "Are you ready to order or will you be waiting on your guest?" She nods to the empty seat.

I know Chari is just stuck in traffic, but I still can't shake the worry that something else might be wrong. Marc must know I want to wait, because he glances at me before saying, "We'll wait."

His gaze lingers on the pretty waitress, and he makes no attempt to hide his interest.

"Chef's choice of appetizers?" I ask her.

"Two? Three?"

"As many as he recommends for three people."

The executive chef at Rochelle's is one of the best chefs in the city. I always leave it up to him. She nods and walks away.

I try to listen to Marc as he starts going on about all of the hot women he's come across in the city, but I can't stop glancing at the archway that leads to the restaurant's entrance.

This is silly. She's on her way. It's just traffic.

"How long have you been dating?"

Caught daydreaming, I return my attention to Marc. For a few minutes anyway, until a flash of red catches the corner of my eye. A lump forms in my throat, and I can't talk or even think. She's fucking incredible.

Chari walks toward us, a red cocktail dress hugging every curve. I stand, heartbeat in my ears, and try not to immediately ravage her as she walks up to me. Instead, I give her a quick kiss on the cheek as the scent of vanilla with a hint of coconut wafts by. Chari sits next to me, and I intro-duce her to Marc.

Who doesn't hide his appreciation for my girlfriend.

Concealing my irritation, I ask Chari about her drive in.

"It was totally fine until I came through the tunnel. You'd swear it's rush hour or something."

"You left your car with the valet?"

She nods. "I did."

The waitress comes to take Chari's drink order. She looks at our drinks and orders an Angel Pale Ale. I try not to smile. And she worried about acclimating to my life? She's a natural.

"So, tell me, Marc"—Chari uses his first name, deliberately I'm sure—"what exactly does a wholesale beer distributor do?"

Marc is all too happy to tell Chari about his business. How he grew up in it, what he's going to change now that he's in charge, and . . . I stop listening. My leg edges ever so slightly toward Chari, and I reach down with my right hand.

She doesn't miss a beat. In fact, she's acting so interested in Marc's relentlessly boring description of sales channels, the green-eyed monster bites. I know what she's doing, but I also hate his appreciative gaze.

From above the table, my shoulder doesn't appear to move. Below it, my hand grabs the hem of her dress and pulls upward. When her voice catches, I try not to smile.

"Fascinating," Chari says.

Our eyes meet.

The only thing fascinating at this dinner table is how clueless Marc is that Chari is merely humoring him.

Keep looking at me like that, I warn her with my eyes, *and this pre-sex dance won't last beyond the first course.*

In fact, as we give our orders, I make a decision.

"Excuse me for a moment," I say, my hand already missing the feel of her after I pull it away from her leg.

I have an idea . . .

28

CHARI

*W*hen Enzo comes back, he has a strange look on his face. I'd assumed he'd excused himself to go to the men's room, but now I'm not so sure. Finally, after what seems like a lifetime of entertaining our pompous dinner companion, Enzo asks for the check.

"I'm glad you were able to avoid your team's affliction and meet us," Enzo says.

He almost sounds as if he means it, which is impossible. Marc Walden is an insufferable braggart. I suspect all of his big talk is a way of compensating for his inability to run the company his father so deftly managed. But I've managed to keep things friendly, and so has Enzo—friendly and professional, except for the way he's been touching me under the table. Except for the way his jaw twitches ever so slightly when his companion flirts with me.

As we prepare to leave, I start fantasizing about Enzo's hands all over me, the feel of him inside me . . .

"Chari?"

I've totally been caught.

"Sorry." Enzo and Marc are already standing. I do the same. "It was a pleasure to meet you," I say to Marc.

"Same to you," he says. "If you ever find yourself in Northern Virginia"—he directs the comment to me—"I'd be thrilled to host you"—finally he looks at Enzo—"both."

There's that tic again in Enzo's jaw, the one that tells me he's about to crack. I've only seen this side of him once before, in Switzerland, and I'm still not sure what to make of a jealous Enzo. Mostly, I kinda like it.

"Thank you." I stick out my hand. "Have a safe trip back, and give our regrets to your team."

He shakes my hand, letting it linger just a tad too long.

Marc shakes Enzo's hand next. Is that a wince? Apparently Enzo's grip isn't very light. Time to redirect that strength to something more useful.

Enzo doesn't say a word as Marc walks off. Also, he doesn't move.

"Are we going?" I ask, confused.

He glances at the entrance to the restaurant.

"In a sec."

We stand next to the table for a moment, unmoving. This, despite the fact that the bill has been paid.

"Enzo?"

He finally starts moving, as if coming back to life, but he's still going oh so slowly. What's up with him all of a sudden?

"I had no desire to ride the elevator with that bozo."

Elevator?

Enzo guides me past the door leading outside, leading me into the connected hotel instead. We go past the front desk and straight to the elevator bank he mentioned. Pressing the up button, he turns to me.

"If you think I'm waiting until we're back at my place . . ."

The elevator dings. Enzo looks me up and down, clearly liking what he sees. I'll have to buy Lisa a drink. I thought the red was too much—it basically screams *take me!*—but she wisely said, "And that's a problem why?"

This is where he went earlier. He got us a room.

The elevator door hasn't even closed behind us yet when Enzo pins me to the back wall, holding my hands above my head in the same tight grip Marc winced over. I can't move. But I don't want to.

As Enzo's entire length presses against me, his mouth blessedly demanding, all of the white noise drifts away. My worry about what Lusanne said earlier. The loneliness I've felt at night, craving his touch. The disappointment of him cancelling his visit last weekend.

His tongue sweeps inside my mouth as Enzo's free hand completes the mission it started over dinner. Under the table, it only traveled so far. Now, as the floors ding past us, it continues to ride up my thigh, his fingers reaching for . . .

I break contact to state the obvious.

"Not here. Someone could get on . . . oh!"

He doesn't listen very well. Enzo's lips part as he plunges two fingers into me, watching my expression. I gasp, the rule-follower in me terrified the elevator might stop at any moment. And also excited. I've told him how much I enjoy being touched this way, and on this, he most certainly listened.

"Enzo," I breathe as he relentlessly works me. This man is an expert with his fingers, among other things.

"I've missed you."

He's watching me, and from his smart suit coat to his crisp white shirt, he looks exactly like the kind of man wealthy enough to book a room in a five-star hotel because he doesn't want to wait a half hour. But those eyes, they're the same ones I've known most of my life.

The small-town guy all the girls adored. Part jock, part nerd, and part all-around nice guy from a family everyone wanted to be a part of.

Including me.

The two sides of him don't seem at odds right now. There's just one Enzo tonight, and he's mine.

"I've missed you too," I admit freely, already feeling myself begin to clench around his hand. "The door," I manage, reminding him we're in a somewhat public place, one of his hands trapping my wrists above my head, his other deep beneath my dress.

The elevator begins to stop.

"Enzo—"

I can't manage to finish the rest of my sentence.

If you don't stop, I won't be able to.

In response, he redoubles his efforts as the elevator comes to a full halt.

"I won't move until you come," he says with unshakable confidence.

"But . . ." I can't speak as the doors begin to open. *What if someone is on the other side?* I mean to say, but the words don't come.

He lets go of my arms, but that's his only concession. I grab his navy sports coat with both hands, clutching it as the spasms come.

Somehow I'm able to gather myself enough to glance out as the doors open. Enzo doesn't even bother to turn and look. Thankfully, no one's waiting in the hall.

Full-on clenching around his fingers, I cry out, hardly able to stand.

Only then does he pull his hand away, turning just in

time to hold the doors open. I don't join him. Instead, I stand there, back against the wall, staring back at him.

The elevator alarm begins to ring, which makes Enzo smile.

"Need some help?" He reaches for me, still holding the door, and I pull my dress down and take his hand. When the doors close behind us and the alarm stops ringing, I pause.

"I could use a second."

Without missing a beat, Enzo reaches for my legs and scoops me up like it's nothing.

"Sorry, don't have a second," he says, stopping to look at the numbers. He turns right, presumably toward our room. "That was just an appetizer," he says.

Being in his arms, being carried by him . . . somehow it's even more amazing than the orgasm he gave me.

What the hell was I stressing about earlier, anyway?

Things are perfect. Beyond perfect. Never better, in fact.

Because I'm in Enzo's arms, and this, I'm figuring out, is exactly where I'm meant to be.

CHARI

"*D*on't freak out."

Devon insisted on having dinner with me, and not at the house. Like he actually suggested we go to Deluca's II. So it's not exactly a surprise that he has something monumental to tell me. But still.

"That's a great segue, Dev," I say.

Devon pops a mozzarella stick into his mouth and mutters something unintelligible. No wonder he doesn't have a girlfriend. My brother's manners leave something to be desired, which is odd being that we were raised in the same house. Although I have noticed a few things, including new additions to my brother's wardrobe. I'll have to keep my eye out for future developments.

I'm thrilled to see Tris's restaurant thriving. I half expected to see Lusanne here tonight, but if she's coming, she hasn't shown up yet. She's been splitting her time between the pizza shop and the restaurant, apparently. Enzo told me last night she was even considering a venture of her own but doesn't want to abandon Tris so soon after the opening.

I get it.

Lisa's been pressing me on what's next for me. She thinks my mother is the only reason I came back to Bridge-water. Apparently my mother thinks that too. But I like my job. I really do. And it's too soon for me to think about making any plans revolving around Enzo.

"Eat your bunny food," Devon says, referring to my salad. Unlike my brother, I actually enjoy a good salad, so I pick at it, waiting for the ball to drop.

It doesn't, and my brother doesn't appear to be in any hurry, so I say, "Spill it, Devon. Whatever you brought me here to say."

Taking a swig of beer, he sits back and looks at me with a *don't kill me* expression that I know all too well.

"Dad called me yesterday."

My fork freezes halfway to my mouth. Did he seriously just say . . .

"Dad? As in your father?"

Devon makes a face. "No, as in our father."

Suddenly, I'm not hungry.

"Hear me out before you say anything."

Although the restaurant's busy, it's definitely slower than it would be on a weekend. There's no one sitting next to us, but enough people are in our vicinity that I ask Devon to lower his voice. Small towns and gossip, and all that.

"It's not like he's some sort of axe murderer," he mumbles. "Just listen."

Part of me wants to make a smart comment, but there's such a strange sensation in my chest, and my throat, and my everything, that I couldn't talk if I wanted to anyway.

"He knows he has been a total shit. And he figured if he called you . . ."

Devon trails off, acting as if the reason is so obvious he doesn't need to supply it. And really, he's right.

"What?" I finish. "That I might not be super receptive? That I would probably ask some tough questions like, 'Is there a reason you failed to pay child support? Or send a single birthday card? Or maybe pop your head in at major events in either of our lives, like, I don't know, our high school graduations? Or college graduations? Or—"

"I knew you'd flip."

Devon was lucky we weren't home. "Which is exactly why we're sitting in the middle of my boyfriend's brother's restaurant. To ensure my freak-out is contained."

My brother can be so annoying.

"Your boyfriend. My best friend," he says, rolling his eyes. "Enzo has a whole bunch of titles these days."

"Oh no you don't." I give him my best *don't you dare* face, hoping for his sake as well as mine that it's enough to dissuade him from shifting the conversation to me. Because this isn't about me. It's about our father. And Dev knows that man is the last person in the world I want to talk about.

"Anyway," he says, which is code for *I know you're right*, "he said there was a story about you in his local paper a while back."

That's not what I expected to hear, and I only manage a very eloquent, "Huh?"

"Yeah, I looked it up online. I'm surprised the *Bridgewater Times* hasn't picked it up, but there's a picture of you coming out of the airport with Enzo. It talks about a 'local woman,' aka you, connected to our very own Enzo DeLuca."

"But that was weeks ago. And I didn't see anything in the press about it." I know it'll happen at some point, of course, and part of me dreads the attention. Another part is eager for the world to know that Enzo is mine.

"Neither did I. But it's bound to come out sooner rather than later."

I simply nod, because the sentiment echoes my thoughts.

Hungry in spite of myself, I pick my fork back up just as the waitress comes by to check on us. She asks if we need anything, which we don't. Except maybe a new topic of conversation.

"He knows you're dating Enzo," Devon says as she walks away.

Like I give a shit about what that man knows. But I don't say as much out loud. Devon doesn't have a relationship with the sperm donor who helped create us, but he has talked to him a few times over the years, unlike me.

"And?" I ask between bites.

"He wanted me to talk to you about a loan."

Devon has the grace to wince before I can even answer.

"You're joking, right?"

He hurries to explain. "Apparently he had no idea Enzo and I are such good friends. When I told him I know Enzo as well as you . . ."

I nearly choke on an almond. The fact that our father doesn't know Devon's been tight with Enzo since the second grade is a pretty good example of why I want nothing to do with the man.

"He said it would be great if either of us could approach Enzo."

"I hope you're kidding. You aren't actually thinking about asking Enzo for a loan for a man who abandoned you? Us," I clarify.

Devon shakes his head. "No. That would be ludicrous."

The first logical thing my brother has said all night.

He scratches his head. "But it's not exactly a loan he's

asking for. He has a business venture, an idea he's been working on for years, apparently. Some kind of natural health drink. So it's more of an investment."

I don't dignify this discussion with words. Instead, I finish my salad, concentrating on the faint sound of Frank Sinatra's crooning in the background. The DeLucas have some sort of unnatural fascination with the guy, Enzo included.

"So there. I told you. I promised him I'd at least do that."

"And you did."

Maybe that's not the most tactful response, but I'm with my brother. I don't have to be tactful.

"Do you know how many 'investments' Enzo gets pitched on a weekly basis? How could you even entertain the idea of helping that man, Devon? He cheated on Mom and then vanished, literally."

Devon winces. "Unlike you, I don't have it in me to hang up on him."

"Actually, I only hung up on him once."

Devon frowns. "You know what I mean."

"Yes, I do."

"Honestly, that's it. I don't expect you to talk to Enzo. I don't plan to either. And I agree with you that it's ballsy of him to ask. But I promised I'd mention it, and I did. So now we can move on."

"That's it? For real?"

Devon nods, smiling like a six-year-old on Christmas. "That's it."

I'm cautiously optimistic. "That was," I hesitate, not one hundred percent sure Devon is finished, "fairly painless."

"Told you. Want another drink?"

I shake my head. "No, thanks. I still have some papers to grade and don't want to wait for an Angel pill."

He gives me a look that tells me he's not yet done with the serious stuff. "This won't be the only request, you know."

My stomach turns at the thought of it. "From Dad?"

"No, just in general. People are going to keep approaching you. Asking you for things. Asking for a piece of his time." He sighs. "Honestly, Char, I hope it works out between the two of you. I really do. You know I think Enzo is a great guy . . ."

Just like Mom. Just like Lusanne. But again, there's a big *but* in there somewhere.

"But?" I prod.

"But it's not like dating the head coach of Bridgewater High."

I give my brother the death glare. The last thing I want is to be reminded of my last failed relationship.

"I mean, there's a picture of you floating around in a newspaper."

I finish with my salad, putting my fork down and eyeing up Devon's chick parm.

"Trust me, I know," I say. Which is only partially true. I've thought about the press, sure, but not about the possibility that people might try to use me to get to Enzo. Still, I'm not sure why Devon's rolling out his big brother speech now.

"And he lives in New York."

I roll my eyes. "No shit, Sherlock."

He's managed to maintain a friendship with Enzo after all these years. Is it so unrealistic to think I can do the same?

Although it's not really the same thing, and I know it.

I don't dare say it to Devon, but I am in love with his best friend. All the way. He's just as good-looking and caring as the boy I loved when I was younger, but a new confidence has been added to the mix that's downright devastating.

And the occasional glimpses through it, to the bits of vulnerability that still exist in him? Even more so.

Not to mention, he likes me. Really, really likes me, if last weekend was any indication.

Sorry, Dev, it's too late for caution. The love train has already left the station—it's currently barreling down a hill without brakes.

Like it or not, I'm in deep. With luck, we won't need those brakes and the train will slow down on its own, taking a more leisurely path to its destination. Because the alternative is a fiery crash that will no doubt consume us both.

"The reports from Europe are in your inbox, sir. And I've moved your two o'clock meeting to one, as you asked. I'll have your car here at two fifteen."

I look up for long enough to thank my assistant, but I'm buried in emails again before she even closes the door behind me. I don't look up until Hayden, now standing behind my desk, clears his throat.

"Jesus. You scared the shit out of me."

He drops a package in front of me.

"Grab two waters."

I look at the wrapping from our favorite deli and shake my head. "I can't stop for lunch. I have a meeting at one, and I'm heading to the lab this afternoon."

Hayden doesn't move.

"The fact that you didn't even notice I'd entered your office is exactly the reason you need to stop for five minutes."

I look longingly at my computer screen.

"Enz." Hayden nods to the refrigerator behind me. Reluctantly, I stand up. No matter how many times I tell myself to do this more often, inevitably I end up hunched over my desk for too long. Stretching, I reach down, get two waters, and hand one to Hayden.

Opening the package, I groan at the smell of tuna salad, suddenly starving. I reluctantly smile at him. "You know me," I say.

"Too well."

We eat in silence, the afternoon and long evening ahead looming over me.

"Did you see the Europe reports?" I ask. "I haven't looked at them yet."

"Yeah," Hayden says after he finishes chewing. "That's part of why I thought you'd be in a more cheerful mood. It's better than we hoped for."

That surprises me. "What makes you think I'm not in a good mood?"

Another mouthful of egg salad prevents Hayden from answering.

"I'm fine. I'm just frustrated by our lack of progress at the lab."

After a swig of water, Hayden says, "You said yourself this was different, that the distillation would complicate things."

I did say that. But still . . .

"It's frustrating. Yesterday I met with Fred Gulerri."

Hayden groans. Neither of us is a fan of Fred, but he's the owner of one of the largest restaurant chains in the U.S. that serves alcohol, which makes him one of our biggest clients.

"He's pressing me," I say. "He's impatient for—"

Hayden cuts me off. "Tell him to fuck off."

"I didn't use those words exactly, but we did have"—I clear my throat—"a heated discussion."

I take a bite of my tuna sandwich.

Hayden gives me a look, and I know what he's about to say before he says it. Because I know him as well as he knows me.

"Don't say it," I groan.

His maddeningly relaxed approach to our business has served us well over the years—a good foil for my own breakneck pace. But sometimes, like right now, I wish he hadn't been born with a silver spoon in his mouth.

"Relax, Enz. We exceeded our goals last year, and this year's looking even better. So the vodka is a bit behind schedule . . . so what. It's fine."

No, it's not fine. But I don't say that. Small failures can easily become bigger ones.

"How's Chari?"

I look at the miniature glass frog sitting on my desk, feeling the corners of my mouth twitch despite my mood.

"Good," I say, meaning it.

"She coming in this weekend?"

Last weekend was a busy one for both of us, so I haven't seen her for over a week.

"She's supposed to."

I glance back at my screen, doing the mental math about the delays this unexpected trip to the lab will cause.

Shit. There's just no way I can take enough time off to make the trip worthwhile for her.

"But?"

"I'll probably have to cancel. No dinner tomorrow either."

Hayden frowns.

Before he can deliver me an earful, I say, "I know the rule. And I acknowledge that you've done a good job of keeping Wednesday sacrosanct with a wife and baby at home."

For years now we've been having our Wednesday non-business dinners, an inviolable tradition we've kept up without fail. Wednesday dinner is sacred. Just like my daily call home to Mom, and now to Chari. But sometimes real life gets in the way. And I'm not in the mood to hear otherwise from the person who understands my schedule more than anyone.

I wrap up the rest of my sandwich. "Sorry to kick you out of my office."

Hayden stands, saluting me. "No you're not. You love working more than any . . ." He stops. Usually my business partner is all smiles, but he suddenly looks way too serious for my liking. "I'd say having lunch with me. But we both know that's not true. Breaking bread with me is your favorite thing of all."

But Hayden's expression doesn't match his joking words.

"What were you going to say?"

Hayden shakes his head vigorously. "Nothing."

And that's it. He walks away.

"Seriously, what?"

"Let me know what happens at the lab," he says, ignoring my question. "Later."

Just before Hayden closes the door, I call out, "Thanks for lunch."

If it weren't for him, I probably wouldn't have eaten anything.

I look at my watch. Forty minutes to wrap things up before my meeting. It'll be tight, but for some reason, I find myself staring at the glare of my computer screen instead of getting to work.

What was Hayden so worked up about? It's not like I've

suddenly turned into a workaholic. Even in college, I sat out most of the parties he went to, choosing to stay home and hit the books instead. Work is important to me, it's what keeps me running, it's . . .

How's Chari?

It's a lightbulb moment. He's worried my work schedule will interfere with our relationship. The idea of Hayden as some sort of love doctor is laughable, or at least it would have been before he met Ada.

I laugh, my empty office the only recipient of the sound.

Sometimes Hayden just doesn't get it. Getting into Cornell wasn't easy for me, and I never took it for granted, not for one second. I still don't. Part of me fears the success we've worked so hard to achieve could be snatched away. That if we don't keep making it better, bigger, it'll drift away like so much smoke. Most of the time I know that's foolish, but I still

remember the look on my school counselor's face when I told her Cornell was my top pick.

"Cornell?" she said, her face scrunching up. "I'm so sorry, sweetie, but I don't think that's going to be possible." She went on to point out that it wasn't the kind of school kids with average grades, or dyslexia, should expect to get into.

Mrs. Forsythe was an old friend of my mother's, so I trusted her. Believed her. More than I should have. Cornell was my dream, and not only because of its kickass science program. My family had visited the campus on our way to one of Tris's playoff baseball games, and it had felt right in a way that no other college had. It had felt like home.

It was only a year later, when I hesitantly mentioned the idea to my mother, that she decided Amelia Forsythe was a *putana,* and I added the new curse word to my expanding vocabulary.

Getting in wasn't easy.

Even my own father had doubts, which Mom seemed to forgive much more easily than Mrs. Forsythe's. But he also wanted all four of us to work for the family business, so he wasn't going to be happy about any college that wasn't within commuting distance of Bridgewater.

After years of busting my ass, not only did I get into Cornell, but I kicked ass there. And I intend to keep kicking ass until Angel, Inc. offers every alcohol known to man and can be found everywhere alcohol is sold, throughout the world.

Maybe then I can ease up, like Hayden keeps telling me to do.

31

CHARI

"*S*eriously?"

I stare at the email for a full ten minutes and then slam the lid on my school-issued laptop. This is bullshit.

The principal denied my request to attend an early-reading training that I know will help my kiddos, and when I offered to use my own money to register, he nixed even that. If I didn't already know he was out of the building today, I'd be heading to his office now to blast him.

Why the hell can't I use my own resources to do something that'll benefit my job performance? He didn't offer an explanation, because he almost certainly doesn't have one. The guy is a total douche canoe. Short man's syndrome combined with an overinflated, and completely unwarranted, ego. He's the worst boss I've ever had in my life.

I can deal, usually. But not when the kids have to suffer for it.

"You look like you can use a drink."

Rob Slater stands in my open door as I clean up my

desk. A phys ed teacher, he's typically not on the second floor so far away from the gym.

"I could," I admit.

"Happy hour?"

It's been ages since I participated in the teachers' long-standing Friday afternoon tradition. I go in waves, hitting Bridgewater Brewing Company every week at times and then not again for months. Since Enzo, I haven't been once.

"Yeah, maybe . . ."

Rob nods toward the door. "No maybes. Let's go, Atwood."

"Now?"

Although the day is over, most people grade some papers or pack up for the weekend rather than bolting for the door.

"Yes, now."

I've known Rob my whole life. Even dated him once in sixth grade, although it was the kind of "dating" that entailed telling a lot of people about it and never actually doing anything together outside of school. He's a real ball-buster, and I've always wondered how his girlfriend puts up with him.

"Fine." I look down at my closed laptop. Screw it. "I'll meet you there."

Rob never did say what he was doing on the second floor, I realize later as I pull my scarf more tightly around my neck and head toward the car. It's less than a ten-minute drive to the bar, and when I pull in, there's only a few cars. One of the perks of being a teacher is an empty bar for happy hour. By the time the rest of the world gets out of work in an hour or so, we'll have filled the entire corner of the tasting room floor.

"There she is."

Rob's already here.

"Angel?" he asks.

If someone drives to a bar alone, there's a presumption that they'll be drinking some sort of Angel product. Funny, just a few weeks ago that name wouldn't have conjured visions of Enzo's naked body straddling me, the muscles of his arms straining as he—

"Chari?"

Who needs a jacket when you have memories like that one? Suddenly hot, I take off my scarf and put it, along with my coat, on the back of the bar seat.

"Sure. Angel Pale," I tell the bartender waiting for my drink order.

Rob already has a lager started, but he pays for mine as well.

"Thanks."

We clink glasses.

"Cheers to another week in paradise," he says. We both drink. Then he adds, "So who were you wanting to murder when I walked by your room?"

I look at him like, *Really?* We both know who drives everyone in that building crazy.

"What did he do now?"

I tell him my tale of woe, and Rob counters with one of his own. I've been so out of touch with the goings-on at school that I had no idea construction had started on the gym. It was supposed to wait until the summer, but much to Rob's chagrin, the principal had the bright idea of moving Rob's classes to the back of the library and breaking ground now. At the end of winter.

"Jackasses," I say. "So that's why you were on the second floor?"

Rob nods to the bartender. Apparently he's ready for another.

"Where've you been, Atwood? We haven't seen you at happy hour for months."

When I don't answer right away, he whistles. "Ah, young love. I did hear about you and Enzo DeLuca."

"I guess it's making the rounds."

That picture of Enzo and me at the airport has been widely circulated now, and it feels super weird whenever people mention it. No one much cared about my comings and goings before. Enzo says it will only get worse, though he'd help me navigate it all, as people realize we are serious.

His words, not mine.

But that was two days before he told me not to come to New York today as planned. Enzo apologized a hundred times, and I told him I understood. But I'm not so sure I do. It's been gnawing at me for the past two days. Even if he's working all weekend, why not have me come up anyway? Surely he could take a break one night to eat dinner? I even mentioned that last night, that maybe I could come and we could both get some work done together. Companionably.

Apparently I would be too *distracting*. Which seems like a compliment on the surface, but if the only time we're together is when he's totally free, we won't be together very much.

"Trouble in paradise already?"

I swat him on the arm. "You're incorrigible. No, there's no trouble in paradise."

The door opens, and I assume it's one of our faculty members, but no one approaches the bar, so it must be someone leaving instead. Luckily, we're far enough away that I don't get blasted with cold air. But the others aren't long behind us. Within fifteen minutes, our party of two turns into ten.

Two beers later, I'm feeling better about my jerk boss—sharing horror stories with my colleagues is a balm second to none—and even about my cancelled trip. I'm not even thinking about Enzo, much, when my phone buzzes with a text from him.

Enzo: Having fun?

For a second, I think he's actually here. That he came to surprise me. But a quick scan of the bar proves otherwise.

Chari: Yes. You?

Thankfully, he's a quick texter.

Enzo: Not so much

"Chari, want another drink?"

Rob points to my empty beer.

"Sure," I say, "but this round is on me."

Enzo is still typing.

I pay the bartender for two drinks and get two drink chips for my friends. Last call for me and then the Angel pill. It's been a long day.

Enzo: So who's the guy?

Four words took that long to type? I look around again. No Enzo.

Chari: ?

Enzo: Gian was there earlier, said he saw you

I would definitely have noticed if Enzo's brother were here. He mustn't have stayed for long. Or maybe he was in the restaurant. Either way, I'm annoyed enough not to text back.

First, he cancels.

Again.

And then he oh so casually turns the jealous boyfriend act up a notch.

I may be losing a bit of myself to him, but that doesn't mean I'm okay with being swallowed up whole.

Enzo: Call me

Chari: Aren't you at the lab?

They have notoriously bad cell reception there.

Enzo: I'll go outside

I waffle between jumping off the barstool—because honestly, the possibility of hearing his voice is the most excitement I've had all night—and telling him the truth. That I'm in the middle of a conversation with some friends, so no, I can't talk right this second about his brother's creepy stalking.

Not that Gian was stalking me. But still. This feels like pretty much the last thing I need to deal with right now. I'm pissy at the moment and self-aware enough to know it.

As I try to decide how to respond, a picture comes through. It's my little glass frog sitting on a lab desk. What the hell?

Chari: Why do you have that with you? Is it sanitary?

Enzo: Reminds me of you. Yes.

So much for making him wait.

"Be right back," I mutter, as if anyone notices. They're all wrapped up in their own conversations, so I grab my beer and tell the fourth-grade special ed teacher she can sit in my chair. Heading toward the bathrooms, I find a semiprivate space and dial Enzo's number.

He answers immediately.

"Hey."

His voice melts my insides. Reminding myself I'm annoyed with him, I answer, "Hey," my tone making it into more of a *what the hell?* than an invitation to chat.

"So you're at happy hour, I take it?"

I'm about to mention his text when I decide to let it ride. For the moment.

"Yeah, decided last minute to come. Shitty day."

He's quiet, thinking about whatever Gian said, no doubt. While I could ease his fears with a few words, I don't want to let him off that easily. So I wait him out.

"Who's the guy?" he finally asks, his tone the opposite of casual. I can hear his annoyance over the phone.

"Maybe Gian should have asked me himself if he was so concerned?"

Silence.

"He was picking up something for the restaurant and left in a hurry."

"Mmm-hmm."

"Char, I'm sorry about this weekend. I really am."

"It's not just that," I venture. Although I don't want to get into a serious discussion on the phone in the middle of a bar, I need to talk to him about this. I need him to soothe my fears. To tell me it's going to be okay. "Where are we going here? If you're too distracted to have me around unless your schedule is totally free, then realistically, how often will we see each other?"

There. I'm damned proud of myself for putting the words into an intelligible string. They've been floating around in my head in one form or another ever since he cancelled.

"So you're not going to answer my question?"

What the hell is he talking about? It takes a solid ten seconds for it to click.

"Rob Slater? Seriously?"

"The gym teacher?"

"Phys ed," I correct him. "With about fifteen other people from my school."

"Oh."

"Yeah, oh. What did you think? That I was so disappointed you cancelled I went and found a new boyfriend to occupy my time?"

I'm definitely being extra pissy now, but I can't help it.

"I didn't know what to think. Gian just said you were sitting at the bar with some guy. I'm surprised he didn't recognize Rob."

"He has a beard now."

"You don't like beards."

"No," I agree. "I don't."

"And I'm getting the sense you don't like me very much right now either."

It couldn't be further from the truth, which is exactly what has me worried.

"I like you enough to be disappointed about this weekend." I take a swig of beer, but it's not going down as smoothly as before.

"I'm a shithead."

I don't argue with him.

"It's not like me to be jealous."

"Really? You weren't just a teensy bit annoyed by your friend Marc from Virginia?"

Enzo groans. "He is not my friend."

"This is where you've been hiding," a friend of mine whispers as she makes her way into the ladies' room. "Party's over there." She points to our gang.

"Go ahead," Enzo says, having clearly overheard her. "I have to get back to the lab anyway."

"Char," he adds. Then stops. My heart starts beating faster. Will he use the L word? And even if he does, will it be enough to keep this long-distance relationship from falling apart before it really gets started?

"Yeah?"

"I'll call you tonight. If," he rushes to add, "you'll be home. And if you're not, it's no big deal."

Nope, no big L word. No real discussion of the conundrum we're in.

"I'll be home," I say. "Give me a buzz when you're done."

Awkward silence.

"Will do. Have fun in the meantime."

"Same to you."

Another short pause, and then he hangs up.

I'm pretty sure that was our first fight. Which is fine—everyone fights—only I don't feel like we resolved anything.

Trouble in paradise?

A week ago I'd have said no way, but now?

Now I'm not so sure.

32

ENZO

"*Y*ou're looking pleased with yourself."

I haven't seen Chari in almost three weeks, but I'm going home this weekend. So yes, I'm pretty pleased. And it looks like we've finally made a breakthrough on the vodka formula.

Hayden winds up a forkful of pasta as masterfully as if he's been doing it every week for years. Because he has.

"You really need to try something else," I tell him. "There's an entire menu, you know."

Hayden doesn't answer, mouthful of food and all.

"I'm going home for the weekend," I admit, knowing Hayden will figure it out anyway. I brace myself for his teasing, and it comes as soon as he finishes his mouthful of linguine.

"Ah, so that's the reason for Mr. Happy-Go-Lucky? And here I thought it was the vodka."

"That too." I take a bite of eggplant. It's good, but not nearly as good as my mother's. Maybe I can convince her to make it this weekend. I make a mental note to ask Tris to put it on the specials menu for Saturday night. Mom splits her time now between the pizza shop and the restaurant, like Lusanne, although her focus is on helping in the kitchen. Tris told me that every time Mom cooks the special, they sell out of it.

"But no work," I remind Hayden.

"Right."

We talk about life with a baby, and Hayden tells me, quite rightly, how lucky he is to have Ada. Which, of course, leads us back to Chari.

"So how long are you going to do this for exactly?" he says, leaning back in his chair.

The waiter takes away our plates. I sit back, full and happy, wine firmly in hand.

"Do what?"

"Eke out a weekend here and a night there to see her?"

It's not like I haven't thought about that. And although she and I haven't outright discussed it, the long-distance nature of our relationship hangs over us. As does the one and only argument we've gotten into so far. Because I'm not sure our problems are solvable.

This is my life for the foreseeable future. And Chari has her own life, back in Bridgewater.

"I don't know," I admit. "I asked her why she moved back home after college, just out of curiosity."

"And to feel her out about possibly moving out of Bridgewater?"

I won't admit it, but yeah. Exactly that.

"She won't do it."

That seems to surprise Hayden.

"Her job?"

My answer is automatic. "No, actually. Chari loves her

kids but hates her boss. And the system, which is set up to reward neurotypical kids. Ones who are good at navigating the kind of learning that happens in most schools."

Hayden knows I struggled in school when I was younger, but I've never explained the extent of it. It strikes me now that it's a little weird I haven't told him. He's like a brother to me. And keeping the secret gives it power, something I don't want to do anymore.

"I'm dyslexic," I admit. I'm not ashamed, not anymore, but I'm still angry at a system that nearly failed me.

Hayden's eyes widen. "Seriously?"

"Seriously." I take a sip of wine, relaxed despite the topic of conversation. Frank Sinatra's "My Way" begins to pipe through the restaurant as if Ol' Blue Eyes himself is commending me for having done, well, just that. I love this song. "So I get her frustrations. If it weren't for my mom, I probably would have slipped through the cracks too."

Hayden looks confused. "But . . ."

Time to dispel some myths. "It doesn't mean I can't read. Just that I had to learn how in a totally different way. The school did squat to help me figure it out. Unfortunately, Chari is now dealing with the same bullshit but from a different angle. Education is slow to change even though we have all of the resources."

"Shit, Enzo. I knew you weren't a fan of grade school, but I had no idea."

There were good teachers too, ones who worked with my mother to find the resources I needed. Too bad it was such an uphill fucking climb for all of them.

"I'm just saying, I get why she's banging her head against a wall. I don't think leaving the job would be an issue for her."

"So why do you think she's unlikely to leave Bridgewater?"

This isn't my story to tell, so I gloss over it as best I can. "Chari's parents are divorced. Her dad just kind of left and never looked back. I think Chari feels like her mom needs her. She doesn't want to take off like her father did."

Hayden's relationship with his parents is . . . complicated. They've never been very hands-on, and Hayden hated being sent away to boarding school. But even he winces at that.

"Ouch."

"Yeah. But the thing is, her mom seems to be doing fine. She has a boyfriend, and according to Chari they're getting pretty serious. The shop does well."

I tilt my head and shrug, as if to indicate I'm not sure what to do with that. I can't tell Chari her mother will be fine without her living there—that's up to Chari.

"Back to my original question," Hayden says. "How long are you planning on doing the long-distance thing?"

That's a great question, and I only wish I could answer it.

"No idea. But I'll admit, I'm pretty stoked to be going home. I cleared my schedule for the whole day Saturday and Sunday, enough time to see Chari and the family. Aside from the car ride, I promised myself no work for two full days. See? I'm balancing work and life. You should be proud."

He looks skeptical.

"I am," he mutters.

"What?" I ask as Hayden makes a face.

"The week is young," is all he says before turning toward the window. It's dark, nothing to see out there. Which means . . .

I look up, groaning. Giovanna Faustini, who I haven't seen in weeks, is sauntering toward us. My good mood sours when I see the look on her face. She's up to something, and I suspect it doesn't bode well for either of us, me especially.

33

CHARI

"*T*his really sucks."

Enzo looks at me through the phone. Thank God for video chat.

"It came out of nowhere, too," he adds.

"It" is a Nor'easter that was supposed to have brought one to three inches but instead dumped more than a foot on us and close to the same in New York City, where they didn't typically see as much snow as in PA.

I shift positions, wishing I'd used my laptop instead of attempting to prop the phone in my lap.

"Is that ours?" he asks when my glass of red wine flits onto the screen.

"Yep," I say proudly, as if being a certified red wine drinker were an achievement. Closest to a Pinot Noir, according to Enzo, Angel Red is *light to medium body with an aroma reminiscent of black or red cherry*—his exact words.

"Impressive."

He's had an effect on me in more ways than one. So much so that I sometimes struggle to remember what life was like pre-Enzo. Boring but with a lot fewer tugs on my heartstrings, some not entirely enjoyable. Like the sinking feeling that came with every new weather report on Thursday into Friday, until it became obvious Enzo wouldn't be able to safely travel home this weekend.

"When we first worked on that," he says, referring to my wine, "Hayden insisted on that particular formula for the red. He said it was the most romantic of all the wines."

"How can a wine be romantic?" I ask, genuinely curious.

"He said it packed a powerful punch, kind of like falling in love."

The word seems to hang over us—me in my home and him in his—maybe because neither of us has said that word to each other. I just can't be the first to do it. Enzo has to know, given our history, I'm totally in love with him. And if he's not ready to profess his love to me, there must be a reason.

Maybe he doesn't feel the same way.

"You should know something else." He looks over his shoulder, as if someone might be watching. Highly unlikely since it's ten thirty at night and he's in bed too. I catch a glimpse of his bare chest, my eyes lingering, and I think Enzo notices. The look in his eyes takes a decidedly more intimate turn.

"What should I know?"

His lips part. I swallow, glad I've locked my bedroom door. Whatever he was about to say before seems to have changed.

"I'm hard as a rock thinking about you in this bed with me."

Yep, that's what I thought.

"Are you now?" I say, my core clenching in anticipation.

"I probably shouldn't tell you this." His liquid brown eyes pull me in, but it's Enzo's voice that clutches me and refuses to let go. The warmth in it wraps around me like a blanket. "But we had reservations for tonight at Chateau LeMonte. Dinner and a room."

My eyes widen.

"For real?"

Chateau LeMonte is a five-star restaurant in a neighboring town. It's housed in a historical building, surrounded by luxury cabins. They're always booked, even in the winter, and though I've passed the place a hundred times, I've never stayed there. My mom and Devon and I did eat there twice, once for each of our high school graduations, but it's not the kind of place you just book for a random Saturday night.

Unless you're Enzo DeLuca.

"How is that possible?"

Enzo's shoulder dips. Is he . . .

"For the right price, anything is possible."

Oh yes, he is. I can't see it, but I can easily imagine him grasping himself while looking at me. I reach my own hand down too, slipping up the hem of the satin nightshirt I really only wear when chatting with Enzo. Usually it's just an oversized T-shirt for me.

"Is that so?"

We've done this before, but there's something about not talking about it, pretending to carry on a conversation but knowing it's really only a front . . .

"Well." His eyes close momentarily. "Most anything. A few things can't be bought."

I've slipped a finger inside. Normally that wouldn't do much to get me off, but this is a special circumstance. I'm staring at my gorgeous boyfriend, who's clearly pumping himself more rigorously now. And the look on his face . . . I just don't know if I can continue the conversation.

But I try.

"Such as?"

He moans, his shoulder dipping down in a steady rhythm that I match, slick and ready to come even though I've only just started.

"Strangely, I can't think straight at the moment." His voice is thick with pleasure and an impending release.

"I wonder why?"

My body heat has risen to like a million degrees. As he moves more quickly, I do the same. Until I feel the spasms start to come. *Not yet.*

"I can't hold back," I manage, licking my lips and willing him to finish.

"Enzo," I fairly beg.

He doesn't need much more prompting. Enzo cries out, dipping his head back, and I swear I've never seen anything sexier in my entire life. Never mind my arm is sore from holding the phone at just the right angle. My spasms come in quick succession, and I withdraw my hand and let the aftereffects claim me.

When they do, I open my eyes . . . which is when I realize I'd shut them.

"Hold on a sec," he says.

He sets the phone down, heading to his bathroom to clean up, I expect, and although I should probably do the same, I don't. I lie back on my mattress, content to let my extra soft pillows claim me as I watch the dark screen. Waiting for him to appear.

"You look relaxed," Enzo says when he finally returns.

"Mmm-hmm," I murmur, content just to stare at him for a bit longer. "I wish you were here."

"So do I, tiger. Want me to stay with you until you fall asleep?"

"It's up to you," I say, more tired than I was when we got

on the phone for sure. I still have to wash my face and brush my teeth. But I do neither of those things.

"I'll stay," he says. "Close your eyes, Char."

I do, saying in my head what I can't yet say out loud.

Goodnight, Enzo. I love you.

34

CHARI

"*A*re you fucking kidding me?" I snap.

Lisa and I sit in our usual spot next to the window in The Wheelhouse bakery. The view is magnificent today. Snow is piled on top of the waterwheel, and it also lines the creek running alongside it. Bridgewater came to life after the snow stopped, but business is still slower than usual for a Sunday morning. After all, everyone still had to shovel out from just under fifteen inches of snow.

Lisa tries to snatch back her phone, which she handed to me without comment, but I don't let her. Even though I read the article once, I need to see it again.

A picture of Enzo with an absolutely beautiful black-haired woman stares back at me. And there's literally zero chance that I'm misreading the look on her face. She's staring at my boyfriend, *my* boyfriend, as if he's the only fucking guy in the entire world.

A Billionaire's Night Out

Enzo DeLuca and Hayden Tanner regularly frequent the small but well-known Italian eatery Faustini's. The owner's daughter, Giovanna Faustini, pictured with the chemist behind

*Angel, Inc., hints at a special relationship that keeps both DeLuca
and his partner coming back each week.*

I look up. "Special relationship?"

Finally successful in reclaiming her phone, Lisa tucks it
back into her purse, going so far as to zip it. Of course, if I
wanted to, I could find the same *New York Post* story myself.
But I have no desire to stare at the woman in the picture any
longer than necessary.

"Explain to me how this is different than when Enzo
jumped to conclusions after Gian saw you with Rob?"

I open my mouth to deliver a retort before realizing that
the situations are, essentially, exactly the same. So I smartly
shovel in a mouthful of eggs instead of replying.

"I'm sure it's exactly how it looks."

I swallow. "Like Enzo is very cozy with a bombshell
attorney who hints at a 'special relationship' with him?"

Lisa clears her throat as our waitress sidles up to the table.
"More coffee?"

"Sure," my friend replies for both of us as I stare at the
snow that kept Enzo and me apart this weekend. When the
waitress leaves after filling our cups, Lisa continues, "No,
like a wealthy, famous man standing next to the daughter of
the owner of a restaurant he frequents every week."

No comment from me.

"Char," she adds gently, "you're going to have to get used
to this stuff with him. Enzo isn't like us. He's a celebrity in a
lot of ways."

I do know that.

"Imagine if Jennifer Aniston got jealous every time she
saw her . . . OK, bad example. Or some other actress.
Imagine if she got jealous every time her celebrity boyfriend
or husband was pictured with another woman."

I stop eating, not really hungry anymore.

"Well, it's kind of their job to 'be with' other people," I say. "Enzo is not an actor."

"No, he's a very prominent businessman in New York, and that paper reports on happenings in New York."

At least the coffee is still tasty. It warms my throat, comforts my stomach, which is sadly tied in knots. This whole love thing sucks sometimes.

"You're right, but . . ."

It's a big but, and we both know it.

"But?"

This isn't really about that article. It's about the fact that I'm in love with a man who hardly has time to pee during the day, never mind to get away long enough to carry on an actual relationship.

"But," I say cautiously, knowing once I say it out loud, the whole thing will become more real. "If we were together this weekend, it would be as simple as saying, 'What's up with this?'"

"Which you can still do on the phone," she says softly as she finishes buttering her toast. She looks at it like it's a lover, then takes a bite, her eyes fluttering shut.

The girl loves toast.

"I know. But it would be different in person. Less of a big deal."

Lisa looks confused, rightly so.

"This weekend, it's snow. A few weeks ago, the vodka formula. Next time, it will be something else."

I hate the heaviness in my chest as I put words to the things that have been swirling around in my head.

"Meaning?"

I shrug, not exactly sure.

"I guess what I'm trying to say is that dating a guy who's building an empire, long-distance, is hard."

She laughs, actually laughs, at me.

"You didn't think it would be?"

I can't say I thought much about the day-to-day of it. "I don't know? Switzerland was just so, so perfect. And of course we can't be on a perpetual vacation, but we have such different lives. A bad day for me is my asshole principal denying a training. A bad day for him is something that can cost his company millions of dollars."

"So?"

I stare at her. "So? We're like night and day."

She blinks.

"And we live two hours apart."

Still nothing.

"And he hardly has time for a girlfriend."

Her brows rise. I toss it all out there now.

"And he hasn't said 'I love you' yet."

The corners of Lisa's mouth actually lift, as if she finds this amusing.

"That's not at all funny."

"Maybe not. But I do wish you could hear yourself."

I'm not sure I catch her meaning.

"Who called off every single relationship you've been in for one reason or another?"

Paying more attention now to my coffee cup than Lisa, I pretend not to have heard the question.

"At the very slightest indication that you might be getting in deep, boom! Goodbye."

I stare into my coffee cup, my attention fixed. I think I might love coffee as much as Lisa loves toast.

"I know you can hear me."

Finally, I look up. "This is different."

"Is it?"

It is. Because I'm not so sure I've been in love before. Probably I have, but right now it's hard to remember. And if I was in love with any of the others, my feelings for them didn't even come close to how I feel about Enzo. If I'm being honest, it's super scary how much thoughts of him have taken over my life.

I hate it.

Want it to stop.

I don't need a man to be happy. My mother didn't have one for years and years. And she was perfectly content to run her shop, raise Devon and me. I don't *need* Enzo, but seeing him standing next to that gorgeous woman, that gorgeous *lawyer*, triggers something in me. It reminds me that I haven't really amounted to anything.

I mean, my profession is a noble one, sure. But I know I could be doing more. I feel it in my bones.

"Call him," she says. And I realize how patient Lisa has been with me. Enzo hasn't just consumed my life, he's consumed hers too. Because of me.

"OK," I say, knowing I will but needing to put the article, and my boyfriend, behind me for the morning. "Enough about Enzo. Tell me about you. How was that big meeting you were nervous about?"

I listen to my friend talk about the contract she was awarded to make signs for a hotel chain as errant flurries fall down just outside the window. It's a beautiful view, really. As I relax into the moment, it occurs to me again that Lisa is right.

I'm a saboteur.

My daddy issues run deep.

And I refuse to sabotage myself again, not this time.

Not with Enzo. He's too important to give up so easily.

35

ENZO

I give up.

After trying and failing to concentrate for the last hour, I jump out of my seat, head to the bedroom, change quickly, and then walk into the hall. While I wait for the elevator, I replay my conversation with Devon a hundred times.

I have a shit-ton of work left to do tonight, and it's almost ten o'clock, but I just can't seem to focus. Arriving at the pool in the basement level of my building, I toss my towel onto a chair, not even bothering with a locker. It's empty this time of night. An hour ago, executives would still be lingering in the lap pool, some having just come home from work, but it's almost closing time, and the pool is silent and empty.

I stare at the still water, at the reflection of the lounge chairs lining the long lap pool, and jump in. The shock of it is exactly what I need. Clearing my mind, I swim back and forth, the only sound an echo of my soft splashes. After a while, realizing I'm exhausted, I hoist myself out and check the time on the wall.

Feeling a bit better, I'm about to leave, but I sink into a plush cushioned seat instead.

Doubt creeps into my consciousness, something that's been happening more often of late.

Who the hell do you think you are?

Swimming a lap pool in the middle of March in an apartment complex reserved for the very wealthiest, I am not Enzo DeLuca, son of a pizza shop owner, a boy who pretended to read by memorizing word configurations and tricking my parents and teachers.

I'm not a kid from a small town in PA.

Or even one of the "lucky" few who somehow got into an Ivy League school.

I am one of the richest men in a city filled with people like Hayden, ones who think having three houses means you haven't made it yet. At least, that's what the reflection in the pool tells me. But I'm not sure how I feel about that. I'm not even sure what it means.

Angrily, I stand and leave, trying to shake the feeling of inevitability that's been haunting me since that call with Devon.

By the time I'm back in my apartment, changed, wine in hand and laptop at the ready, I know the swim hasn't worked. My problems haven't gone away, or even retreated.

I grab my phone, scroll to her number, and press the button.

"Are you all right?"

My mother has trained Lus well. The girl has a PhD in worry.

"Yes, geez. I can't even call my baby sister?" Standing, I move to the very same couch that evokes a not-so-innocent memory of Chari every time I look at it.

"At ten o'clock at night on a Thursday?"

"OK," I say, stretching out my legs. "I'll give you that one."

"What are you looking at?"

This is something we've done on our calls since I left for college. Just Lusanne and I, no one else.

"The Manhattan skyline," I tell her. "If you look really close at the lights' reflection on the water, you can see purples and pinks and not just white. It looks so calm, from here at least."

In fact, it's beautiful. One of the biggest cities in the world, sitting just outside my window, so deceivingly serene.

"You?"

"I can see the water too," she says. "Hold on."

There's rustling in the background, which is when I realize it is indeed Thursday and Lusanne is working at Tris's.

"I'm sorry, Lus, I totally forgot. You're working."

"No worries," she says as the noise behind her ceases. "It's snowing again, so it's kinda slow. But I can see it now, Lake Shohola. Mostly it looks like a black abyss with a few lights here and there. But I can see the snow coming down if I look hard enough."

Funny, it's not snowing here.

"Sounds pretty."

"It is. What's wrong, Enz?"

I don't try to deny that something is. "I talked to Devon yesterday."

Her silence tells me to go on.

"He said Chari won't tell him anything about us. But he knows there's something wrong."

"And is there?"

I'm almost at a loss for words, which is why I was hesitant to make this call. But I needed to talk to someone, and

Lusanne gets me better than anyone. She always has, at least since we were teens. I think it has something to do with her own struggles with severe ADHD.

"I don't want there to be," I say, knowing that's not really an answer.

"But?"

"She deserves more than I can give her at the moment."

There, I said it.

"And what the hell is that supposed to mean?"

I knew Lus wouldn't mince words. I relied on it.

"I haven't seen her in weeks. And she has a bachelorette party on Saturday, so she can't come to New York this weekend."

"So come here."

I brace for it. "I can't. We're having some problems with the vodka antidote. Not to mention, once the issues are resolved we'll have to work overtime to get it approved by the FDA so we can stay on track."

"Work. Of course."

"Lus, if I wanted a lecture, I could have called, well, lots of people." Hayden. Mom. Probably my father is the only one who would say something to the effect of, If you have to work, then work.

"So you can't come home, and she can't come to New York."

"Last week there was the storm," I say.

"And it's still friggin' snowing," she says, echoing basically every Pennsylvanian's sentiment by mid-March. "What else did Devon say?"

Lusanne is a goddamn clairvoyant.

So I get right to the punch line.

"He reminded me of the first talk we had about Chari

and me. The one where he told me not to screw around with her emotions."

"Hmmm." I never told her about that particular discussion. "So are you?"

"Screwing around with her emotions? No," I answer emphatically. Because I'd never do that.

"So what's the problem?"

"You have to get back to work. We'll talk about this some other time."

"Enzo DeLuca. Spit it out."

That's my mother's tone, and Lusanne wields it like a sword.

"I like her, Lus. A lot."

"I'm not sure I get the problem?"

What am I supposed to say? That I like my work more?

Or not *more* precisely. It's just that the two strands of my life don't jive very well.

"If it were five years from now, after all of the dust settles—"

"Oh, you mean when Angel, Inc. is international? And your vodka is more popular than anyone else's? When you're working on other spirits. Angel Bourbon. Angel Whiskey. Then, you mean?"

I'm really starting to wish I hadn't called my sister. Although I'm not sure what I hoped she'd say.

"Enzo, there won't be a good time to fall in love. Not for you."

I don't argue that I'm not in love with Chari Atwood. I don't want to lie. But that doesn't mean it will help anything to acknowledge it out loud either.

"There couldn't be a *worse* time," I point out. "And it's not like she's here, in New York."

"I'm in here," she calls out to someone. "Enz, I gotta go."

"That's fine. I should get back to work too."

I can almost feel her eyes rolling from Bridgewater.

"Thanks for listening to me, at least."

"Not that it did any good. There's really only one person who can give you the answers you need. But for what it's worth, I like her too. A lot. Call you tomorrow?"

"Sure," I say. "Love you, Lus."

"Love you too. Ciao."

The phone goes dead. I stare at it, agreeing at least with her last point. There really is only one person who can figure this out, and I'm staring at him in the reflection of my big picture window.

36

CHARI

The black screen lights up beside me. Picking it up, I answer wearily. It's the first time all weekend Enzo and I have video chatted, but this time it was because of my schedule, not Enzo's. For the last week, I have forced myself to stop waiting for my life to start.

My mother didn't raise me to be dependent.

Not on my boss.

Not on my boyfriend.

Lisa was right about one thing. I am a saboteur. Or at least I have been in the past. All day last Sunday, I thought about what she said. I turned off everything, made myself more coffee than one person should drink after noon, and contemplated what I want from my life, where I'm going with it, and where I've already gone.

Do I push people away out of a fear of rejection? Out of a fear of being left? Sure. It doesn't take a genius to figure that one out. Am I doing it with Enzo too? Just a week ago I vowed to fight for him, and I still think he's worth it. But even more worthwhile? Not losing myself completely. Which is totally what I've done.

Most teachers don't leave public education and willingly give up a pension. But that's exactly what I plan to do. As much as I love these kids, I'm not so keen to operate under this twisted, arcane institution that cares more about preserving itself than it does about progress. Nope, I just can't do it anymore.

So what's the alternative?

I'm not positive, but I'm determined to figure it out. Joining a private education company? Starting my own? Even researching the possibilities gives me more hope about my future than I've had in a while.

And then there's Enzo.

My path forward is clear. I need to start accepting invitations from my friends again. Stop planning my life around a nightly video call. While he moves forward with his life in New York, I need to do the same here.

But we've paid the price. There's a new distance between us, one I don't like, but I'm not sure if there's any hope for spanning it. For making this work. I can't sit around waiting for him to toss me a scrap of himself. He tried to warn me weeks ago, but the high of Switzerland and being with him kept me from actually processing what he said on the plane back to the States.

"I work a lot, Chari."

Of course he does, I thought at the time. *That's totally fine.*

"You can ask Hayden when you meet him. Or talk to my family. Even your brother. Any one of them will tell you, Angel, Inc. is like my baby."

And still, I shrugged off his words. *We'll make it work*, I thought. *He cares about me, and that's all that matters.*

So naive.

"Hey, tiger," he says, Enzo's handsome face flashing onto the screen.

I prop the phone on my computer.

"Hold on a sec."

Turning off the show I was watching when he called, I take in the casual navy T-shirt and damp hair.

"Went for a swim?" I ask, wishing I could run my hands through that tousled mass of sexy darkness. It seems I do a lot of wishing when it comes to Enzo.

"Yeah," he says.

Looks like he's sitting at his dining room table. Working, no doubt.

"How was your weekend?"

I relay everything since Friday, including possible plans for my future. He fills me in on what's happening with Angel.

On one hand, it's a comfortable conversation between two people who know each other's daily lives well. On the other, there's a tension between us that hasn't totally eased since our fight about Rob. But I'm determined not to go there, to take this as it comes and stop overanalyzing what could be. I've decided my life is not going to be about Enzo, but that doesn't mean Enzo can't be a part of my life.

But then he drops a bombshell.

"I do have some bad news," he says. His frown is more telling than his words. He looks as if the lab tech just told him there was a problem with the formula. Part concerned, part thoughtful, and definitely not at ease.

"What's that?"

I fluff a pillow behind my head, waiting for him to continue.

"Chari?"

Looking back at the screen, I realize I've been purposefully avoiding him. Sensing something was happening and knowing I wouldn't like whatever he has to say.

"Unfortunately, I'm going to have to cancel next weekend."

I knew it before the words left his mouth. He was supposed to send a driver on Friday. The plan was for me to spend the whole weekend in New York. Maybe that's why I've been able to focus so much better this last week, knowing we'd see each other soon enough.

But my carefully built house of cards comes crashing down with his words.

"I have to head up to Rochester. Long story, but it has to do with the vodka antidote. I swear, moving into spirits will be the death of me."

And Enzo will be the death of *me.*

Don't say it, Chari. Don't.

"Maybe I could come with you?"

Ugh, what is wrong with me?

"I'm actually going with Hayden."

Which means it's serious. Hayden doesn't travel as much anymore, and they usually split up Angel, Inc. duties whenever possible. I know there's another lab they work with in Rochester, and while a part of me wants to ask what happened, the other part knows it doesn't matter.

This just isn't working.

"I have a baby shower the weekend after that," I say, grasping at straws. "But maybe you could come to Bridgewater?"

I know his answer even before he gives it.

"I can't get away, not with everything going down at the moment."

And there it is.

But I promised myself not to give up easily on him. So I keep trying.

"The weekend after?"

His eyes, always so expressive, give me the answer. He at least has the decency to look as devastated as me, although I doubt it. Only one of us is in love here, as far as I know. I'm beginning to wonder if Enzo is capable of loving anything like he loves Angel, Inc.

"So much for that," I say, not even feeling the need to ask why that weekend won't work either. Ultimately, it doesn't matter.

"I told you, on the way back from Switzerland . . ."

I don't blame him for sounding defensive, but I do blame him, maybe irrationally, for not making the situation clearer before he took complete control of my heart.

"You told me . . ." There's a definite edge in my voice now, the kinds that cuts, but I can't help it. ". . . you work a lot. Not that you work every waking moment."

He grinds his jaw tight.

"But I suppose it's my fault."

If I'm lashing out, it's because of the disappointment that feels like a lead weight in my gut. All the progress I've made this week, all of the grand promises to find myself, and it's glaringly apparent I've failed. One cancelled weekend, and my world is shattered.

"I should have known better. If you can't find time to come home for your family, then why did I think you'd find time for me?"

Enzo is getting angrier by the second, which is fine by me. Because I'm good and angry too. How long was he planning to jerk me around, exactly?

"I'm not gallivanting around New York with my new friends and leaving my family, or you, in the dust, Chari. I'm working. Building a company. Aside from Wednesday night, I don't go out. I live in my office. You know that."

I hate that I'm saying this. "And your special relationship with Faustini's daughter?"

It was a stupid thing to toss in his face, but my anger has taken over.

"We've talked about the press, Chari. That was nothing."

"I know." And I really do.

But my chest feels like one of Devon's prized bucks is lying on it. I can't breathe right, because another thing I know is where this conversation is heading.

Maybe we can avoid it. Enzo is worth fighting for. I still believe that. I *know* that. Maybe . . .

"There are trade-offs," he says. "I bring my family on a cruise every year. Tris got to open his restaurant ten years earlier than he would have on his own. And we"—Enzo looks me straight in the eyes, or as close as he can through a piece of glass and metal—"we have Switzerland. Or anywhere else in the world you want to go, Char."

So that's his peace offering.

We may not see each other very often, but when we do, fancy dinners and 5-star hotels await. Does he seriously not know me at all?

"I don't care about any of that," I say earnestly, angry again. "Your billion-dollar date in Switzerland, you can keep it. No view in the world, no royal treatment, as awesome as it is, can compete with time with you."

How does he not get that?

"So what are you saying?"

What *am* I saying, exactly? OK, time to bring it down a bit.

"We can't see each other for the next few weeks, which sucks. But what about after that? Are there any concessions you can make at all, any way you can maybe be a bit more like Hayden, who seems to balance work and family successfully? Anything at all you can change to make this feasible?"

I wait for him to consider it. Come up with a plan to meet me halfway. Enzo's broad shoulders rise and lower as he watches me. Thinking.

And then . . .

"No."

Is he freaking serious?

"No?"

He seems to have made some sort of decision and digs in.

"No, Chari. I've been through this with my family. Not now when we're expanding. Hayden's family lives in New York, so that makes a big difference. I can't come running to Bridgewater at ten o'clock at night after things wrap up for the day."

"Come running? I'm not asking you to come running. Just to think of something, anything, to make this work better than it has this past month?"

Like saying *I love you*, or promising we'll make a plan together.

Like saying, *Maybe I can try to avoid working Saturday nights so we can be together at least one night a week.*

Like saying, *I can deal with you distracting me if it means you're here, with me, even if I'm working and you're lying near me, reading a book. But at least we'll be together.*

There are so many things he can say right now, and I hold my breath, waiting for any of them to come out of his mouth.

"I'm sorry, Chari. I really am."

So his answer is still no. There's nothing he can do to meet me halfway. He won't even try.

"This isn't just a business to me. It's . . ."

I wait, but he doesn't finish. Because Enzo doesn't know what it is, exactly. He just knows that nothing is more important to him at the moment than turning Angel from a gazillion-dollar global enterprise into an even bigger gazillion-dollar global enterprise.

And if I'm not high on his priority list, then Enzo just isn't the guy for me.

"Then . . ." A lump in my throat prevents me from saying it, so I shake my head a little until the words come out. "I don't think there's a ton more for us to say."

Contradict me. Please, Enzo, contradict me.

"No, I guess there's not."

We stare at each other for another few seconds, and then I gather up whatever modicum of self-respect I have left and hover my finger over the end button.

"Bye, Enzo."

He blinks, and maybe he regrets how this went down? It's hard to tell.

"Bye, tiger."

The endearment doesn't make it any easier to click the button and hang up.

37

ENZO

"*H*ello, Enzo."

This is just what I need. We're going to have to find a new restaurant soon.

"Evening, G."

I step inside, wondering why the high-powered attorney is playing hostess tonight. After her little maneuver a few weeks back, I'm even less keen on being in her presence. She asked for a small press opp, a photo together, and I caved. Should have known she'd put her own little spin on the story. My fault, but it's a mistake I won't make again.

"I hate to say it, because you know how much I adore you." Giovanna walks us toward the table even though she knows full well we sit in the same spot every week. "But you look like shit."

Not what I was expecting.

"Thanks," I say wryly. "Appreciate it."

Instead of leaving me with my menu to wait for Hayden, the brazen woman sits across from me. I seriously can't catch a break.

"Can I be honest?" she asks.

"More honest than telling me I look like shit?"

The look on her face, a blank slate, makes me think of all those days she spends in a courtroom, playing whatever part is necessary to convince everyone around her that her client is innocent.

Giovanna herself, not so much.

"You don't like me."

I'll give it to her, G managed to surprise me with that one.

"I can come on a bit strong."

This time I'm the one who delivers a poker face. I don't much like her, but I'd never say, or even hint, at such a thing. So I remain as impassive as possible.

"You're one of the only men I've ever met who hasn't jumped at the chance to be with me."

I can't help but laugh.

"I love your humility, G."

She smiles. Not a predatory, come-hither smile, but a genuine one. Who knew she was capable of that?

"I also don't like beating around the bush. But you know that."

I glance toward the door. No Hayden yet. "I do."

"After I saw the pic of your girlfriend"—at the mention of Chari, I'm on high alert—"I realized we were never going to be a thing."

I don't deny it.

"I'm not your type."

No, not at all.

"So you can stop looking over your shoulder, waiting for me to pounce. I've moved on."

"Have you?"

Sure enough, there does seem to be something different about G tonight. Maybe she really is giving up on me, which, to be perfectly honest, is the best news I've heard all week.

"Yes, I have."

Giovanna stands up as a couple enters the restaurant. "Helping out Dad tonight," she says by way of explanation. "Enjoy your dinner."

She's about to walk away, but I stop her.

"G?"

As she turns to face me, I wonder if I'm going to regret this question.

"What do you mean, you knew after seeing that picture of Chari and me?"

She looks at me as if it was the dumbest question in the world.

"Because I've never seen that expression on your face before. And I've known you for a long time, Enzo DeLuca." Winking, she turns away.

She winked at me, and it wasn't even flirtatious.

Will wonders never cease?

"You look confused."

Hayden.

"And you look—" How do I put this? "—dapper?"

When he wants to, Hayden can fit in with the crustiest of the upper crust. No suit in his closet is off the rack—he's sporting one of his finest tonight.

"We have a sitter later. Ada's coming into the city for a date night."

That's unusual. "On a Wednesday?"

He sits, unfolding the napkin from the table and putting it on his lap. "Got two tickets for the Black and White Pre-Ball."

Ah, that made sense. The Black and White Ball is one of the city's most coveted events. But the Pre-Ball, always held the Wednesday before, is a sneak peek held exclusively for a select few celebrities and, in Hayden's case, the crème de la crème of the New York City elite.

"So why are you here? Aren't they serving dinner?"

Hayden gives me a strange look.

"It's Wednesday."

The waitress comes over with our drinks, having known what we'd ask for without taking our order, looks at the menu on the table, then at Hayden, and smiles. "The usual?"

"Yes, please," Hayden says.

"Eggplant for me."

She scribbles on her pad and walks away.

"Ada said she doesn't mind, she had a late lunch anyway. I'm meeting her there at eight."

Which gives us plenty of time to eat, but still.

"You could have cancelled."

Hayden cocks his head to the side. "Nope. No need. Besides . . ."

He doesn't say it, but I know exactly what he's thinking.

"I'm fine," I lie.

I told Hayden about Chari yesterday at a lunch meeting. He wasn't able to say much then, but I'm bracing myself for the second degree now that we're alone.

"Clearly, you're not."

I've never seen that expression on your face before.

"Why did you look so confused when I came in?" Hayden presses.

I relay the conversation with G, minus her parting statement. He looks properly taken aback.

"Well, that's interesting."

"I'm relieved, to be honest. It was starting to get uncomfortable."

"At least you managed to get out of it without screwing up Wednesday nights . . ."

"I would never screw up Wednesdays."

And it's true, for the same reason Hayden never cancels.

Because in our own messed-up way, we're not just business partners or friends, we're family.

"But you did screw up with Chari," he says.

The fact that I knew it was coming doesn't make it any easier.

"I don't want to talk about it."

Hayden looks like he might try anyway, but when the waitress comes with our salads, he lets up. We talk about basketball instead. At least, Hayden talks. I listen. Feeling like shit but knowing there's no help for it.

This is my life, and what's worse, I chose it.

38
─────

CHARI

"*I*'m going to kill him."

"And you wonder why I had Mom tell you instead of talking it out," I say with a sigh. It's why I considered staying home tonight. But as much fun as the prospect of sulking on my couch while my mom got dressed for a date sounded, I decided to put on my big-girl pants and meet my brother and his friends instead. Plus, Devon has been less available lately, so I'll take this chance to hang with him.

Lisa is also on a date. Because the universe is basically making sure I'm one hundred percent aware I am now single.

Five days.

It's been exactly five days since I last talked to Enzo. When my phone buzzed with a new text in the middle of the day on Thursday, every ounce of resolve I had mustered up on Sunday was erased. But my hopes of a reunion were quickly dashed.

Enzo asked if I was OK. I said yes. His response: *Good.*

And literally, that was it.

So I've been attempting to interpret his text. A worthy activity, kind of. If you are as pathetic as me.

The amount of time I've spent obsessing over Enzo, and crying while obsessing over Enzo, over the past five days is just embarrassing. It's not like we were dating for very long. And I was perfectly content—if not thrilled—with my life pre-Enzo. But still . . .

"You knew I'd find out eventually," Devon says as I jump in his car and immediately turn up the heat. We're picking up his friend Mike, the bartender at The Wheelhouse, and heading to Mill Creek, a neighboring town with even fewer people than Bridgewater. They do have a brewery though, and apparently that's worth the twenty-minute drive. Never mind that Bridgewater Brewery is just as good or that Devon won't be able to sample beers since he's driving home. It's Angel's Brew for him, but I'm swearing off the stuff. Forever.

Yeah, not being petty at all.

"You are not going to kill him," I say, putting my gloved hands in front of the heater. "It was my idea to break up."

To be fair, I was kind of forced into it, but I leave that part out. I really don't want to ruin their friendship.

Devon grunts.

"Enzo was a perfect gentleman. There wasn't any big fight or anything. He just . . ." I try to find words for what happened, but it's hard to do that around the big lump that has formed in my chest. I can't help but wonder what he's doing. How his day was. I've gotten used to talking to him, if not seeing him, every night.

"He works too much," Devon guesses. It doesn't take a genius to figure it out. "And he lives in New York, while you're out here."

But he's still angry.

I look at Devon's profile. My big brother, always protective.

"Please don't be mad at him, Dev. Enzo didn't do anything wrong. Seriously."

It would probably be easier if there had been some big blowup. If one of us had stopped caring. Instead, he just picked Angel, Inc. over me. It's that simple.

"Except date you in the first place. A person would have to be blind not to have seen this coming."

That stings.

"Sorry, I didn't mean you."

He turns the corner, snow dotting every surface from a dusting earlier in the day.

"I knew this would happen, though."

Yep, I'm starting to regret coming out.

"I guess I was naive to think he could build an empire and carry on a long-distance relationship. But what do I know about billion-dollar businesses? I'm just a small-town schoolteacher."

So much for not being a bitter Betty.

"Char, don't."

I can't help it. I've felt out of my league since the beginning. Because I was out of my league. Maybe Devon's right —maybe this was inevitable.

I bite my cheeks as they start to tingle. If I cry in front of my brother, he'll go on a the warpath.

"You are *not* just a small-town schoolteacher. You are an amazing woman who cares more about her students than anyone I know. You're the one who's always talking about the third grade benchmark. How it's your job to make sure your kids can all read as they should so none of them fall through the cracks."

My chest rises and falls as I listen, unable to answer.

"Maybe if he'd had a teacher like you . . ."

Devon closes his mouth like a crocodile feasting on a fresh fish. He clearly regrets the words, but it's way too late for him to take them back now.

"What are you talking about?"

We pull onto Mike's street.

"Nothing. Forget it." He pulls out his phone to text his friend. When Devon looks up, he finds himself staring down at my best *tell me right now* look.

"You can't say something like that and then take it back."

Apparently he can, and he will.

So I pull out the big guns.

"I'll tell Mom you have a girlfriend."

Devon whips his head toward me.

"How do you—"

It's my first smile of the week. There've been clues, but my brother just confirmed it. My guess is Colleen.

"I can hear her questions now. 'Where did you meet? Why didn't you tell me? When are you bringing her to dinner?'"

"Char." I don't heed the warning in his tone.

"Maybe I'll call Mom up now before her movie . . ."

"You are such a pain in the ass."

"And you need to spill whatever you were going to say. Now," I press, seeing the lights flicker off in Mike's house.

"If you tell him . . ."

"I assume you mean Enzo? The man I am no longer dating?"

Saying it aloud sucks.

"He doesn't tell people. I'm serious, Chari."

Normally, I wouldn't press my brother to break a confidence. But he's the one who offered it up. And I'm way too curious to let this go now.

Mike's front door opens.

"Enzo . . ." He hesitates. ". . . couldn't read."

I sit up in the seat and turn the music down.

"He got to fifth grade somehow before they figured out he had dyslexia. His mom went on a tear trying to figure out how to help him. She finally convinced the school to get some special program . . ."

I was barely listening.

Enzo? How is that possible? He went to an Ivy League school, for God's sake.

"I'm not sure who worked harder to help him at that point, Enzo himself or his mom. I just remember they had to get a lawyer. It wasn't pretty."

Having dealt with the system for the last several years, I completely get it. Well-meaning teachers (myself included) are still fighting the good fight to help the kids who need it. To get money diverted from new gyms or sports equipment for the expensive research-based programs that might help kids like Enzo learn to read more quickly. The exact program Devon's talking about.

"Don't mention it to him," Devon pleads as Mike opens the back door. "I could tell you a few horror stories, but I won't. All I'm going to say is that I think it's part of the reason he pushes so hard."

"Hey, Atwoods," Mike says. "Ready for a night on the town?"

I turn to greet him, trying really hard not to look as if my heart wasn't torn out twice this week. Once when Enzo decided not to make room for me in his life, ad again upon learning that the man I know, the paragon of confidence, was once a fourth- or fifth-grade kid who pretended he could read because he thought he had to. Who feared being called on by the teacher. Whose parents were shuttled from one conference to another to be told about how he was struggling with the curriculum. As if everyone involved didn't already know that.

I know that kid, because I see him or her every year. I lie awake at night wondering if, despite my best efforts, that kid has left my class without the skills needed to progress to the next grade even though I did my very best to help close the gap.

I know that kid because I was just dating him.

I just didn't realize it . . .

39

ENZO

"*A*da?"

Hayden is as surprised to see her as I am. She never comes to Wednesday dinner.

"I didn't know if I'd catch you."

I stand, reaching her before Hayden does. As I kiss her on the cheek, I realize it's been much too long since I last saw Hayden's family. I tell her so.

Hayden looks at her the same way he always does, his expression full of as much reverence as love. She saved him. I may have helped set the course for Hayden to be the man he is today, out from the shadow of his father's expectations, but Ada provided the sail. And the wind. And my friend knows it.

"Come sit. We were just finishing." He turns to look for a seat.

"No, that's OK, you guys finish up. I know you don't check your phone during Wednesday-night dinner, but I figured it would be nice if I picked you up so we can send Henry home."

Henry is their driver.

Hayden looks at his wife curiously. "But won't we need him later?"

Ada makes a face at me, and I can't help but laugh. Clearly she knows something Hayden does not.

"Today is his daughter's birthday. Please tell me you didn't forget to give him the gift earlier?"

His expression says otherwise.

Ada shakes her head, but she has a bemused expression on her face.

"It's in my coat pocket," he confesses.

"Finish your drink. I'll grab it and give it to Henry before I send him home."

Rather than wait for a response from Hayden, she heads straight for Giovanna, who guides her to the back of the restaurant.

Hayden finishes his wine and looks at me sheepishly.

"Oops."

Poor Ada.

"I know you realize you're a lucky bastard," I tell him in earnest. "If she hadn't come along . . ."

Hayden snatches the bill. It's my turn, so I'm not sure why he takes it.

"If she hadn't come along, you'd be left to pick up the pieces," he says. "Which is why I'm paying tonight."

As if it really matters. Our money is tied as closely together as our fates. Even without Ada—I shudder at the thought—there's no one I'd rather be in business with. Faults and all. But I still enjoy teasing him.

"If you're trying to make up for all your bad behavior, I hate to tell you, but a sixty-dollar bill isn't going to cut it."

Hayden's smile reaches the corners of his eyes. He knows I'm telling the truth. But I don't think that's the reason for his sudden giddiness. He's looking at his wife. Who just saved his ass, and not for the first time.

"I know it," he says. "Sorry to skip out on you. Talk to you tomorrow."

I nod to him and wave to Ada. "Have fun. And keep your pants on."

His laugh echoes through the restaurant. The last Black and White Ball went particularly well for Hayden, which is why he won't miss it. Only a guy like Hayden, who is the very opposite of shy, revels in getting caught in an extremely compromising position with his then girlfriend. He pays and leaves with Ada, but I don't get up just yet. The only thing waiting for me back at my apartment is a laptop and more work.

"More wine, Mr. DeLuca?" the waitress asks.

I'm about to say no but decide otherwise.

"Sure."

Which is how I end up sitting alone, watching a restaurant full of people and the few brave souls scurrying by outside, bundled up against the cold.

You know what? I'm done for the night. The budget approvals can wait until morning.

Hayden doesn't seem concerned about them. Instead, he's with the love of his life, enjoying a night out. But I really don't begrudge him that. I never do. Hayden works hard in his own way, and no matter what his dad says, Angel, Inc. would never be what it is today without my partner.

So why do you begrudge yourself the same happiness?

I shove the thought away.

Only for it to be replaced with another.

I've never seen that expression on your face before.

And my least favorite: *Cornell? I'm so sorry, sweetie, but I don't think that's going to be possible.*

I've hated the word "sweetie" my entire life.

Certainly I don't work too much because of Mrs. Forsythe or any of the other teachers or adult figures who have doubted me because of my learning disability. That would be giving them too much power over my destiny.

I do this because . . .

I'm proud of what we've built. Of how far we've come. And the possibilities are so exciting that I can't help but push further, faster. Want to go further yet.

Being competitive isn't a weakness. It's a strength. One I shouldn't have to apologize for.

Right?

"More wine?"

The waitress looks at me curiously. I don't usually stay for long after Hayden leaves, and never for this long. "No, thank you," I say. "Just the check please."

She shakes her head. "On the house. See you next week, Mr. DeLuca."

"Good night, Julia."

But I still don't want to leave. My apartment is the last place I want to be, because everything in it reminds me of Chari. I see her everywhere. Standing by the windows, looking out at the view. In my bed, on my couch . . .

But it's not just my apartment.

I see her in the office, the glass frog she gave me staring at me in judgment all day long because I can't bring myself to move him.

I see her when I close my eyes, and in my dreams and daydreams, she's wearing an oversized sweatshirt, coffee mug in hand, with the Swiss Alps rising behind her.

How could she ever think she's anything but magnificent? A country bumpkin indeed.

I don't want a woman who's coolly sophisticated, like

Giovanna. Or fake, like so many of the people I meet on a daily basis.

I want Chari Atwood just as she is. Or was, until I slammed the door on what could have been, in favor of my own ambition.

I've never seen that expression on your face before.

Because I'd never been in love before.

Until now.

OF COURSE IT'S SNOWING.

The weather isn't bad enough to keep me put—it just means the drive will take three hours rather than two. If I'm lucky. It doesn't help that I'm leaving at the worst possible time of day. Unfortunately, there's no help for it—I finally finished rescheduling the last of my meetings, and I couldn't bring myself to wait.

I flip open my laptop as the car moves slowly out of the city.

Another few hours and that's it for an entire week. My driver has strict orders to take this bad boy back to my apartment. I'll be honest: I struggle with the thought of being without my laptop for so long.

Which only tells me that I've let this—not the laptop, necessarily, but what it represents—take over my life for too long. Others are addicted to things far worse. But some, like me, are addicted to their jobs.

And just like those other kinds of addictions, this one has cost me more than I'm willing to pay. Certainly it has damaged other relationships in my life. Thankfully, my family doesn't have the luxury of breaking up with my ass. They're stuck with me. Chari, not so much.

My phone lights up.

Lusanne.

"Hey," I say, answering.

"Are you seriously coming home? For a whole week?"

So Lus talked to my mom. I wondered how long it would take her to call.

The fact that she sounds genuinely excited is one of the many reasons I know I'm doing the right thing. After talking to Hayden on Thursday and then Devon last night, I'm feeling pretty good about this. So good, in fact, that I can't help but kick myself for not having done it sooner. This is the first full week I've taken off since we started the company.

"Yes. I'm even sending my laptop back to the city."

Silence.

Then, "Um, couldn't you have just left it there in the first place?"

"Pfft. Crazy talk. I'm stuck in this car for at least a few hours. An extended vacation might be necessary, but I'm not about to willfully waste time."

I look out the window. "Is it snowing there too?"

"A little. But, oh my God, Enzo, this is so cool."

A lump forms in my throat. I have so much to say to her, to my parents. To my brothers. I plan to start making amends this week, tonight actually. I plan on working along-side Lusanne at the restaurant, but she doesn't know about that yet.

"What do you see?" I ask instead. There are plenty of important things to say, but I'd rather say them in person.

Including the fact that I've been a total schmuck.

If losing Chari hadn't slapped some sense into me, how long would I have gone on this way? Pushing away the people who care about me.

"I see Tris kicking my ass if I don't get a move on. I'm working at two tonight."

My family now calls the pizza shop "one" and the restaurant "two."

"I'm surprised you're not there already."

When Lusanne's ready to move on to a venture of her own, I suspect Tris is going to have to search high and low for a replacement who will do half what she does. He's more chef than restaurant owner. He's talked about asking Mom to manage the place, but we all know she has her hands full with the pizza shop.

"Mom's at two tonight."

Ah, that makes sense. Our mother runs a tight ship, so Lus wouldn't feel the need to hurry.

"All right, I'll talk to you later."

I'm about to hang up when Lusanne stops me.

"Wait, you never told me what you see."

I look out toward the traffic, light snow falling as we make our way out of the city.

What do I see?

"I see a long road home, Lus. But one that's long overdue."

40

CHARI

"No, Mom, that's enough . . ."

I stop, knowing she'll put as much butter as she damn well pleases on the English muffin. To her, "just a little" means coating something thoroughly and completely.

"Why don't you just call him?"

She caught me staring at my phone, again, and I look up at a plate with an overbuttered English muffin on top of it.

"Thanks, but I can't call him. Nothing has changed in the last week."

Actually, tomorrow will make it one week exactly, but who's counting?

I take a bite of the muffin, realizing how much I'll miss this when I move out. But it's time. It was probably time a while ago, actually.

"So," I hedge, grateful to think about something other than the hole in my heart. "I was thinking . . ."

My mother whips her head around. She knows me too well to misinterpret my tone, which was probably a whole lot less light and breezy than I was going for. "Things seem to be going well with you and Jeff."

Her expression confirms it. She really does like this guy, and I've given up trying to find something wrong with him. Much to my satisfaction, I haven't discovered anything.

But I can tell my approach is making her nervous, like maybe I have her thinking I discovered his secret life, or secret wife. "What is it, Char? You're scaring me."

"Sorry," I say. "Nothing awful. I was just thinking, it may be time for me to move out."

Her shoulders sag in relief.

I take another bite, grateful now for all that butter.

"And here I was thinking something was wrong."

Well, something is wrong, but it has nothing to do with me moving out. Or maybe it does. I felt a little fearless when I was with Enzo. He thinks so big and . . . maybe it's time for me to do the same. My mother is strong, always has been. She doesn't need me here, living at home. She never did. I came back because I craved security, but I'm ready for what comes next.

"So where are you thinking?"

That's a great question.

"For now, maybe Lakeside?"

There aren't many apartments to be had in Bridgewater, and even though Lakeside would practically bankrupt me, I can swing it. "I'm going to give the realtor a call next week."

"You said, 'for now.'"

I muster my courage and say it out loud for the first time.

"I'm keeping my options open, you know?"

But clearly, she doesn't know. My mother gives me a strange look, so I just spill it.

"I know I have a great job, and am grateful to have it. But"—I swallow—"I don't feel like I'm having enough of an impact. I'm going to keep my eye out for . . . something else maybe."

Yep, she's confused.

"Not teaching?"

"I'm not sure. I want to do something to help kids, for sure. But in the public school system? I don't know. All I know is that it's not working for me here."

"What about your pension?"

The golden handcuffs. The idea behind the pension is that teachers make most of their salary after they retire. Yeah, it'll suck not to have that security blanket. But it's no reason to stay.

"I know. But I can't do this forever for that reason alone."

I can tell Mom is concerned, and maybe I am too. Just saying it out loud is scary. But I know myself, and I honestly don't think I can work in this environment forever. I have crazy respect for my colleagues. Teachers work so much harder than most people realize. Especially the good ones. But I'm not a good fit for the system.

"Don't quit because of your boss. He'll move on . . ."

"It's not just that. I mean, yeah, he's a total douche, but even with someone great in that position, I still feel like I'm in a constant battle, and I don't want to put armor on every time I go to work. I want to actually make a difference."

"I can understand that. Maybe you'll find yourself somewhere a little bigger than Bridgewater?"

How many times have I said this town was just too small for me? My mother smiles, supportive as always. And I love her for it. I'm about to stand and give her a hug as my brother makes his presence known in his usual not-so-subtle manner.

"Jesus, Chari, your phone is right there. Why don't you check it?"

"Good morning to you too," I mutter.

Sure enough, as Mom stands up to get Devon an English

muffin, I turn my phone over and see my brother tried to call me. Numerous times.

"I turned it over," I say, not explaining why. "Where's the fire?"

"No fire." Devon kisses Mom on the cheek. "Just wanted to see if you're interested in grabbing lunch."

My mom and I both look at him with a healthy dose of skepticism. It's not even nine in the morning. Why the push for lunch plans? I can't remember the last time we grabbed lunch. Dinner, sometimes. Drinks, for sure.

"Why?"

My mother looks back and forth between us. "I have to open the shop." Then to Devon, she adds, "You better not be up to anything."

"Up to anything?" says Devon the Innocent. Not a look he pulls off well. "Me?"

Which means he is definitely up to something.

"I got it, Mom." She was making a moves to clean up the mess, but I shoo her out of the kitchen. "You go ahead."

She looks at me with a combination of gratitude and concern, but overall, I'm pretty pleased about how our talk went down.

The minute she leaves, I look at Devon, demanding an explanation.

"Lunch? Really?"

"Yes. Lunch. I owe you for winning our bet, as you so astutely called me on the other night. Why so prickly this morning?"

Sometimes I really want to slap him.

When I don't answer him, he shrugs. "Never mind, I already know. Pick you up at noon? OK, see you later."

Devon doesn't bother waiting for an answer. Armed with the English muffin he commandeered from my plate as if he doesn't already have one, he walks out of the kitchen, yelling back, "Next time look at your phone."

Leaving me with no doubt Devon is being sketchy. Though I suppose there are worse things than having your brother forcing you to lunch. Besides, maybe it will distract me from thinking about Enzo.

I look at my phone again.

And then again, maybe not.

41

ENZO

"*W*elcome to Chateau LeMonte, Mr. DeLuca."

"Thank you"—I look at her name tag—"Sarah."

"It says here you will be staying with us for a week?"

"Until next Sunday, yes."

She looks at her computer as I take in the eclectic mixture of woodside lodge and French country decor. This place always reminded me of our region's coal mining past, but that might be only because I know the original proprietor was a mine owner. He opened Chateau LeMonte in the early '40s, the French decor nothing more than his desire to class the place up.

When I was a kid, my parents took us here for dinner a few times on special occasions. For a long time, it was the fanciest place I'd ever been. As Sarah checks me in, I look past the log cabin interior to the empty deck. No one sits outside now, the cold keeping the few guests indoors. But the view is perfect, the setting as close to Montreux as I can get in Pennsylvania.

She'll be here soon.

After I take my key card from the attendant, I grab one of the hotel notecards and scrawl a quick note.

Chari,

I'm sorry for tricking you into coming, and so much more. Join me for lunch, please. Give me a chance to explain.

Enzo

"I have a guest coming at around noon. Can you give this to her with directions to the Boathouse Cabin?"

"Of course, sir. It is prepared as you asked."

"Thank you."

I pass the restaurant and head back outside, following Sarah's circle on the resort map. Eight individual cabins dot the lakeside around the building containing the lobby and the restaurant. Walking along a path, I find our cabin and head inside.

They did a good job.

Flower petals everywhere. Chilled champagne.

I drop my bags, chuckling to myself as I imagine what Hayden would say about me carrying them myself. For such a great guy, he can be an insufferable snob. Before Ada, I considered it my duty to bring him back down to earth, but now she's taken up the torch. Though I'm not sure she's always entirely successful.

Climbing the stairs, I take in the contrast between the log cabin walls and bright white and pale blue decor. The large, cozy-looking bed. Opening the sliding glass door, I'm reminded this is no Montreux—the weather is still very much that of PA in late winter. I stand on the deck anyway, taking in the lodge's famous twenty-mile view of Lake Shohola surrounded by the Pocono Mountains. It's no Swiss Alps, but it's beautiful in its own right.

I'm lost for a time, playing my speech over and over in my mind.

I started with my family yesterday, begging them for forgiveness. They all claimed no apologies were necessary, but I still feel regret over the time I lost with them as I built what I thought was my legacy.

A movement in the distance catches my eye.

Chari came.

I wasn't sure she would. Devon agreed to help get her here after I told him all the things I planned on saying, on doing, but that doesn't mean she'll be receptive. Even now, as I hurry down the stairs to open the front door of the cabin and she walks slowly toward me, I can feel her skepticism.

A look passes between us, and I curse myself for the umpteenth time for how foolishly I handled that phone call. The thought of offering any concessions put me into a panic. It would have been the equivalent of admitting I had a problem, that I had let my work habits spiral out of control. It felt like she was asking me to leave everything behind, even though the logical part of my mind knew better.

I'm a goddamn idiot.

"Come in," I say. "It's freezing."

I know that from standing outside on the deck for the last fifteen minutes. Since Chari hates the cold, I open the door a little wider to show her the roaring fireplace in the corner of the downstairs living room. That might not be playing fair, but I'm desperate enough to use the resources available to me.

"I don't understand. What are you doing here?"

She might not understand yet, but she follows me in

anyway. When she stops at the entrance, I turn to look at her. Her cheeks are red, and I can't see much of her bundled in a down coat and scarf. But she's never looked more beautiful.

"Come warm up. I'll explain."

I hold out my arms for her coat. After a brief hesitation, she takes it off and gives it to me, revealing an outfit of skinny jeans and a chunky beige sweater. Chari's eyes rest on the champagne stand next to the beautifully set wooden table just off a kitchenette.

She doesn't move.

"Devon . . ."

"I asked him to get you here. I was afraid that if I asked you directly, you might say no."

"Enzo"—my name on her lips sounds as sweet as it did that first night at the bar—"I'd never do that. We've known each other forever. We've been friends for years."

I nod toward the fire, mostly because I'm still cold, and she follows.

"I don't want to be your friend, Chari."

Shit. That didn't come out right. I'm usually slicker than this.

We're standing by the fire now, close enough that I can smell her perfume. Vanilla and coconut. I want to skip to the part where she takes me back and lets me kiss her senseless. I want to slip my hands underneath that sweater and warm us both up more effectively than this fire can.

But we're not there yet.

And if you fuck this up, maybe you won't ever be.

"I screwed up."

I asked my sister for advice, and she was very clear on one thing: be honest. The words fumble out of me with all the confidence of a teenage boy, but at least they're true.

"I should have said so many things last week. But I honestly couldn't see a way forward. Angel, Inc. is my life, has been for years."

"And you were honest about that from the beginning."

Chari's so detached, it's scaring me. It's as if she's already made her decision. And although I've talked myself into and out of hundreds of business deals, I'm scared shitless I won't be able to change her mind.

"At the beginning I figured I could try to have it all. That I could work as hard as I'd been working and have you too. The reality of it was just . . . so much more difficult."

She's already shaking her head. "I'm not sure what all of this is"—she sweeps her hand around the room—"but nothing has changed. You're still in New York, busy running an empire. I'm still here, wanting more than you're able to give me. I'm sorry you thought for a second I wouldn't see you. In some ways, you're like family. My brother's best friend. I'll always have a soft spot for you. But . . ." She frowns.

This is not going well.

I want to reach out for her so badly, but Chari isn't mine right now. And I have to respect that. But still . . . fuck, this is hard.

Tell her you're committed, that you'll find time to be together.
Tell her you love her and should have realized it sooner.
Tell her something, you idiot.
Be honest.

"Remember the night you turned twenty-one?"

Chari's brows draw together as she nods. "Yeah."

"After your twenty-one shots . . ."

"Many of which were beer," she adds.

"Thankfully, yes."

Her smile loosens something in my chest. This *has* to work.

"I stayed at your house that night."

I was sure she couldn't possibly remember, but as the fire crackles next to us, Chari surprises me.

"I know. We ate bacon the next morning. At least, you and Devon did. I don't think I ate all day."

"You passed out on the couch," I recall. "Devon took off your shoes and put a blanket on you before he went to bed. I went into the kitchen and drank some water first, like a responsible young man."

Chari smiles, clearly having no clue where I'm going with this story. But to me, it's like the whole thing happened yesterday.

"When I came back out and walked by the couch, I thought about the raging hangover you'd have the next day. And I wished I'd made you drink more water too. Even if they weren't all real, you did your share of actual shots that night."

"Raging hangover," she mutters. "That's an understatement."

"I watched you, feeling guilty. It was the first time I really saw you as anything other than Devon's little sister. All night, I'd imagined what I might say to you if you weren't. And while I watched you sleep, your hands folded so neatly on your chest, your hair splayed out everywhere." I shrug, acting like it's no big deal to confess this, when in fact I never planned on telling anyone other than Hayden. "You looked like an angel to me. I thought about that night for years, wondering what Devon would think if I told him I thought his little sister was hot as hell."

"Oh my God," she says. "You did not think that?"

But I can tell she still doesn't get it.

"After my discovery, when Hayden and I decided to move forward with the company, one of the first decisions we had to make was to name it. Something that could work well with beer, wine, and who knew what else."

It takes her a second.

"Hayden's dad hired a marketing team that would make most Fortune 500 companies jealous. They were the best in the business. Charts of names and market research . . . but it was one thing I refused to budge on."

Her eyes, like saucers, tell me she's finally made the connection.

"Are you saying . . . ?"

I nod. "It's named after you, Chari."

"No, there's no way. Devon . . ."

"Has no idea."

She still doesn't believe me. I pull my phone out of my pocket, pull up Hayden's number, and hold it out. "Text Hayden. He'll tell you."

Chari doesn't take the phone. "Angel, Inc. is named . . ."

"After the beautiful, caring girl who turned into a woman right before my eyes."

"Why didn't you ever tell me? Last week . . . how could you?" She stops, but I know what she's trying to ask.

"How could I screw up a chance with the woman I've harbored a secret crush on for years? My only real defense is that I'm an idiot, and it's not a very good one. Why did I think it was OK not to go home for Christmas last year when my family lives two hours away? Or that buying my dad a few new pizza ovens would make up for missing his surgery last year."

How could it have gotten so bad?

"I don't know, Char. I really don't. But I do know one thing." I swallow, mentally crossing my fingers. "I need someone to remind me never to do it again. Never to take the people I love for granted. And I'd really like for that person to be you."

42

CHARI

From the minute Devon dropped me off at the front door of Chateau LeMonte, I've been caught up in a whirlwind of confusion. Of course, it makes a whole lot more sense that Enzo, and not Devon, would want to meet me here. To say this is not my brother's scene is to put things mildly. I knew something was fishy before I showed up, but I hadn't put two and two together.

Enzo is here.

Devon is not.

I've tried all week to harden myself against the possibility Enzo might change his mind (although I was admittedly close to caving when he sent me that check-in text). At the end of the day, Enzo chose Angel. He will always choose Angel.

There just isn't room for us both in his world.

Or so I thought. The realization that Angel was named after *me* . . . that's something I hadn't prepared myself for. And honestly, I don't know what to say.

Thankfully, a knock at the door gives me a stay of execution. Within minutes, the table is set with lunch, reminiscent of the breakfast Enzo ordered for me that morning in Switzerland. Of course, I don't miss the parallels.

The view.

The notecard.

He's recreating the date that put me on a collision course with disappointment and heartbreak.

Still, I don't react to Enzo's announcement. We talk casually over lunch, as if the bombshell he dropped on me in front of the fireplace never happened. I'm buying time to figure out what to do next. He knows me well enough to realize that, and he's very politely allowing it.

I want to throw myself in his arms, obviously. But then what? Will it be another three weeks before I see him again? Longer?

"More champagne?"

"It's not yours," I tease. Forgetting for a second this isn't a date. It's a . . . I don't know what exactly. "Angel doesn't have a sparkling wine."

"Yet."

He refills my glass as we exchange glances. I hate to be a mood killer, but this has to be said.

"And that's the reason why, as much as I want to forget dessert and have my way with you, it just can't happen."

Enzo hears only one thing in all of that. His chocolate brown eyes darken. As they do, I force myself to look away, only for my traitorous eyes to shift to his bare forearms instead. Throughout the meal, I've cursed the fact that I once told him I have a weakness for rolled shirtsleeves. And I'm sure he did it on purpose.

Jeans and a button-down. He knows it's my favorite of his looks.

"Tell me, precisely," he says, standing, "why 'this' can't happen?"

So he did hear me.

Oh crap, he's walking around the table toward me.

"Sparkling wine. Vodka. Gin. Rum."

I know there are a ton of other liquors, but I can't seem to name them at the moment. He's standing so close, I have to look up.

"There will always be another thing to conquer. More markets to expand into. And you're still in New York. And I'm"—my heart is doing a little dance as Enzo just watches me, his expression intent and serious—"still distracting."

He leans down, gently pulls the glass from my hand and sets it down. Wrapping his fingers through mine, Enzo pulls me to my feet.

I don't even consider stopping him. My body and mind are not communicating.

"That you are," he says, letting go of my hand. We're standing so close, I can almost feel the heat from his body.

"I have this cabin for a week."

My chest rises and falls as every muscle in my body screams to touch him. This is going to happen, probably, regardless of whether or not it should.

"My laptop is in New York."

His words take a moment to penetrate.

"A week? You took off the entire week?"

"I did."

This is terrible timing for him to be off from work. And no laptop? Enzo doesn't go anywhere without it. The thought of him leaving it behind, for a week . . .

"Why?"

He takes the final step, closing the gap between us.

Enzo reaches behind my head, fists my hair and pulls me into him. Our lips find each other's as if starved. And as his tongue swirls with mine, Enzo's words flit through my mind.

A week.

No work.

"Enzo," I mutter with the very last vestiges of restraint left in me. "Why?"

In answer, he begins to unbutton his shirt. Oh dear Lord, this man is the devil. He knows what he's doing to me right now. With each button that comes undone, we're one step closer to a reconciliation with no resolution.

But he stops for long enough to say, "To convince you to take me back. To convince you I realize how fucked up my priorities were. But that's about to change."

To convince you to take me back.

He undoes the final button, and before he even tosses his shirt aside, my fingers itch to touch him, to trace the ridges of his abs and . . .

His shirt is off, and I'm a goner.

43

ENZO

I'm not gentle.

Chari's sweater is off, her jeans unbuttoned before we can make it past the couch. There's no way in hell I'm waiting to get upstairs. Discarding my shoes and socks, I slip a package from the back pocket of my jeans and then lose them too.

Chari hasn't agreed yet. The fact that she wants me now, in this way, doesn't mean she wants me back.

At least she's listening. I know my confession shocked her, but it was the only way I could think of to make her understand.

As much as I want to forget dessert and have my way with you . . .

When she said that, she flipped a switch in me, and I can't turn it off. Don't want to turn it off.

We're both completely naked in front of the fire. My hands are everywhere at once, grabbing and caressing. I pull us down onto the plush carpet as the wind picks up outside, bending and snapping tree limbs, as tumultuous as my emotions.

I want to be inside her.

I want to love her, to show Chari how wrong I was to push her away.

But I also want to worship her with my hands, cherish her with my mouth, give her more pleasure than she dreamed possible.

So I slide down, push apart her legs, and squeeze her thighs with my first taste. When she tries to push upward, into me, I push her back down, knowing what she likes. This strong, fierce woman enjoys being controlled in bed, and I'm more than happy to oblige.

So when she grabs my hair, none too gently, I reach up, without missing a beat, and hold her wrist down. I'm throbbing with the need to be inside her, but I ignore it. I also ignore her plea for me to fuck her.

With both of her wrists pinned now, I look up.

"When you come," I say, "and not a second before."

She shudders, Chari's entire body telling me it's ready.

Too bad.

I'm not.

Another taste, this time with Chari knowing full well I'm in control. Her hips lift as she screams my name. A sweeter sound, I've never heard.

"For God's sake, Enzo."

When I look up, it's to see Chari's blessedly naked body sprawled out above me like the grandest feast known to man. I don't waste any time. Reaching for the package and tearing it open, I make eye contact with her.

I can see it in her gaze: she's forgiven me.

She's willing to try again.

The knowledge of it makes me impatient. I know she's ready, and I'm beyond so. As I slip inside her sweet wetness,

I position myself to free up one hand. I'm relentless with it, caressing her breasts, her clit. Soon Chari's pulling me toward her, a good sign . . .

But I'm not ready for this to end.

I have a powerful need for this woman, one that's built up for weeks, made fiercer by the knowledge that I almost lost her for good.

"If I'm hurting you . . ."

"You're not. Not now, at least."

The reminder is a potent one. The fact that she's allowed me back into her life, back into her body . . .

"Never again, Chari. I swear it."

Each thrust is another promise, but before long I'm having a hard time holding back.

"Yes, Enzo. Yes!"

She's close, and so am I.

Of all the things I've told her today, there's only one thing I left out. The most important thing of all. And now seems like the perfect time to correct that lapse.

"Chari. I am so in love with you."

Her eyes widen, and she comes in a great, powerful rush. So I let go too, wanting to squeeze my eyes shut against the sweet pain of it but also wanting to watch her expression. Needing to. Her lips are sweetly parted, and I have no choice but to capitalize on it.

I kiss her, our tongues tangling for what seems like forever. Until a loud crackle from the fireplace reminds me of where we are. Of what I still need to ask her.

"Give me another chance," I say, pulling away.

She's so damn expressive. The love she has for everyone —her family, her students—I want some of it. I want her to cherish me that way too.

"I love you," I remind her, just in case she didn't hear me.

She's an angel, my angel.

Please, Chari . . .

"I love you too."

44

CHARI

*E*ven though we still have four days left, it's starting to feel like the day we left Switzerland. Like I know we're going to be parted soon, and a piece of me will go with him.

We're still in bed, Enzo having convinced me to take a "wellness" day. After a very pleasing bout of morning sex, I'm lying next to him as we watch yet another round of snow fall outside. I can even see the lake from this vantage point, and that reminds me of Switzerland too.

"I actually don't mind the cold so much from in here."

He pats his chest, and I happily oblige. Laying my head down, I can hear Enzo's heartbeat thunder beneath my ear.

"So you wouldn't be opposed to having a house or an apartment in Montreux?"

I laugh as his fingers trace across my shoulders. "Not at all."

His hand stills. I pick up my head to see if something's wrong.

Propped up on white pillows, with his jet-black hair, I

swear Enzo has never looked hotter than he does at this moment.

"I'm not kidding," he says. I wait for him to crack a smile. But he doesn't.

"You're serious?"

"I am." He pushes my hair back behind my ear.

"A house in Montreux?"

He runs a finger down my back, something I refuse to let distract me. We haven't talked about the future yet, but both of us know the discussion is inevitable.

"You love it there."

"I do, but . . . we can't buy a house in every place I love."

His slow smile refutes my words.

Again. Not getting distracted.

"So maybe we can meet up in our vacation homes?"

Sadly, his smile fades. But we need to talk about this. Although I know he's willing to make this work, and so am I, the details matter.

"Chari, I'd never ask you to give up your job. But you've talked about being unhappy with your boss. With the whole public school system."

I know this is a serious discussion, but before we go any further, I have to ask, "Are you tracing a heart on my back?"

He winks. And I think I might melt right into the bed.

"Feel free to tell me I'm crazy," Enzo continues.

"You're crazy."

He gives me a look.

"But do continue."

"I've been thinking a lot about what you do. What I went through as a kid."

Enzo opened up about his struggles in school this week, and rather than pretend I'd had no idea—I am so not a good liar—I did admit to having pulled that particular bit of information from my brother.

"You're right. The kids who are struggling need help. Our help. But maybe we can do it another way." His hand slows to a stop and now just rests on the small of my back. "What if . . ."

Enzo rarely gets nervous. But I can tell he is right now, and it's freaking me out a bit.

"Enzo?"

He swallows. "What if you had unlimited funds to create something of your own for struggling readers? A program. A school. It would be totally up to you. But you'd have all the resources you need to get it started. Sky's the limit."

Create something of your own.

"Or you could do advocacy work to get the right reading programs into schools. Honestly, whatever you think would help kids the most. And"—he looks straight into my eyes —"you could do it from New York."

Oh my God.

"Are you asking me to move in with you?"

I just want to be sure I'm not getting this wrong.

"I know it's a big ask. You love Bridgewater. Your family is here. Your job is here."

Is he serious? Move in with him? Start my own reading outreach program?

"And you're so close with your mom. Not to mention Lisa and your friends. But . . ."

Holy shit.

Spread your wings, Chari. Like an angel.

I smile so hard my dry winter lips are ready to crack.

"Yes! Enzo, yes."

He flips me onto my back, and I find myself looking up

into his beautiful face, his smile reaching the very corners of his eyes.

"One thousand percent yes."

———

"I can't believe you're going to work Monday."

It's hard to hear Lisa over the drunken shouts that fill the bar as Enzo and Devon win another round of shuffleboard. Apparently neither has lost their touch, and no other duo in The Wheelhouse can best them.

"Another round?" Mike asks from behind the bar.

"Sure," I respond as Lisa shrugs her shoulders in the universal gesture of *why not?*

Since I still haven't responded to her about the whole work thing, I shift my gaze to her and say, "I can't just up and leave. They need to find a replacement for me."

I watch as Enzo leans over the shuffleboard table.

"You are not being very subtle," Lisa comments with no small measure of amusement.

"Thankfully, I don't have to be," I respond. Enzo moves aside for his brother Gian, who's on the opposing team.

Lisa takes two Angel Pale Ale bottles, along with the small white pill packages accompanying them, from Mike. After thanking him and handing me one of the bottles and pills, she asks, "So when will you move?"

"As soon as they replace me."

I've already told everyone. It was especially hard to break the news to my mom and brother. I'm so close to them both that it's difficult to imagine a week without either of them. But the trade-off is pretty sweet. As if he can hear my thoughts, Enzo looks back at us.

At *me*.

"He's crazy about you," Lisa says with a smile.

Gian gives his brother a nudge. It's Enzo's turn.

"I'm crazy about him too."

Thankfully, people are a bit more used to seeing Enzo here than they were that first night. And although we spent most of the week at Chateau LeMonte, whenever we emerged I was reminded that my boyfriend isn't just any guy. Everywhere we went, people watched, some more subtly than others.

And now I'm a part of that world.

As if dating him weren't enough pressure, I now have my own business to build. The possibilities keep me awake well after Enzo falls asleep at night. And for the first time, I think I understand him a bit better.

I won't be working for someone else. Every idea, every success or failure, will be mine. There's a certain power to that. It's also intimidating as hell.

"You OK?" Lisa asks, giving me a nudge.

"Yeah. It's just . . . this whole job thing is scary."

"I bet. But exciting too, right?"

Exciting. That's a good word for it. Before Enzo came back into my life, it had fallen into a routine that was both safe and boring. Now I'm plunging into uncertainty, head-on. All week Enzo has been preparing me for life as a business owner.

"Super exciting," I agree.

"Finally," Lisa says, gesturing to the shuffleboard table. "I didn't think anyone was going to beat them."

Gian and his friend pump their fists into the air in victory and then shake hands with Enzo and Devon. They've lost, but there's an upside to it.

As Enzo approaches me, I shift on my barstool to face him. He stands between my parted legs, kissing me as if my best friend and brother aren't two feet away.

"Get a room," Devon quips.

I'm not usually one for PDA, but all bets are off. Enzo and I are still celebrating our reunion and savoring each other. I hope we never stop.

"We have a room," Enzo says as he ends the kiss, stepping out from between my legs. Nodding to Mike for another drink, he stays firmly planted next to my stool, one hand on my upper thigh. Taunting me.

"I'm gonna have to get used to this," Devon says. "It's still hard to believe."

"Chari and Enzo?" Lisa asks. "What's it like to have your best friend dating your little sister?"

"Ouch." Enzo reaches across my body to grab a beer from the bar. When he leans this close, I can smell his cologne. Resisting the urge to taste it too, I let his neck pass by untouched. "You make it sound like I'm robbing the cradle. She's only two years younger than Devon."

Enzo moves his hand up to rub my arm.

"You cold?"

"Nope." I might have shivered, but it wasn't from the cold.

As Devon and Enzo verbally spar with each other, I listen to them, realizing with something like wonder that the two friends will actually be related someday. Last night Enzo asked how I felt about the idea of getting married. He quickly assured me that he wasn't rushing me—he was just curious.

I told him I liked the idea, a lot. But we both agreed we have a lot to do in the interim. Including one business to launch, and another to launch further into the stratosphere of success. So I have no idea what the timeline will be, but I do know I'm not letting this guy get away anytime soon. Our short brush with a breakup felt like it lasted a lifetime.

"Excuse me?"

The four of us turn toward a man who approached Enzo from behind. None of us know him. He walks with conviction, his salt-and-pepper beard somehow making him look more ominous.

"Enzo DeLuca, right?"

Enzo reaches out the hand that previously rested on my thigh.

"Yes, and you are?"

"Kenny Bradford. I live in Stratton."

Two towns away, Stratton is even smaller than Bridgewater with, from what I can remember, maybe two bars, tops.

"My dad lived there when he first came over from Italy," Enzo says. He's gotten so accustomed to chatting with strangers that I swear he could run for political office. Except for the fact that he hates politics.

"I don't want to intrude," says the man as his gaze skates around the group. "I just wanted to thank you."

I can tell we're not the only people paying attention now —although people aren't being obvious about it, I can tell they're listening.

"My sister was hit by a drunk driver a few years ago. Her back is so messed up, she still can't work. But she's alive and we're grateful for that. When we first heard about Angel, Inc., both my sister and I were thrilled. So I just wanted to say thanks, in person. You guys are doing amazing work."

Enzo shakes Kenny's hand again. I can tell he's moved by this stranger's gratitude. I know better than anyone his work ethic has much less to do with making more money than it does with improving quality of life for people, avoiding drunk driving accidents. He takes the social responsibility part of his business very seriously.

"It's my pleasure," he says, and I know Enzo is being sincere.

"I won't take up any more of your time."

Before Enzo can stop him, the stranger walks away, calling over his shoulder, "Angel is a great name, by the way."

Everyone else has gone back to their conversations. But I can tell Enzo is pleased. As he should be.

"Angel," he says, looking at me. "It's not bad, but if I had to rename it, I think I'd go with a different name."

"Would you really?" Lisa asks. "What would you call it?"

Enzo doesn't break eye contact with me while answering her. "Tiger." He smiles. "I think I'd call it Tiger, Inc. instead."

I laugh, not even remotely cold, even though some ding-dong is holding the door open for all his friends. I hold up my beer.

"Cheers," I say. Lisa and Devon raise up their drinks. "To Angel, Inc."

Enzo raises his beer too. "And to its namesake, the woman I love."

I'll drink to that.

EPILOGUE

Enzo

"I'm so nervous."

It's hard to believe Chari is so worried about tonight. Within the last month, she upended her life, quit her job, and moved to New York. But she's seriously worried about meeting Hayden for the first time. We're stuck in traffic, and every minute that goes by, Chari fidgets more and more. Before long, she's going to pull the buttons off her coat without realizing it.

"He's going to love you."

I take her hand, staying her nervous twisting of the buttons. Taking advantage of the fact that neither of us is wearing gloves, with it warming up a bit now that April has come. I rub circles into her palm.

"I still can't believe you've never connected before. He and your brother get along great.

Unlike Chari, Devon has been to New York often enough over the past few years to get to know my friend and business partner. Hayden has been to Bridgewater before too, but those weekend visits coincided with occasions when Chari was either away or busy.

"I know, but Devon's a guy."

I'm not sure what to do with that.

"There's a different dynamic between men. I just . . . I know how important he is to you, and I want him to like me."

This is so unlike Chari. Her concern would almost be laughable if it weren't so genuine. I haven't met a soul who doesn't like her. Chari's ability to blend seamlessly into any crowd is one of her many remarkable qualities.

"He'll love you. Like I do."

"Wednesday nights are your thing," she says, biting her lip. "Maybe we should have arranged this for another time."

"Are you kidding? Hayden is dying to meet you."

Chari just moved her stuff this weekend, and Hayden was out of town. So I'm bringing her to dinner tonight. But it's very clear to me she's as nervous as she claims, and nothing I say seems to help.

"Talk to me."

Chari licks her lips, so of course I can't resist the urge to do the same. I lean forward, intending to make my kiss comforting. Instead, it spirals quickly out of control. Thinking of those buttons she played with earlier, I find them easily, using them to pull her even closer.

One minute, I'm kissing my girlfriend to distract her.

The next, my hand is up her sweater, the distraction becoming very real. I find her hard nipple and roll it between my thumb and forefinger. Her low groan encourages me to continue until I'm throbbing with need for her.

I pull away and look out the tinted window. The traffic is

basically at a standstill, and another soundproof tinted window conceals us from the driver.

Fuck it.

Moving with the speed of someone who knows traffic can lighten up any time, making our drive to Faustini's quicker than anticipated, I fish out the condom in my wallet and go to work. It's not easy maneuvering all of that in the back seat of a car, even a roomy one like this, but a little determination can go a long way.

It takes just a few minutes, Chari staring at me, open-mouthed, clearly surprised at the quick turn of events, and I'm ready.

"You can't be serious."

But she knows I am. Already Chari's boots are off, and her black leggings are halfway down her legs. I don't need to pump myself. I don't need to prepare at all. The thought of her sliding onto my lap, me filling her as we inch toward the restaurant, is all the enticement I need.

"Hurry."

I don't say it because the car is moving closer to our destination, but because I really want—need—Chari closer to me. When she does finally manage to wrestle off her leggings, it takes me less time to pull her on top of me than it will for another horn to honk outside the car.

"Chari." I can barely get the word out as she slides onto me. My hands palm both cheeks, spreading her wide. Thankfully, being caught isn't a concern. I could come now if Chari were ready.

"I can't believe we're doing this."

I set the pace, Chari follows. At first. When she takes over, I'm lost.

Tossing my head back, I close my eyes, unable to watch her any longer.

"Are you OK?" she says in an undertone.

If I'm being honest? No.

I feel like a horny teenager.

"Oh God," I say as she writhes over me.

"You look really hot right now," she says, panting.

Me?

I open my eyes. Chari's hair falls down between us as she moves, faster now. My hand lowers in between us, and because of the angle, I use my thumb.

Chari bucks up for a brief second and then presses into me. We're close. Both to the restaurant, and to finding our release. When I lean up and kiss her, using my tongue to match the pace between us, a blessed moan accompanies Chari's unmistakable wetness, so I stop holding back.

It's only after we pull ourselves together, as much as we can, that I realize how we must look. When she gets out of the car a little while later, I smooth down a strand of her hair.

"Is it that obvious?"

I take her hand and lead the way into Faustini's, leaning in close to whisper, "You look like a woman who was just properly fucked. So if that's what you mean by obvious, then yes."

Which is exactly how Hayden sees us.

Chari, still slightly disheveled, and me, the very opposite of cool and collected. I'm heated, adrenaline coursing through my veins even now. Of course traffic eased up just in time to make our re-dressing an exercise in haste.

Hayden has selected a corner table instead of our usual table for two by the window. I'm sorry to see Ada wasn't able to make it because I know she and Chari will get along great. At least Chari doesn't look worried anymore.

Instead, she looks like a woman thoroughly pleased. Just the way I intend for her to stay. Whatever it takes.

"If I weren't a gentleman," Hayden says as we approach, "I would say what you two look like right now."

"A gentleman," I mutter. "Why start now?"

With mock indignation, he turns toward Chari. "Be nice, Enzo. What will Chari think of me?"

He sticks his hand out, and as Chari takes it, Hayden covers their joined hands with his free one. And I know, despite Chari's worry, this is the beginning of a beautiful new relationship.

I've only seen my partner shake someone's hand that way a few times before, once when Ada was still a business associate and not yet his wife. To Chari, it's nothing more than a simple greeting. But I know better. For all his shortcomings, Hayden Tanner is more fiercely loyal than anyone I've ever met. And he's just accepted Chari as a part of our family.

"It's great to meet you," she says. "I've heard so much about you."

Hayden lets go of her hand. "Unfortunately, most of it is true."

He looks back and forth between us.

"It's a good thing you went back home for Tris's opening," he says. "See what happens when you listen to me?"

I can't help but laugh at that. Leave it to Hayden to take credit for sending me home. But I will make one concession.

"It *is* a good thing I went back home."

I grab Chari's hand.

"I found myself again." I take a deep breath, knowing I shouldn't say this without having talked to her about it first, but unable to help myself. It's all I've been able to think about ever since Chari agreed to come to New York. "And I found my future wife."

WANT a bit more of Enzo and Chari? Re-visit Montreux, Switzerland with them. Visit BellaMichaels.com/BDD to read a bonus epilogue.

ABOUT THE AUTHOR

Bella Michaels is the pen name of a steamy contemporary romance author debuting her first billionaire novel with this book, Billion Dollar Date. While not writing historical, paranormal and contemporary romance, Bella loves dreaming up new sassy heroines and alpha heroes for readers to enjoy. Firmly Team Gryffindor, Stark and Reylo, she lives with her husband and two pre-teens in chilly Pennsylvania.

Sign up to be a Bella Michael's to receive book news and updates via email by visiting BellaMichaels.com.

Connect with Bella on:

Made in the USA
San Bernardino, CA
21 July 2020